Whispers from the Grave

Whispers from the Grave

Kim Murphy

To Debbie,
Best wishes,
Kim Murphy

Published by Coachlight Press

Published by Coachlight Press March 2007

Coachlight Press, LLC
1704 Craig's Store Road
Afton, Virginia 22920
http://www.coachlightpress.com

Printed in the United States of America
Cover design by Mayapriya Long, Bookwrights Design

This is a work of fiction. Names, characters, places, and incidents either are the product of the author's imagination or are used fictitiously, and any resemblance to any actual persons, living or dead, events, or locales is entirely coincidental.

Library of Congress Cataloging-in-Publication Data

Murphy, Kim.
    Whispers from the grave / Kim Murphy.
        p. cm.
    ISBN-13: 978-0-9716790-5-4
    1. Supernatural—Fiction. I. Title
    PS3613.U745W47 2007
    813'.6–dc22

                                                        2006033630

*To Ginger
and Magic*

Also by Kim Murphy

Promise & Honor
Honor & Glory
Glory & Promise

Prologue

Near Charles City, Virginia
May 1867

GEORGE CRUSHED THE WILTED ROSE between his fingers, letting the pieces fall through his hand to the oak desktop. He poured another Scotch, took a sip, then gulped the rest. He opened the desk drawer to the Colt .44 revolver and set the gun on the desk.

Margaret.

He closed his eyes and sniffed the air, swearing he could smell her perfume lingering in the room.

Honeysuckle.

She had ordered it from Paris along with the blue silk gown she had worn. She had only been attempting to revive the carefree days of dances and parties before the war. Out of shame, he had given her the rose. Reopening his eyes, he brushed the remnants away.

He picked up the gun and fingered the trigger.

"George?" With a worried smile, Catherine entered the library. "There you are."

He stood, shoving the gun behind his back. *Too late.* She had seen it.

She clamped a hand over her mouth and muffled a cry. His nerve vanished, and he sank to the leather chair, returning the gun to the desktop. Her skirt rustled as she moved closer. She gripped the chair opposite him, and her knuckles turned as white as her face. "George . . ." Her voice wavered. "That's not the answer."

"I made a vow that I would love her forever."

"That was before the war. You've done everything possible to help her, but she's as much a casualty of war as those who fought and died."

He pondered her words, but nothing could absolve him from his shame. Margaret had found *him* with Catherine. He withdrew a crystal pendant on a gold chain from the desk drawer. "It's time that you reclaim what is rightfully yours."

"Are you certain?" Catherine reached across the desk and stroked his moustache with a finger, then clasped the chain in her hand. Tears entered her eyes as the crystal pendant caught the lamplight and cast a rainbow on the wall. "Now do me a favor." Swallowing hard, she held out her free hand. "Give me the gun."

George grasped the gun. "I carried one just like it during the war."

"I know. We'll put it away for safekeeping until you're feeling better."

Death was nothing new—only one more life to claim. But he relaxed his vise-like grip and pushed the gun across the desk.

"You have to stop feeling guilty for what's happened. It's not your fault."

"I wasn't here when she needed me, and I promised to never love another. Catherine . . ." His gaze met hers. "I think I knew when we first met that I loved you."

Catherine came around to his side of the desk and wrapped her arms around him. "What do you think you would have done to me if I had found you . . ." Her voice cracked.

Dead. She didn't need to say the word. He drew her on his lap and kissed her, realizing how close he had come to dying. He shuddered. Not since the war had he felt anything similar. No matter how much he had loved Margaret, he couldn't face his wife's melancholy state alone. In the air, he smelled the delicate scent of honeysuckle, and he was delighted that Catherine liked the same fragrance.

Chapter One

Near Charles City, Virginia
Late September 2004

RELIEVED TO BE RID OF BICKERING attorneys and whiny clients for five days, Christine Olson turned onto a paved country lane leading to the Cameron estate. Oak and pine canopied the path, guiding the way like heavenly arches. Trilling sparrows flitted among the brambles and shrubbery, and the red flash of a cardinal darted in front of the silver Integra. She was pleased to see the area had escaped the wrath of the recent hurricane and wondered how twisty, rural roads were more efficient than hour-long commutes on freeways.

After nearly a mile, the path narrowed to a single, graveled lane. The car hit a pothole and thumped. Swerving to avoid a downed tree, Chris brought the Integra to a halt. She got out and cursed at the flat left, front tire. Perhaps the area hadn't escaped totally unscathed from the storm after all. Still a couple of miles from her friend's house, she withdrew a cell phone from her purse to warn Judith that she'd be late. *Nothing.* She could have sworn the battery had been fully charged. Ringing phones all day at the office, and as soon as she found herself stranded in the middle of nowhere . . . She tapped the phone and tried again. *Dead.*

Should she walk or wait for help? The wind picked up in gusts, hinting at an evening cloudburst. As much as she disliked

the idea of being caught in the darkness alone, she liked the
thought of walking through a potential thunderstorm even less.

Resigned that someone would eventually come looking for
her, she returned to the Integra. After twenty minutes of waiting
and no sign of help, she tried the phone again. *Nothing.* Clouds
were building, and daylight faded in the western sky. Chris decided that she'd rather not wait all night and opened the car
door.

A classic red Mustang pulled up behind her. A blond-haired
man, with a very Southern-looking goatee and sparkling blue
eyes, rolled down the window and leaned out with a wave.
"Are you in need of some help, ma'am?"

Ma'am—Southern men certainly were polite. "I have a flat
tire and my cell phone is dead. If you could call the auto club, I
would be grateful."

But he was getting out of the car and walking toward her. A
very wolfish-looking black dog followed him. "There's no need
for an auto club. If you have a spare . . ."

Unable to imagine anyone stopping to help a stranded mo-
torist in Boston, she opened the trunk. "I'll pay you, of course."

He flashed a friendly smile and lifted out the jack. "That
won't be necessary."

The muscles in his arms bulged as he jacked up the car. She
surmised from his casual attire of a T-shirt and faded blue jeans
that he must be a hired hand for one of the estates. "Do you
work around here?"

Groaning, he loosened the lug nuts of the flat tire. "You could
say that."

The flat tire was on the ground and the spare, on the car. She
watched while he finished and lowered the car to the ground.
"Then you know the Camerons?"

"I do." He returned the jack to the trunk and wiped his dirty
hands on his jeans. "I'm Geoff."

Geoff Cameron. Why hadn't she realized? Feeling a tad foolish, she offered her hand. "You're Judith's brother. I'm . . ."

"Ms. Olson. Judith has mentioned you often."

As he shook her hand, she was drawn to his robust, masculine grip. "Please, call me Chris."

"Chris," he agreed. His hand lingered. Finally, he let go, and she cleared her throat. "Judith has spoken about you on occasion."

A devilish gleam entered his eyes. "All bad, I'm sure." Chris laughed. "As a matter of fact, she admires your horsemanship."

"She's never bothered to tell me that."

Another laugh. Chris pointed to the dog, which, appearing more like Geoff's shadow, was smaller than a wolf. "Who's your friend? He looks like a black coyote."

Geoff winced. "His name is Saber. He's a Belgian sheepdog or *Groenendael,* as they're called in Belgium."

A rare breed. She should have guessed a family like the Camerons wouldn't own a simple mutt. "I meant no insult."

Excited, the dog wagged his tail and barked. Geoff gave a hand signal, and Saber quieted and sat.

"Well trained, too."

"Chris," he said, becoming serious once more, "will you be able to make it to the house now? Judith is looking forward to seeing you, but I see we have yet another tree to worry about. Since it's on the road, I'll need to clear it before the storm moves in. We had a few trees down when Ivan came through."

The recent hurricane. "I hope things weren't too serious."

"Fortunately, most of it went north of here."

"That's good. Yes, I'll be fine. Thank you, for everything."

Giving her a dazzling smile that sent a shiver along her spine, he picked up the flat tire and put it into the trunk of his car. "I'll see this gets fixed." One more smile, and he climbed into the Mustang.

They had met before. But where? She couldn't recall.

"Geoff?" Foolish thinking. She waved a hand in dismissal, letting him know that it wasn't important. She got into the Integra, and the cell phone rang. *Odd*—she could have sworn it wasn't working. Even stranger, no one was there. The upcoming storm must have caused a glitch.

Chris put the car in gear and started forward again. Behind her, Geoff turned off onto a side road. The trees thinned, and black cattle grazed in a field. Although rural Virginia was great for a getaway, she was uncertain how anyone tolerated living in such isolation. She preferred the city's theaters and multitude of museums.

The road wound its way through another forest. Wind whipped in increasing gusts, and oak and sycamore trees swayed. At the top of a ridge, a zigzag rail fence lined the road. After several hundred yards, prancing bronze stallions atop brick pillars marked the lane. Green patina revealed the statues' age. A massive sign with a Colonial-looking script hung to the side—Poplar Ridge.

Turning onto a road lined with poplar trees, Chris traveled another mile before braking. White marble columns lined the portico at the lane's end. The three-story red brick mansion had adjoining two-story wings. Ivy climbed the bricks, and black shutters surrounded the windows of the graceful Georgian architecture. Aware that Judith's family possessed wealth, she hadn't realized just how much. Feeling even more foolish about asking Geoff if he was a hired hand, she let out a breath and released the brake. The drive circled to the front of the estate.

Arriving none too soon, she swung the door open as rain began to fall. She threw her jacket over her head and ran through drizzle to cascading steps. On the door hung a brass knocker in the shape of a horse head. Everything screamed of horses. But then, hadn't that been the cement that had tied her to Judith during college? The knocker barely dropped from her hand before Judith squealed with delight and drew her into a wooden-floored hall covered by a burgundy Persian wool rug. An immense hand-painted vase stood on one side of the entryway, and a bouquet of yellow flowers sat atop a Colonial table on the other. Halfway across the hall, a polished walnut staircase wound its way to the second floor.

After an exchange of hugs and greetings, Judith led the way down the hall.

Eighteenth-century oil portraits lined the walls. Eyes from the past followed Chris as if monitoring her movements. In the drawing room, flower and leaf designs encircled the plaster ceiling. Similar plaster moldings ran along the top and sides of the fireplace mantel. A warm fire invited her. Rubbing her hands, Chris held them over crackling flames.

Judith handed her a brandy snifter. "Here," she said in a soft Virginian accent, "the house gets drafty this time of year. This will warm you. I've told the cook to bring a late supper."

"That won't be necessary. I've already eaten." Chris sipped the amber liquid. It tingled her throat. "Judith, has it really been four years?"

"Five."

"Impossible." Chris wrinkled her nose in disbelief. "But you haven't changed."

Judith's heart-shaped face had retained her dimpled smile, but her blonde hair had been shoulder length in college. Now it stretched the length of her friend's back, down to her waist. *Five years?* How could she have let that much time slip away? She turned to set the brandy snifter down, but the fine red wood of the table made her hesitate. Genuine mahogany.

Judith motioned for her to have a seat, and Chris sank to the sofa. The tapestry covering with horses and hounds on a hunt seemed vaguely familiar. She traced a hand over it.

"How did we finally manage to get you down here, Chris? I've lost track of the times that I've invited you."

Chris glanced up from the tapestry design. "I finally got a break in my caseload."

Relaxing her shoulders, she settled back and told Judith about a hopeful promotion to senior associate at the law firm, as well as her unfortunate circumstances in meeting Geoff.

Judith traced a finger over her brandy snifter. With a feverish smile, she brought Chris up to date on the special man in her life. Just as they had during college, they once again shared their deepest secrets.

Swirling the amber liquid, Chris sipped from the snifter and gazed into the firelight. As the flames danced, they grew soothing. Almost hypnotized, she thought of a chilly autumn day after a carriage ride. A hot cup of apple cider, not brandy, was in her hand. A man sat beside her. His deep laugh reassured her, but his face ... His features remained hidden in the shadows, but she sensed a quiet male strength.

"Chris?" Judith snapped her fingers. "Are you all right?"

She blinked back the scene, and Judith's concerned face came into focus. "I'm fine. Why do you ask?"

"You looked lost."

Chris shrugged. "I guess I was. Sorry, Judith. You were saying?"

"Nothing important. Is something wrong?"

She shook her head. "But I was wondering if you still have the stallion Raven?"

Judith peered over the rim of her snifter. "Raven? We've never had a horse by that name."

Certain the horse would be here, Chris frowned. "A black stallion—he has a white star on his forehead. You've shown me a picture. He used to pull the carriage."

"Chris, you may have seen a picture, but it wasn't here. I only wish it were. He sounds wonderful."

"I could have sworn ..." Baffled, Chris settled back again. How could they have sold Raven? He might have been a bit of a rogue, but ... *But what?* Unable to finish the thought, she forced a smile. "I must have been thinking of someone else." Dismissing the idea with a wave, she said, "Never mind, it wasn't important."

"You're exhausted from the drive. If you're not hungry, why don't we call it a night? We'll go riding in the morning. I'll show you the stallions, and you'll see for yourself there's no black one."

Judith rose and led the way. Carpeting muffled the creak of the wood stairs. A porcelain lamp bathed the landing in light. Hand-painted gold birds fluttered across the base in an endless circle. For some reason, Chris imagined oil lamps. Yes, that was it—oil lanterns, and candles on special occasions. All of the rooms had been alighted in a brilliant blaze. Judith continued past the first door, but Chris stopped by the door to her left. A hint of a sweet floral fragrance lingered in the air.

"Chris, your room is over here."

Chris placed a hand to her head and blinked. *Where was she?* Poplar Ridge. "The trip must have been more tiring than I thought."

Judith went into the bedroom and switched on a light. Chris joined her. Her leather bag rested on the cedar chest at the foot of the canopy bed, and the sheets were turned down.

"Feel free to hang your things in the wardrobe or put them in the dresser. If there's anything else you need, let me know." Judith gestured to the door at the far corner near the fireplace. "The bathroom is across the corridor in my room, or if you prefer, you can use the one down the hall to the right. I'll warn you ahead of time, that's the one Geoff uses, so I won't vouch for its tidiness."

"I'll be fine," Chris replied with a laugh. After exchanging goodnights, she withdrew her toilet bag. The coarse, uneven wood of the dressing table suggested a homemade antique. A heavy-bodied mirror with horse heads hand carved in the frame was attached to the dresser. As she touched one, she imagined hot breath on her palm. An unknown sculptor had truly captured the horse's spirit.

The tired-looking woman in the mirror was another matter. A wrinkled blouse and tousled hair confirmed the day had indeed been a long one. She had better attend to necessities and get some sleep. Chris stepped into the corridor. A door across the way led to Judith's room. If she used the other bathroom, she just might run into Geoff again. Suddenly relishing the thought, she headed that way.

Several stairs guided the way down to the west wing. In the hall, mounted to wallpaper with a floral design, brass sconces lit the way. The frosted upright globes hinted they must have once been used as gas lamps. Chairs and tables blended into the wall like shadows, but she easily found the bathroom. At the opposite end, another door opened to a darkened room. *Geoff's room.* She resisted the temptation to peek and closed the door. Rumpled towels lay over the rim of the claw-footed bathtub. More towels and washcloths had been hastily thrown in the wicker hamper. A brown-tinted prescription bottle sat on the counter, and a ceramic crock filled with water for Saber was on the floor. Judith needn't have worried. The disarray wasn't overly problematic. At least the toilet seat was down.

Curious about the prescription, Chris reached for the brown bottle but withdrew her hand. She had come here hoping for the opportunity to see Geoff, not pry. As she brushed through her cinnamon-colored hair, she sensed someone behind her, staring intently. In the mirror, an outline of a reflection appeared. A man—the same man she had envisioned by the fireplace, only this time she could make out his features. His blond hair touched the top of his collar, and a moustache swept up slightly at the ends. His blue eyes were identical to Geoff's. Startled that he had entered without knocking, she spun around. *No one.*

Chris took a deep breath and returned her gaze to the mirror. The image had vanished. Either her imagination was working overtime, or the brandy had been extremely potent. Swiftly, she readied for bed and returned to her room. Pressures at work had caught up with her. After a good night's sleep, matters would seem clearer. Slipping beneath the bedclothes, she turned out the light and listened to the house creak in the wind. An hour of tossing and turning must have passed before she drifted.

Clad in a gray uniform, Geoff stood outside the red brick mansion. Extending an arm, he helped her from a carriage drawn by a large black horse. The hem of her light-blue, silk dress rustled against the brick walk. His firm, but gentle, hand caught her arm playfully and tugged her to his embrace. With a smile, he brushed his lips against hers and whispered in her ear, "I love you, Margaret."

Enveloped in darkness, Chris sat up with her heart racing. The dream had been incredibly real. A sweet fragrance lingered, like an expensive perfume. Sniffing the air, she tried placing the scent. She had smelled it earlier in the evening outside the other bedroom door. *Honeysuckle.*

She hopped out of bed. Beneath her bare feet, the wood floor felt cold. Breaking out in goose pimples, she donned a robe, went into the main hall, and knocked on the door to Judith's room.

Opening the door, her friend stifled a yawn. "What's wrong, Chris?"

With a shiver, she rubbed her arms. "I've had a weird dream."

Judith gently squeezed her arm. "You're in a strange place. Why don't we make some tea?"

Chris nodded, and Judith led the way to the east wing. Less lavish than the west wing, the walls were painted off white, and Chris surmised this section was the servants' quarters. The stairs wound down to the kitchen. In the new surroundings, Chris breathed easier. A long, unused hearth fireplace was the only sign of age. Soft fluorescent lighting had a calming effect, and the visions even seemed humorous and unreal.

After placing a copper kettle on the stove, Judith sat beside her at the butcher block table. "I think your difficulty sleeping goes beyond the long day. What's troubling you?"

Not surprising—even during college, Judith had the uncanny ability of seeing through her. "I'm not sure. It may sound strange, but ever since arriving, I've had the feeling of déjà vu. Even Geoff, it's like I should know him. I regret not visiting before now."

The kettle whistled. Judith poured water into rose-patterned china cups and dunked the tea bags. She brought the steaming cups to the table. "You've refused my invitations."

"There was always something going on, and I never found the time." Chris blew on the tea, then cautiously took a sip. With a laugh, she added, "But now I seem to be working overtime dreaming up ghost stories."

Judith's eyes widened. "Ghosts?"

Clapping a hand over her mouth, Chris snickered. "Judith, you never told me that you believed in ghosts."

"I don't," Judith responded, becoming indignant. "Still, I have seen some mighty strange things around here."

"What sort of things?"

"Another time. I doubt my tales of unusual happenings will help you sleep."

"You're right, and I'm fine now." With Judith on her heels, Chris made her way to the stairs. Unlike the main stairway, these steps were cloaked in darkness and they creaked—almost groaned—with age. Barely able to see a hand's length in front of her, she stumbled but caught her balance. She should have let Judith lead. They passed through an unused bedroom to reach the main hall. A light cast the landing in shadows, and another flight of stairs led the way to a third story. "Judith, where do those stairs lead?"

"To the third floor. There are a couple of bedrooms up there, but we use them for storage now. I don't think anyone's been up there in years. When I was little, I used it as a play area. You'd probably find some of my toys still up there. It does have a spectacular view of the grounds and river. I'll show it to you before you leave."

Chris looked forward to seeing the view. As she glanced up the stairway, a chilling breeze ruffled her hair. She was drawn to it. Something or someone awaited her. Without thinking, she placed a hand on the banister and took a step up. Judith tapped her on the shoulder, reminding her that it was the middle of the night.

Yawning, Chris nodded. Exhaustion had gotten the best of her. Yet she was unable to move. *Exhaustion*, she silently repeated to herself.

As she was about to turn away, the breeze swept through her hair again. A man whispered in her ear. She easily recognized the voice as belonging to the man in her dream. His little prank had gone too far. Chris whirled around to confront him. But only Judith was there.

Judith blinked in confusion. "Chris?"

Determined to find him, she scanned the hall, wondering where he could have disappeared to so quickly. Maybe he had slipped into a nearby room. Certainly Judith had seen him, but her friend kept staring at her, blinking. She had better not bring the incident to Judith's attention. It would only give her added cause for concern. "Never mind. Shouldn't we be getting some sleep?"

"An excellent idea," Judith agreed.

By the door to her room, Chris glanced to the staircase leading to the third floor. Though his words were unintelligible, the man spoke. *Not real*, she told herself. She bid Judith goodnight. Shutting the door behind her, she groaned in frustration. While Judith may believe in ghosts, she didn't. Could Geoff have been playing some sort of trick? She hated puzzles with no answers—mysterious ones even less. Without switching off the light, she jumped beneath the sheets. No further dreams disturbed her.

The grandfather clock in the hall struck twelve times. In the drawing room, Geoff stood near the fire. Relieved the long day was finally over, he poured a cup of tea and rubbed his eyes.

"Geoff . . . "

Judith stood by the doorway in a pink robe with matching threadbare slippers. He suppressed a laugh. "I wish your pompous boyfriend could see the lady of the house now."

She arched an eyebrow. "Leave David out of this. You don't look so great yourself, but then you never do."

"It's chilly out there." He rubbed his hands together for emphasis.

Dropping the sisterly jabbing, she continued, "The storm came up about the same time Chris arrived."

"I met her. It's good that she got here when she did. There are flash flood warnings now." He took another sip from a mug. "You obviously have more on your mind than the weather."

Judith edged closer, then upon seeing Saber curled on the sofa, her face reddened. "I wish you wouldn't let the dog on the furniture. Saber!" She pointed to the padded dog bed in the corner. Tucking his tail, Saber hopped from the tapestry sofa and slunk over to the bed. "Geoff, you know I don't like him up there. His nails catch on the fabric."

Geoff hung an apologetic head. "Okay, I'm appropriately reprimanded. What's on your mind?"

All too aware that he wasn't sorry, she scrunched her face in annoyance. Her expression faded, and she took a deep breath. "Have you noticed anything unusual?"

"Unusual?"

Judith swallowed noticeably. "Umm . . . you know . . ."

"No," he answered a little more abruptly than he had intended. He cleared his throat. "Why?"

She shook her head. "It's not important. By the way, Chris told me about her little adventure. Thanks for helping her."

Geoff nodded, and Judith giggled. "Heaven knows why, but I think she likes you."

With a sarcastic laugh, Geoff winked. "It must be my charm."

"Brothers," Judith hissed.

Now he had her really riled and couldn't resist upping the stakes a little more. "Then you shouldn't mind if I ask her out to dinner one of these evenings. I've heard about Northern girls being wild women with loose morals."

"Geoff!" She raised a finger in protest. "I expect you to be on your best behavior."

He held up a hand in Scout's honor. "Best behavior."

"And get that smirk off your face."

His smile faded. "You needn't worry, sis. I can't think of anything I might have in common with a city girl."

"Geoff . . ."

He overheard her mutter something about insufferable brothers on her way from the drawing room. With another laugh, he placed his empty mug on the mantel and caught a whiff of honeysuckle. Geoff sucked in his breath. God, he hated that scent and had hoped to never smell it again. A warning— sickeningly sweet to the point of intoxication. *Get a grip.* He checked Saber for a reaction. Unmoving, the dog sprawled upside down on his padded bed. This delicate fragrance wasn't like before, but more like a woman's perfume. A logical explanation. He breathed out in relief. Judith must have bought a new perfume.

* * *

Raindrops tapped against glass as Chris stared at the gray fog hanging over the area. While horseback riding might be out of the question on such a dismal day, the dull morning would be a perfect opportunity to explore the mansion. Perhaps, even the third floor. Suddenly cold, she wondered why the upper story made her uneasy.

Breathing deeply, Chris dressed in a plain brown, calf-length skirt and matching jacket. Business casual. *Ugh.* She had promised herself to leave work at home. Attempting to smooth travel wrinkles from her skirt, she sighed in resignation. It hadn't helped much. She opened the door as Judith was about to knock.

An exchange of greetings masked Chris's low spirit, and as Judith showed her to the dining room, Chris grew absorbed in the surroundings. The crystal chandelier accented glass in the china cabinet, and oil paintings of the Virginia countryside decorated the walls. An African American maid seated her at the massive oak dining table. Freshly cut pink and white flowers brightened the room. "Do you have breakfast like this every morning?" Chris whispered across the table.

"Only on special occasions and when we have guests."

"I'm honored." Chris unfolded her napkin. As she smoothed the linen across her lap, she noticed the fragrances of honeysuckle and bacon. Her mouth watered as she tried to recall the last time she had eaten such a forbidden treat.

But a familiar masculine laugh from across the table distracted her. Her heart ached. He would be leaving soon. Perhaps, they could go riding later in the day. At the cottage, she would surrender to him in a tearful goodbye.

Chris blinked the image away to Judith's frown. A fanciful daydream—that could be the only explanation. "Sorry. I was thinking about the case I'm working on." The honeysuckle had all but faded. She hated resorting to lies to keep her friend from thinking she had gone crazy. She leaned forward and asked, "Have you started wearing a new perfume?"

"No. Why do you ask?"

"I thought I smelled honeysuckle." With a shrug, Chris shook her head. "It wasn't important." She settled back. "A rest in the country is exactly what I need."

A tall man, wearing a russet blazer, strode into the room. His straight stance and broad-shouldered frame reminded Chris of a sixtyish Geoff with striking gray hair.

"Chris," Judith said, "I'd like you to meet my father. Daddy, my friend from college, Chris Olson."

Judith's father held out a hand. "Winston Cameron."

Chris shook his hand. "A pleasure to meet you, sir."

The maid that had seated her popped in carrying a silver tray, while Judith's father seated himself at the head of the table. "Judith tells me that you had some difficulty prior to your arrival yesterday."

"I had a flat tire." The maid set a plate on Chris's linen place mat. "Fortunately, Geoff happened by and helped me."

"That explains why he was late returning from Richmond yesterday."

Surprised by the elder Cameron's gruff response, Chris detected she had touched on a father/son conflict. She glanced at her plate. *No bacon.* Puzzled, she looked at Judith's plate. Ham, eggs, biscuits, but no bacon. Winston Cameron's plate held the same fare. But she had smelled bacon. Slicing some ham, she reasoned the bacon must have been burned. A perfectly good reason—there was no need to get bent out of shape.

She reached for her water glass and took a sip, when Geoff entered the dining room. *His face.* His hair was shorter, and he had a goatee instead of a simple moustache. But there was no mistaking his identity. His face was the same one she had seen in the mirror. Choking back water, she clenched the glass to keep from dropping it.

He rushed to her side. Catching her breath, Chris waved that she was fine. His dazzling blue eyes—their familiarity was uncanny.

"Are you all right?" he asked.

"Yes." Her voice rasped, and she cleared her throat. "Fine . . . yes, thank you." *His eyes.* Her heart fluttered, but she couldn't stop thinking about the dream. *Get a hold of yourself, Chris.* After he had helped her with the tire, her mind must have conjured up the dream. Satisfied with the explanation, she recovered and said, "You seem to have a habit of catching me at awkward moments."

"As long as you're fine, that's all that matters." He sat across from her.

She had never dreamed that a Southern drawl could be downright sexy. The warmth in her cheeks warned her that she must be blushing. With a giddy tingle, Chris felt more like a teenager. Stealing a glance at Geoff, she recalled the strength of his grip. Calloused hands suggested he wasn't afraid of hard, manual labor, like changing a tire. Yet, she couldn't shake the feeling they had met before. Not yesterday, but in another place. She envisioned his arms around her and him kissing her deeply. *His strong but gentle hand traced along her bare side . . .*

Chris shook her head before the fantasy played out. As if reading her mind, Geoff smiled. Every muscle in her body froze. His eyes locked onto hers and held her captive. She swore he must be able to read her mind. Certainly, he must feel the attraction. She had no doubt that her body language betrayed her.

Finally, she blinked, and the spell was broken. Judith nodded knowingly. No longer hungry, Chris smiled to herself and picked at her breakfast. Perhaps she could arrange a few moments alone with Geoff during her visit.

Chapter Two

AFTER BREAKFAST, JUDITH GAVE Chris a tour of the house. Overwhelmed by its sheer size, Chris lost count after five bedrooms and at least an equal number of bathrooms. Her friend ran the entire household with only the help of a cook and the maid she had met earlier, and as Chris had guessed the previous evening, the servants' quarters were in the east wing on the second floor above the kitchen and breakfast room. The main section of the house included the dining and drawing rooms, as well as a formal reception room and parlor.

In the far west wing, Judith opened the door to the library. "Until Daddy retired, this is where he spent most of his time." Bookcases full of hardcover books lined the walls. "Most of the ledgers from before the War Between the States were destroyed, but all accounts since then are in here or stored away for safe-keeping." Judith giggled. "There's even mention of moonshine during Prohibition."

War Between the States—Chris had only half believed the stories that the Civil War was alive and well in the South. The massive desk with acorn carvings was made of fine oak. The modern computer with a flat-panel monitor sitting on the highly polished surface spoiled her image of Geoff attending to paper-work in the black leather chair. "Does Geoff use this room as well?"

"Usually in the evenings. He has a more hands-on approach to farm operations than Daddy ever did, so you'll tend to find him outside during the day."

When Chris touched the chair's worn leather, it molded around her fingertips.

"Go ahead. Sit in it, if you like."

Chris swiveled the chair around and eased in. It creaked under her weight, and she smelled the strong, masculine scent of aged leather. She visualized a woman writing in a slow, even hand, addressing an envelope in a fancy old-style script.

"Chris?"

She looked up at Judith's bewildered face. "Sorry, I was lost in thought. You were saying?"

"I wasn't saying anything. I grew concerned when you became distant again."

Leaning back, Chris ran a hand along the desk's wood grain. "I'm overwhelmed. I've never seen anything as elaborate as this house."

"I've shown you pictures."

"Pictures can't do a place like this justice. And I certainly don't remember any of your brother. Why have you been keeping him a secret?"

"Secret? Geoff? I only wish I could hide him away somewhere."

Mildly amused, Chris leaned forward. "Until yesterday, I thought chivalry was dead." She snuggled in the chair once more. "Besides, he has a nice butt."

Judith merely laughed. "I can't say that I've ever thought of him in that manner, but I did notice how you kept stealing looks."

"Okay, so what's wrong with him? All of the nice guys are either married or gay."

Judith held up three fingers. "Try divorced for *three* excruciatingly long years, and I'm reasonably certain that he's not the latter."

"Now you're playing matchmaker."

Judith batted her lashes in a wide-eyed, innocent routine. "You didn't say you were dating anyone."

"I'm not." If she could arrange an evening out with Geoff, it would lend her the perfect opportunity to speak with him alone.

She envisioned his arms around her and their partially clad bodies pressed together. His kisses on her bare skin tingled, while his hand moved with agonizing slowness along her inner thigh. Swallowing hard, she blinked back the image. Chris shook her head furiously. "No, Judith, it's a bad idea. It wouldn't be right. After all, he *is* your brother."

"It's *already* worse than I thought. You meant for him to notice you during breakfast." Judith's mouth formed a sly grin. "So why should the fact that he's my brother make a difference?"

"Because it could lead to awkward situations." Chris stood. "Let's continue the tour."

In silence, they stepped into the hall. True, it had been several years since she had been seriously involved with anyone. Geoff's hand moved from her thigh, touching her in the way she liked. Chris suppressed a laugh. She was horny—for Judith's brother, no less.

"Chris, if I intruded where I shouldn't have, I apologize. I only thought for the short time you'd be here, you might be good for one another. From everything you've said, or elected not to say, you haven't been serious with anyone since Dan from college." Chris nodded that Judith had guessed correctly, and her friend continued, "Geoff would kill me if he knew I was telling you this, but the divorce took a couple of years to settle. I just thought with you being here, you might get him out of the house and socialize a little."

"If the divorce was that messy, then money or kids must have been involved."

Judith produced an angry scowl. "Both. Beth eagerly takes the support money, but we rarely see Neal. It just goes to show that sometimes you don't know a person as well as you think. I thought of her as a sister." A smile returned to her face. "Never mind our family strife. I want your stay to be relaxing."

Relaxing, *indeed*. At least Geoff wasn't married, but he did have a son. Wondering about the circumstances, Chris kept quiet. She hadn't visited to poke her nose where it didn't belong. A numbing cold seized her as it had the previous evening.

With a shiver, Chris hugged herself. She glanced around, checking to see where they were. Off to the right, the flight of stairs led to the third floor. She pointed.

"There won't be much of a view today."

"I'd still like to see it." Chris touched the banister. *See—no ghosts or goblins.* She gripped the rail, and an icy chill radiated from her hand through the rest of her body. She hesitated. *Coward.* The nip could be chalked up to a drafty, old house. She forced herself to take a step. There—she was feeling more like her old self. But the chill remained, like deathly fingers touching her neck. What could be making her feel this way? She'd never been the nervous sort before.

Chris blew out a breath and collected herself. At the top, Judith had arrived by the door. Forcing her feet forward, Chris pushed on. Judith swung the wood door open. As it creaked on ancient hinges, a smell of must rushed out. They went into the room.

Toys lay scattered on the floor. At the sight of a doll with a missing arm, a reminiscent smile crept to Judith's face. Beside the door was a full-length mirror and a covered sofa. Storage crates were stacked in the far corner. Nothing—absolutely nothing—was out of the ordinary.

A round, multipaned window overlooked neatly manicured grounds. Judith had been correct. The view was dismal on such a gray day. Fog blanketed the river and grounds. From the stable area, Chris heard a neigh. Peculiar—why would anyone be riding on such a miserable day? Her heart pounded, and she edged up on tiptoes. Hoping to see further, she craned her neck but saw nothing. Convinced her mind was playing tricks again, Chris relaxed.

Out of the mist, a black horse galloped across the grounds carrying a man in some sort of gray uniform. He brought the horse to a sliding halt and let it graze on seeding grass. He looked her way. *Geoff.* No, this man had longer hair and a moustache. A smile crossed his face, and he reached out. "Margaret."

He said the name again, and Chris ducked away from the window. Short of breath, she jabbed a finger at the window. "Judith . . ."

Judith rushed over and looked out. "I don't see anything."
"I saw Geoff riding Raven." Bolting for the stairs, she'd
prove once and for all that she hadn't imagined all of these
weird events. Geoff was outside with Raven.

By the door, Judith caught her elbow and drew her back.
"Chris, Geoff had business in Richmond this morning. And I've
already told you there's no stallion by the name of Raven."

"But he's outside on a black horse." Pointing to the window,
she turned back. No Geoff . . . or black stallion. The grass was
neatly mowed. "I could have sworn . . ."

Hysterical—she had become a sniveling, whiny female. Re-
pulsed by the image, she concluded that she was losing it. Work
hassles hadn't been troubling her *this* much. Suddenly light-
headed, she placed a hand to her temple. "I don't know what's
come over me, but ever since arriving, strange things have been
happening. You said there were ghosts."

Her friend's face paled. "The only ghost I've ever seen has
been a Civil War soldier."

Calm now, Chris agreed, "That's him. He was wearing Confederate gray."

"The ghost I've seen doesn't look anything like Geoff," Judith said, swallowing hard. "You'll never forget him if you see
him. He's missing an eye. Poplar Ridge was a Union field hospital during the war. I presume he was wounded in battle."

Her explanation certainly sounded plausible. "Then it's possible there might be other Civil War ghosts?"

"It's possible, but I haven't seen any. It also doesn't explain
why this one looks like Geoff."

"True. Give me some time, and I'll figure it out."

"I'm sure you will," Judith responded with a relieved smile.

"Ghosts," Chris muttered. "I've never even considered the
possibility they existed before."

"This old house has that effect on a lot of people."

Chris debated whether that particular thought was comforting. As they strolled toward the door, she spotted an old-
fashioned wardrobe. Odd—she hadn't noticed it before. Horse
heads with flowing manes were etched in the surface. A chilling

breeze brushed her face. She reached out, but her hand stopped in midair. "Judith?"

"Nothing's in there." Judith stepped in front and opened the wardrobe. "See, there's nothing but old clothes."

Chris searched through them. Long skirts and bodices with matching pagoda sleeves, shawls, capes, and . . . a light-blue silk dress. Her knees weakened, but she kept her composure. "Judith . . ." With glistening white pearls sewn to the bodice, the dress hung in the wardrobe. "It's the same dress as in my dream."

A branch scraping the window woke Chris from a troubled sleep. Visions of the day's events kept replaying through her mind. *Dreams,* she reminded herself. *They were only dreams.* But how could she have envisioned an elegant ball gown down to every detail?

Throwing off the bedclothes, Chris wandered over to the window. In the wind gusts, the branch scratched the glass. Irritated with the sound, she went over to the heavy-bodied mirror. Dark circles had formed under her eyes. She would have been better off remaining in Boston, listening to her bald-headed boss harp about briefs that she was supposed to conjure up by the snap of her fingers.

Chris resisted the urge to crawl back under the covers. Besides, the mystery intrigued her. Certain there had to be a logical explanation, she changed into a dressy pair of pants with a sheer yellow blouse and matching scarf. She brushed her hair and dabbed makeup under her eyes to hide the bags. If she hurried, she might be able to speak with Geoff before dinner.

Comforted by the thought, Chris went into the hall. Empty. For some odd reason, she had been expecting someone. Geoff? The porcelain lamp with birds circling the base cast the landing in shadows. Suddenly, she held doubts. She looked up and down the stairs to make certain she was alone.

Convinced no bogeyman lurked behind any closed doors, she made her way down the stairs. At the bottom, the pint-sized maid by the name of Laura advised her to check the drawing room for Judith. Snuggled in a wing chair by the fire, Judith sat reading *R is for Ricochet*.

Her friend smiled a warm welcome. "You look more rested. Geoff phoned a few minutes ago. One of the mares injured herself, and he won't be in until after the vet arrives. Daddy says he'll join us, though."

A frown formed before Chris could suppress it.

With a growing grin, Judith closed the book. "Obviously you were hoping Geoff would be here."

"I had hoped to speak with him," Chris admitted.

"No more black horses?"

Chris shook her head.

"At least that much is good. Don't worry, Geoff will be here, and I bet he knows a remedy or two that will keep you from worrying about any ghosts; but first, shall we have dinner?"

"Judith," Chris chastised, "I merely wish to speak to him to see if he knows anything about the mysterious happenings."

Judith snickered. "Whatever you say."

Well aware what Judith was hinting at, Chris sighed and followed her to the dining room. A simple evening out would leave her unsatisfied. Once she was in his arms, his eyes would sparkle in approval as he traced a strong, calloused finger over her lips before kissing her. His free hand touched and fondled. Startled by her intense attraction, Chris forced the vision away. She certainly couldn't share such details with Judith.

After dinner, Winston Cameron stood in front of the fire and poured snifters of brandy. During the meal, Chris had decided that she had mistaken his earlier gruffness. He was actually quite polite, and she couldn't help but notice his pride when he spoke about Poplar Ridge. She sat on the sofa and sipped her drink. As flames sputtered and crackled, her whole body relaxed.

More than an hour passed, and the grandfather clock in the hall struck ten. The elder Cameron set his snifter on an end table and gave a slight bow. "If you ladies don't mind, I'd like to bid you goodnight."

Goodnights circled the room, and Chris stifled a yawn. "I think I'll retire as well."

Judith motioned for her to stay put. "He'll be here."

"You're taking my wish to speak with him out of context." Chris relented and sat back, occasionally glancing at the door. The clock chimed eleven. She drained her brandy snifter and stood. "Judith . . ." Unable to keep the yawns at bay, she covered her mouth as a black dog with pointed ears trotted into the drawing room. Geoff was close behind. Unless he had a twin, he was definitely the same man she had seen on the grounds earlier in the day. No two people could look that much alike. Determined to find answers, she reseated herself.

Judith greeted him, then placed her brandy snifter on the mahogany table. "If the two of you don't mind . . ." Stretching her arms, she yawned. "I'll retire. It's been a long day."

Leaving the room, Judith shot a wicked glance over her shoulder. Alone—she was finally alone with Geoff. Unable to look at him, she shifted in her seat. What should she say? If she started a conversation by mentioning the day's events, he would think she was stark, raving mad.

Geoff saved her the bother. "Would you like another brandy, Chris?"

"Please." He poured amber liquid into the snifter. "Thank you." As she took a sip, she summoned the courage to look in his direction. His blue eyes were smiling—familiar, yet different. She reverted her gaze to the brandy snifter. "Saber doesn't seem to leave your side," Chris said, taking great care to keep her voice even.

The dog sat at Geoff's feet and stared attentively up at him. "Rarely."

"I'm sorry that I said he looked like a coyote."

Geoff made a quick motion with his hand, and Saber trotted over to the dog bed. "No harm done."

"And how is your mare?"

"She'll be fine. Something spooked her and she put a leg through a fence."

With his casual manner, Chris felt her muscles relax. She finally got the courage to look up. He had a knowing smile, and his eyes were definitely laughing. *Damn him!* He was enjoying her discomfort. Determined not to surrender to nerves, she took a deep breath and met his gaze.

His smile faded, but he continued to study her. For a brief moment, she sensed a similar familiarity. Could the feeling be mutual? She dared not hope. Finally, he poured mineral water for himself and began speaking about farm life. Before long, she was telling him about the hectic pace of Boston and her career.

The clock chimed midnight. She needed to steer the conversation to the strange events before it got much later and took a sip of brandy for strength. "Judith tells me the house has ghosts."

"Ghosts?" He laughed. "Did she mention any by name?"

"Geoff, I'm serious."

He stopped laughing. "I wouldn't think a sophisticated career woman such as yourself would believe in apparitions."

"I'm curious about old legends," she responded nonchalantly.

He was silent a moment before speaking. "During the war, the house was used as a field hospital."

"Yes, the Civil War. Judith mentioned it."

That condescending smile of his was back. "We prefer to call it the War of Northern Aggression here."

He was attempting to get a reaction from her. Time was too precious to indulge him in any sparring. "Then there are legends from the war?"

"They're not just legends."

For some reason, his words made her shiver. "Have you seen the ghosts?"

"Ghosts, spirits, whatever you want to call them. They're here."

Ghosts—plural. Uncertain whether he was teasing her or telling the truth, Chris continued, "Are there any legends surrounding a woman by the name of Margaret?"

He stared at her as if not really seeing her.

"Geoff?"

He blinked. "Did Judith mention Margaret?"

Her heart raced. She was onto something. "In passing."

"Margaret is our great-, several times removed, grand-mother."

Attempting to give a calm appearance, she leaned back and crossed her legs. "Can you tell me about her?"

"Why the interest?"

Suspicion registered in his voice. She may have pushed her luck. "Never mind, it wasn't important. Forget that I brought the subject up." Chris set the empty brandy snifter on the mahogany table. "It's late. Goodnight."

She stood and came face-to-face with Geoff. His eyes suddenly held her captive. The reflection in the mirror had an upswept moustache. Chris caught her breath. From the moment she had met him on the road, she was drawn to him and wanted him to look further.

An amused smile crossed his face. He knew. Damn him, not only was he aware of the attraction, but he took pleasure in the situation. "I think there was more that you wanted to tell me."

Suddenly annoyed by his cockiness, Chris held her ground. "Is this where I'm supposed to bat my eyelashes like some demure Southern belle and pretend my will is no longer my own?"

His grin widened. "You don't strike me as the sort befitting of such a role."

Her hands went to her hips. "And what role do you think would be more appropriate?"

Geoff held up a hand in a truce. "I think I had better take the Fifth, counselor."

As he lowered his hand, Chris thought he might kiss her. His gaze remained fixed on her face as if he struggled to keep his eyes from wandering the length of her body. The attraction *was* mutual. She reseated herself on the sofa. "A wise choice."

He sat beside her. "I meant no offense. You acted like you wanted to talk about something."

So, he had reverted to the Southern gentleman. She ached to tell him everything—the house's familiarity, the third floor, the silk dress, and the black stallion, Raven. Unable to keep quiet any longer, she blurted out the whole story, carefully omitting the detail of the ghost that looked exactly like him.

As he listened, his leg brushed against hers. She wanted him to touch further. His hands would be strong, but gentle beneath her blouse.

Geoff's brow furrowed in confusion. "I don't know whether this makes you feel any better, but the only ghosts I know about are soldiers."

His remark was similar to what Judith had said. His leg remained in contact with hers, and she envisioned the shift of his weight atop her. She swallowed hard and blinked back the image. "Can you tell me about Margaret?"

"There's not much to tell. She married my grandfather, and they obviously had a son to carry on the family name."

There had to be more to the story. Was he withholding the information or did he truly not know? Collected again, she inquired further, "Did she live during the Civil War?"

"Margaret helped with the wounded when the Yanks—I mean, Union—occupied the area."

"*Yanks.*" She giggled. "I thought the war was over."

He smiled slightly. "Southerners have a long memory. There was more that you wanted to ask?"

"Do you know anything else that might explain what's been happening to me?"

He shook his head. "No. You might want to ask Judith about Margaret, but most of the records before the war were lost."

Frustrated that she had reached a dead end, Chris pondered his words. At least, she hadn't gone completely insane. There had been a Margaret. "Thank you for your help. Now if you don't mind, I'll be returning to my room."

"Of course." Geoff stood. "I didn't mean to keep you up so late."

Holding out a hand, he helped her to her feet. As she had known, his grip commanded strength. His hand lingered.

"Goodnight," she said.

His hand fell to his side, but his smile returned. "Goodnight, Chris."

The whisper of her name caressed her cheek as if he had touched her there. She needed to keep her wits, or she'd wind up in bed with him. The last thing she wanted was to complicate her life by sleeping with her best friend's brother. When she turned, she felt his gaze follow. Quickening her pace, Chris rushed into the hall and shot a glance back to the drawing room.

With the water glass in hand, Geoff remained standing in front of the fire. Staring at the flames, he was probably trying to make sense of her outlandish stories. She had been foolish to trust him—all due to a physical attraction. *What next?* Throwing herself at his feet and begging him to ravish her body? That thought made her snicker.

As if detecting her stare, Geoff looked in her direction and smiled curiously. He stepped toward her. Turning swiftly, Chris hustled up the stairs. She continued past her room until reaching the stairway to the the third floor. Her only solid clue to the mystery was the silk dress hanging in the wardrobe. At the top of the stairs, she cracked the door open and searched for a light switch.

Barely cutting through the darkness, a naked light bulb flickered on. She went over to the wardrobe and searched for the ball gown, locating it among the musty clothes. The blue silk shimmered. More than a century old, the handmade lace and pearls on the bodice had yellowed, yet its elegance remained intact. She pressed the dress against her body and started to dance across the floor.

After much thought, Geoff left the empty water glass on the mantel. Chris didn't seem like the type of woman who would ordinarily give into hallucination. Uncertain what to make of her story, he hoped he hadn't given himself away. While they sat on the sofa together, there had been a distinct tension—more like a rush of hormones on his part. He thought about her asleep in the guest room. So close, but Judith would serve his head on a platter if he touched Chris.

Was Chris's nervousness due to a mutual feeling or the strange events? At any rate, she would be returning to Boston soon, never to be heard from again. How long had Judith said Chris was visiting? A few days? He thought of her naked. It was going to be a hell of a long week, so he had better take a cold shower and clear his head.

A feminine voice called his name. *Chris?* As he was about to respond, the scent of honeysuckle filled the room. Goddamn it—not honeysuckle. Judith's perfume, he reminded himself, but she was nowhere to be seen. The fragrance grew stronger, but Saber remained curled on his bed. He now knew the scent would lead him to Chris.

The ball had been a magnificent occasion. Every man had shared a dance with her, but she enjoyed waltzing with her husband the most. When he led her to the dance floor, no other couple existed. His gentle smile was what she lived for. Tipping her head, she sniffed the rose he had given her before the dance. Placing it in front of the heavy-bodied mirror, she smiled at his reflection and whispered his name.

Geoff called her name. With a blue dress pressed against her body, Chris kept staring at the full-length mirror. "Chris, are you all right?" he repeated.

The scent of honeysuckle grew stronger. All this time, Chris was the source of the sweet fragrance. Drawn to it, he resisted the urge to take her into his arms. She traced a finger along the lace of the gown, then threw an arm around his neck and kissed him on the lips. Surprised but pleased with the reaction, he drew her closer.

She stepped back. When she finally spoke, her voice was barely a whisper. "It's made of the finest imported silk, but the dance is over." Her hand moved to return the dress to the wardrobe.

The honeysuckle. A warning bell rang in his head. He must leave, but with Chris here... Under the faint light, flecks of green glittered in her brown eyes. Her hair fell to her shoulders in a wavy, untamed wildness. He longed to kiss her full lips more intimately. Geoff grasped the hanger. "It would look better with you wearing it."

"I'll put it on if you promise not to peek." Chris waved for him to turn his back. "Promise?"

With a nod, he turned around. A sheer blouse fell at his feet, then a pair of pants. A lacy bra. His body reacted, but he resisted the temptation to look. He heard a rustle.

"You can help me now."

Swallowing hard, Geoff turned. Faced away from him, Chris held up her hair with the dress opened down the back. He reached for the pearl buttons. Instead, he brushed her bare skin. She straightened. He kissed her back and ran his fingers through her hair, catching the soft scent of wildflowers as he did so.

Her breath quickened, and she faced him in a low-cut gown, without revealing cleavage.

He hadn't misinterpreted her signals. She wanted him to touch her. More than willing to oblige, he cradled her head and bent down to kiss her. As he probed the depths of her mouth with his tongue, his right hand stroked the sloping curve of her neck. The silk fabric spread taut across her erect nipples. His pulse raced. He lowered the gown to her waist, exploring velvety skin with his lips and tongue.

"Geoff..." Through the denim of his jeans, Chris stroked his groin.

The soft fragrance of honeysuckle drifted over him. With every breath the scent intensified, almost to the point of intoxication, yet no less alluring. Only aware of the woman in his arms who had shown every indication of wanting him, he lifted her chin. Her lips parted. As he kissed her, he thought of the cottage. Away from the main house, no one would discover them. "Catherine," he whispered in her ear.

Chris struggled against his hold, but his arms remained locked around her. "This isn't right."

He didn't want to let go.

"Geoff, you're hurting me."

The scent vanished with her plea, but his head continued to spin. Gulping for air, she quickly covered her breasts and stood transfixed.

He loosened his grip. "I'm sorry. I thought..." He wasn't positive what he had thought.

"You called me Catherine. Did Judith tell you my middle name?"

"Your middle name? No, Judith never said..." As his head began to clear, he shook it, hoping that it would help. Still light-headed, he knew he couldn't look at Chris. If he did, his desire for her would return. The scent of honeysuckle returned. He had ignored the warning and could feel it now. "Chris..."

"Don't say anything."

She placed a hand on his arm. He closed his eyes. Her touch was no longer sexual, but he couldn't move.

"I'm leaving. Will you be all right?"

Stray thoughts flashed through his mind. The cottage... and a woman with light-brown hair. Unable to catch his breath, he felt the honeysuckle smother him alive.

"Geoff?"

Lights sparked, and a wave of darkness captured him.

Chapter Three

AN EMPTY STARE CROSSED GEOFF'S FACE, and he swayed on his feet. Something was wrong—terribly wrong. "Geoff!" Chris reached for his arm, missed it, and he collapsed to the wooden floor with a thud. She called his name again.

His muscles quivered violently, and his eyes rolled up in his head while his body writhed.

Was he having a stroke? A heart attack? A seizure? She had never witnessed a seizure. Should she run for help? Or stay with him? What if he didn't come out of it? "Geoff..."

Helpless to do anything but watch, she stayed by his side. The spasms continued. No, she wasn't helpless. She rolled her blouse and placed it under his head. At least, if he had injured himself in the fall, there would be no further harm. A minute passed. *When would it end?* Another long minute. He groaned, and his frantic thrashing finally ceased. Thank God, his breathing was returning to normal.

"I'll get help," Chris said, attempting to sound calm.

His hand wrapped loosely around her wrist. "No," he gasped.

"But you had a..."

"I..." He swallowed. "...know."

"Are you hurt? What can I do to help?"

The grip on her wrist remained, and he laid his head to the floor. "Tell me... where I am."

"The third floor."

"What?"

"Geoff, you're not making much sense. I should get help."

His grip tightened. "No... I'll be... fine." As if trying to prove his point, he sat up. None too steady, he tried getting to his feet.

"At least let me help you." Chris drew his arm over her shoulder. Thankfully, he gave no further protests and accepted her aid. With her help, he stood. Though he was wobbly, they made it to the door. She thought about her clothes strewn across the floor and decided that she'd retrieve them later. She hoped that, in Geoff's groggy state, he remembered nothing about their interlude.

Geoff braced against the banister for the stairs, and she tightened her embrace around his waist. Bearing the brunt of his weight, she took one small step at a time. The going was slow, but they reached the landing. Instead of cutting through her room to get to the hallway in the wing, she halted beside her bed. He slumped and promptly fell asleep.

His breathing was even, and she pressed a hand to her chest in relief. Now was her opportunity to return the silk dress to the third floor and recover her clothes. But as she turned, she worried he might suffer another seizure. She couldn't leave, not until she was certain he would be all right.

Chris drew a blanket over him, then sat in the rocking chair beside the bed, carefully monitoring his every move. Her hands trembled. The seizure had frightened her so much that she hadn't had time to think. Maybe Geoff had epilepsy. He seemed aware of the fact that he had a seizure. Judith had never mentioned epilepsy in the family. Maybe it was a recent affliction. Or maybe the family was embarrassed, or... *Stop guessing.*

When Geoff recovered, he would tell her. And how did she feel now that the crisis was over? Fingering a pearl on the gown's bodice, she recalled his caresses. She certainly was attracted to him, but not so much that she would unthinkingly have sex with him. Yet, she had given him signals to the contrary. *Damn it—what was happening?* Maybe the seizure was a blessing in disguise.

She leaned back, rubbed her eyes, and drifted. A groan from the bed made her jump. "Geoff?" Enough light flickered through the window to see by, but dawn was at least another hour away. She must have fallen asleep.

Geoff tossed the blanket to the side. She knelt beside the bed, and his eyelids fluttered open. A hand went to his head with another groan.

"How are you feeling?" she asked.

He rubbed his temple. "Like my head has been twisted off."

"You..." Unsure whether he would appreciate being reminded of what had happened, she whispered, "...seizured."

"That's right, say it like it's a dirty word. The correct term is seized. I seized, not seizured. It must have been a mild—*seizure*," he whispered the word as she had, "if you didn't run in disgust."

Confused by his reaction, Chris repeated the word, "Disgust?"

"That's when bodily fluids make a mess of things. You know—blood, drool, vomit..."

"What are you accusing me of?" She raised her voice. "I'll have you know, you scared the hell out of me."

"Welcome to the club," Geoff replied dryly.

He continued rubbing his head, and Chris realized he was in pain. "Can I get you something?" He shook his head. "Then you have epilepsy?"

With a groan, Geoff sat up, looking around the room as if trying to get his bearings. "Since I was five. The car hit a tree. My mother died, and I got this wonderful malady."

A family tragedy. Chris felt ill to her stomach. A five year old—going through what she had witnessed. "I'm sorry. Judith never told me."

"People don't tend to air their family's dirty laundry. Besides," he said, lowering his voice, "I don't remember anything about the accident or before then for that matter. I was in a coma for nearly a month, and when I woke, I had to learn everything all over again."

Without a mother to help. "It must have been very difficult for you. Do you take medication?"

"Dilantin—once a day—religiously." He laughed in biting sarcasm. "Even then, the evil spirits occasionally take over."

His answer explained the medicine bottle in the bathroom. "I've never known anyone with epilepsy. Give me a chance to learn."

"Sorry," he quickly apologized. "For all the doctors know, it might as well be evil spirits, and part of my reaction is defensive. I usually get the opposite response when people find out."

"Then you're all right now? I worried you had hit your head."

"A few bruises and a headache—not from hitting my head."

Chris blew out a breath. "Does it happen often? I mean the . . ."

"Seizures. You can say it. It's the first in a couple of years. Obviously, I had hoped they wouldn't be back."

There was no mistaking his disappointment. She squeezed his hand. "If it's safe now, I can help you to your room."

Still disoriented, Geoff glanced about her room once more. "I don't mean to sound indelicate, but why am I here?"

"What's the last thing you remember?" Chris bit her lip.

He rubbed his head. "You left the drawing room, and for some reason, I came upstairs."

"You collapsed, and I brought you to the closest room." This answer seemed to satisfy him, and she let out a relieved breath. "Will you be all right now?"

He nodded. Although he remained a bit shaky, he got to his feet. Chris grasped his elbow to help. "I'll be fine. I can make it on my own."

She let go of him. "Then we'll talk later."

Thankful that he hadn't noticed she still wore the silk gown, she watched him as he wobbled to the door beside the fireplace. When he stumbled, she rushed over to help, but he waved her away.

"Chris . . ." Her heart skipped a beat when he glanced over his shoulder. "Thanks."

"You're welcome," Chris replied, breathing easier. He stepped into the hall and closed the door behind him. Confident that he remembered nothing about their interlude, she hurried from her room. No one was in the main hall. Appreciative of her good fortune, she clambered up the steps to the third floor. After changing her clothes, she left the gown in the wardrobe.

Upon returning to her room, the first rays of dawn glimmered through the part in the drapes. Chris stopped in front of the mirror. With her brush, she took long, soothing strokes through her hair. Settling down from the night's events, she studied the hand-carved horse heads surrounding the mirror. She stroked one. Had she really imagined the horse's breath on her palm? Then she thought of Geoff. She had wanted to have blatant, unrestrained sex with him. Had the seizure disgusted her? No, she had been caught off guard when he had called her by her middle name. If Judith hadn't told him the name, how could he have known?

A rap came at the door, startling her from her thoughts. "Chris."

Grabbing a robe, Chris smoothed her hair and cracked the door to Judith's beaming face. *Bright eyed and bushy tailed.* Unlike Judith, Chris had to apply a ton of makeup just to look halfway civilized the first thing in the morning. She sighed.

"I didn't mean to wake you." Judith's grin faded. "I thought you'd be up by now."

"You didn't wake me. I merely didn't sleep well."

Mumbling her apologies, Judith invited Chris to breakfast. "Do you want to talk?"

Chris opened the door wide enough for her friend to enter. "Last night . . ." How could she tell what had happened without leading to uncomfortable questions? "Geoff had a seizure."

Judith's eyes widened with worry. "A seizure? Was he hurt? Is he all right?"

"He's fine. I know your mother died when you were small, but why didn't you ever tell me about the accident?"

Tears formed in her friend's eyes. "I was only one at the time, so I obviously don't remember anything about it. Geoff says he doesn't either, but a couple of doctors think he's blocked the memory. Who really knows? Daddy wasn't in the car, but even now, I know he's hurting. He keeps a stiff upper lip, but Geoff's seizures are a painful reminder. Over the years, we've simply learned not to talk about it. Didn't Saber warn Geoff?"

"Saber?"

"I have no idea how—maybe it's the bond between them, but Saber always knows when a seizure is coming. He gives Geoff a warning. The only time that I know of those two being apart is when Saber needs to go out. I'm sorry you had to find out that way, but now you know why my brother doesn't tend to be a big socializer." Her tears abated, and she checked her watch. "I'll call the neurologist after breakfast."

"He'll be all right, won't he? I mean, can't people die from seizures?"

Judith gave her a smile of reassurance. "I'll check on him to be on the safe side, but the call is merely a precaution. Nothing more. And I doubt he'd do it himself."

Suddenly doubtful, Chris asked, "Then I did the right thing by telling you?"

"He probably won't think so, but yes, you did the right thing."

"What a way to start a visit. He's going to be furious with me."

"Stop worrying. He'll get over it." Judith squeezed her arm. "I'll see you downstairs."

After changing, Chris hurried to the dining room. Outside the door, she halted. How could she pretend ignorance to the passage of events? Pasting on a smile, she stepped forward. Only Judith and her father were seated at the table. The elder Cameron immediately stood. "Good morning," she said in as cheery a voice as she could muster.

After an exchange of greetings, Winston Cameron withdrew a chair for her and helped her to be seated. She could easily grow accustomed to Southern manners. As Chris spread a linen napkin across her lap, she continued to worry about Geoff. Would he have been able to get help if he had suffered from another seizure? "Judith . . ."

Judith shook her head and glanced to her father, then back again.

So, Judith didn't want her father knowing about Geoff's seizure. If there was a family wedge, Chris now understood the crux of the problem.

Ten minutes later, Geoff charged into the dining room. Startled by his appearance, Chris knocked her fork to the floor with a resounding clang. She reached down to retrieve it, but Geoff beat her to it.

With a glare, he handed her the fork. "Does the whole estate know by now?"

"Geoff, that's not fair," Judith said, piping up in Chris's defense.

"I'm sorry," Chris muttered.

"Sorry? Do you realize . . ."

"Would someone please tell me what's going on?" Winston Cameron demanded.

Geoff gestured to Chris. "Why don't you tell him?"

"Geoff!" Judith stood to confront him.

Among accusing stares, Chris tossed her wadded napkin on the table. "Tell him yourself. I get enough bellyaching from clients, without being dragged into family squabbles." With an about turn, she headed for the door. In the hall she resisted the temptation to pound a fist against the wall. But she sensed someone standing behind her, watching intently. Even before she looked, she knew it was Geoff. Sympathy, not anger, registered in his eyes. Shouldn't she be the sympathetic one? Suddenly embarrassed by her little tantrum, she replied, "I truly am sorry."

"I'm the one who should apologize for losing my temper." A wild-eyed gleam appeared in his eyes. "Besides, I doubt you told Judith everything. You looked lovely wearing the dress."

He *did* remember the events before the seizure. "I didn't mean to lead you on."

He sighed in disappointment. "I understand."

"Geoff, the seizure has nothing to do with this. I'm apologizing for giving you the wrong impression."

"I see." Letting out a breath, he laughed. "Well—I suppose we're even. I don't usually make a habit of trying to ravish my sister's friends."

Chris wondered how he could still laugh with the blows life had dealt him. "And I don't usually solicit total strangers, whether they're my best friend's brother or not."

He held out a hand in a truce. "Friends?"

She grasped it lightly. "Friends."

A grin crossed his lips. "That doesn't mean it wouldn't be a perfectly pleasurable experience."

Chris jerked her hand from his grasp. "Now we'll never know, will we?"

"You seemed to like the idea until I fell to the floor in a goddamned twitching heap."

"Geoff . . . don't."

He lowered his voice. "I'm doing it again. You have my humble apology." He checked his watch. "Judith is likely to be busy trying to get hold of the neurologist for at least a couple of hours. Would you like a tour of the estate? You can even choose which grand style you'd prefer to travel in, my Mustang or a pickup truck."

Drive? "Is it safe for someone like you to drive?"

He blew out a frustrated breath. "Whether you say the word or not doesn't change the fact that I have epilepsy. I won't seize while driving, nor in front of you again."

With a twinge of guilt, Chris wondered how he could make such a claim. "I told you I'm just learning. I won't know unless I ask."

"Agreed. Virginia law allows a person to drive when they've been six months seizure free. DMV may have a few questions, but with a neurologist's report, they'll likely consider it a breakthrough seizure after going two years without one. I also have Saber to warn me."

With his ears perked, the black dog trotted over to Geoff and sat at his feet. "Judith told me about him. Why wasn't he with you last night?"

"I let him outside, then got distracted."

And she had been the distraction. She pointed to herself. "Did I cause . . ."

With a growing smile, Geoff shook his head. "If you're guilty of anything, it's diverting my attention so I forgot to let Saber in. Now about the drive . . . I'd offer horseback as an alternative, but the day is rather dismal."

Her feelings hadn't changed. If anything, the seizure had drawn her closer to him. Not out of pity—he'd hate pity—but through a secret she shared with him, bringing them more intimacy. "I'd like the grand tour in the Mustang."

Morning drizzle made visibility difficult, but Chris was relieved to be temporarily away from the mansion in Geoff's vintage '67 Mustang. Cobblestones led from the west wing. As they traveled along the lane, she heard the clip-clop of horse's hooves. A spirited stallion raised his head and cried, and she saw a sleek, black shape dart across the road. "Geoff!"

Chris reached over and grabbed the wheel, swerving to miss the horse. Tires screeched and the car careened to the ditch. Geoff hit the brake, narrowly missing a tree. He caught his breath. "What the hell are you doing?"

"I saw . . ." Chris pointed to the poplar grove where the stallion had disappeared.

Calmer now, Geoff asked, "What was it?"

Chris searched up and down rows of poplar trees. No horse. He couldn't have vanished into thin air. "I saw Raven."

Doubt flickered in Geoff's eyes. "Someone must have been out riding," he reasoned.

"After last night, I thought *you* believed me."

His hands twitched on the wheel. "You know as well as I do there's a logical explanation." As Geoff shifted gears, they grated. He uttered a curse under his breath as the car lurched back onto the lane.

Collected once more, Chris leaned back in the seat. It was an explanation, but logical? She had begun to wonder. Even Geoff had admitted to seeing ghosts.

* * *

Rows upon rows of prone forms sprawled across the grass, saturating it with blood. A cannon rumbled in the distance, shaking the ground beneath her feet. A low moan from the wounded echoed. Many were missing limbs. She felt queasiness in the pit of her stomach. Her husband could be among them. She calmed herself. These men wore blue. She bent down to a soldier with reddish peach fuzz. He licked his cracked lips with a blackened tongue, and she held out a dipper of water to help him drink.

"Chris?"

Geoff's voice made Chris blink. She stared out the car window. The Mustang had come to a halt outside an octagonal barn. The engine softly hummed and the wipers brushed the windshield. "I saw them."

"Saw who?"

"Soldiers—wounded soldiers. There were so many they covered the ground."

"When the place served as a hospital."

"Then you've seen them?"

"Once or twice." Geoff pulled the keys from the ignition and swung the car door open.

The window steamed as he slammed the door behind him. Chris wiped the moisture from the glass. *Of course, during the Civil War.* Everything seemed to point to the time period. And how did Geoff fit into the strange events? He looked so much like the man wearing the Confederate uniform. Like Margaret, could he have been Geoff's ancestor? It would certainly explain the resemblance.

Geoff rounded the car, and Chris lowered the misted window. "Why have you brought me here?"

He opened the door for her. "It's the stallion barn. I wanted to show you there's no Raven."

That definitely sounded like a good place to start. She joined Geoff, and they sprinted through the rain along the cobblestone path to the barn. A man with a graying beard waited inside.

"This is T.J.," Geoff said. "He's our stable manager."

Chris thrust out her hand. "Pleased to meet you, T.J. I'm Chris."

T.J. eyed her hand and remarked in a thick Scottish accent, "In my day, a man kissed a lady's hand." He shook her hand. "T.J. MacGillivrey, an' a pleasure it is ta meet ye. Geoff, she's a mighty fine lookin' lass. If ye know what's good fer ye, ye'd latch onto her."

For some reason, Chris overlooked T.J.'s blatant sexism and took an immediate liking to the salty gentleman. She noted that he had called Geoff by his first name, rather than addressing him more formally, like the maid in the household had. "I'm here to see the stallions."

"Aye, we presently have five. If ye'd like ta look at any o' them closer, I'll bring them out o' their stalls."

Chris passed each box stall—a bay, a gray, another bay, a chestnut. By the last stall, she halted. Her heart nearly stopped. The stallion was black. "I'd like to see him."

As T.J. withdrew a leather lead line and led the stallion from his stall, her heart pounded. He had no star and was more of a dark bay, rather than black. *Not Raven.* With a sigh, she moved toward him.

The stallion flattened his ears and bared his teeth. "Lass, be careful, he might bite."

"Thanks for the warning, but . . ." Chris scratched behind the stallion's ears. The threat changed to a nicker. "He appears tame enough."

Mystified, Chris studied the horse. Raven's image remained imprinted on her mind. She exchanged gazes with Geoff. Another haunting image. So much like the man in the mirror. Because of the similarity, she had let him touch her bare skin. Even now, she wanted him to explore further.

Geoff's eyes glistened, and he met her gaze with a smile spreading across his face. Her body language had betrayed her. "Thank you for your time, T.J."

The whole venture was nothing but a folly. She hurried for the barn door and retreated along the cobblestone path.

Morning drizzle had given way to sunlight poking through the clouds. She looked back on the path to see if Geoff was coming. The stallion whistled from his stall. Frustrated, Chris rushed to the car.

"Chris," Geoff shouted. She reached the Mustang when he caught up with her. "Did he resemble Raven?"

Out of breath, Chris folded her arms across her chest. "He's not Raven. Are you satisfied? Just pitch me in the loony bin."

Chris got in the car, slamming the door after her, and Geoff slid in behind the wheel. "I believe you."

Did he really, or was he trying to placate her? "Why?"

"Because I've already admitted to seeing ghosts."

"But no black stallions?"

"No black stallions." He checked his watch. "It'll probably take Judith a while longer before she can get through to the doctor."

"Why don't you want her to call about the seizure?"

"Because you can't know what it's like."

"I'm trying to understand."

"I appreciate that . . ."

"But?"

Staring at the road, he drummed his fingers on the steering wheel. She had been mistaken. He wasn't angry.

"You're embarrassed. There's no reason to be. I wasn't disgusted."

His eyes flickered in a strange way. "It's more than embarrassment."

Fear. The brave front had been for her benefit. How could he possibly worry about her trivial misgivings when he had serious health threats to deal with? "The time before last night, did they—the seizures—happen often?"

"Sometimes."

Choosing her words carefully, Chris hoped not to upset him further. "You're concerned this wasn't just a . . ." What had he called it? ". . . a breakthrough?"

"A breakthrough is when someone has been seizure free for a year or more. Doctors begin reducing medication levels. At this point, they can only guess if last night was caused by the lower dosage, or..." He blew out a breath. "...a sign of things to come."

His frustration was evident. Chris squeezed his hand. "Why hasn't it scared you off?"

"It does scare me—a little, but I was still hoping to discover what's been happening..." She shook her head. "Sorry, that wasn't fair. I don't mean to downplay what you went through. It's just that everyone is beginning to think I'm crazy."

He laughed, and a mad gleam entered his eyes. "If you associate with me, they'll be certain of it."

His ability to shrug off the situation lifted her spirit. "Then tell me what *did* happen last night?"

His gaze returned to the road. "I knew I'd find you on the third floor. Your perfume..."

"Perfume? But I wasn't wearing any."

His eyes widened as he looked her way. "I *know* what I smelled. Believe me, it's not a scent I can forget. It was..."

"Honeysuckle. I've smelled it too, before I've had a vision."

Geoff's face paled.

Damn—another seizure. She patted the back of his hand. "Geoff?"

He held up his hand, and she stopped tapping. "What are you doing?"

"I thought you were having another seizure."

"It's not the same as fainting. There's nothing you can do to stop a seizure. I was about to say that honeysuckle is my aura."

"Aura? I get them with a migraine." Coincidence? "So when you smell honeysuckle..."

He rubbed his temple as if the headache had returned. "I know a seizure is imminent, but it doesn't always give me enough warning, like..." He gestured to Saber curled up on the back seat. "It wasn't until he came along that I had enough warning so as not to make a public spectacle of myself."

She glanced back at Saber. "His ability to detect them is amazing. It's strange how a dog can sometimes provide more than modern science."

"Isn't it?" Geoff's hand reached under her chin, tilting her head until she was looking into his eyes. "I've lived with epilepsy most of my life. Because of people's normal reactions, I don't broadcast it, but I accepted it a long time ago."

"I knew you wouldn't want pity." The memory of him in the throes of a seizure faded as he leaned across and kissed her. No longer frightened, she parted her lips to reciprocate. He reached inside her coat, tracing his fingertips along her side. She ached for him to touch further with feverish kisses to her bare skin. In response, she would run her hands through his thick blond hair and squeeze the muscles of his shirtless shoulders. She wanted him inside her. With a gasp, Chris drew away.

"Too abrupt?"

She couldn't look. Certainly, he knew. "I need to keep my head clear. When you're around, I can't. I feel like I know you. The visions have been about a woman named Margaret, the horse, Raven, or . . . " She looked over at him. ". . . you—in some past time."

Intrigued, Geoff gestured to himself. "Me? In a past time?"

"The man who looked like you wore some sort of uniform. Civil War gray, I think. Margaret wore a hoop skirt under the gown in the wardrobe, and her perfume smelled like . . ."

"Honeysuckle." Geoff's ensuing laugh was laced with sarcasm. "Next thing you'll tell me, I have epilepsy because I'm possessed. That theory is a little out of date."

"I said nothing of the kind." Thrusting her chin out, Chris folded her arms across her chest. "For the record, I've never believed in ghosts, but some of the things around here have made me begin to think otherwise."

"I'll take you to a place where you'll be convinced." Geoff started the car, shifted gears, and returned to the road.

Chris was unsure whether to be relieved or not. "Thank you for your help."

A slight grin formed on his mouth. "You haven't bothered asking what I accept in repayment."

"My sincerest gratitude," she said dryly. As he laughed, she sat back.

The road wound away from the barn until they were beside the mansion again.

With a flashlight in hand, Geoff showed her to the back of the house. Marble columns with a balcony lined the door, while rows of boxwoods led the way to the river. The couple strolled along the grassy path. Magnolias and dogwoods spread across the lawn. A screened-in gazebo stood on her right side. "That's odd," she commented.

Saber dashed ahead of them, and Geoff glanced in her direction. "What's odd?"

"The columns are larger on the river than around front."

"That's because this is the 'front.' During Colonial times, most guests arrived by boat."

And she had worried that she might miss Boston's history museums. Poplar Ridge *was* a museum. A small brick building stood to the far left. "What's that used for?"

"That's the necessary. It even has a built-in fireplace to warm your backside during the winter," he answered with a laugh.

"Always so proper. *Backside?*"

"What would you rather I'd say?"

"Do you really think I'm so delicate that I might melt because you used the word that was really on your mind?"

His grin widened. "That thought had never occurred to me, ma'am."

"Ma'am," she muttered. "You certainly had me fooled when I arrived." To this, he gave no response.

They continued strolling. Finally, they reached the mist-covered river. The waves lapped against the bank. Chris meandered along, and the breeze numbed her face. While the house and grounds were certainly beautiful, she couldn't imagine living this far from civilization. She looked in the direction where Geoff's gaze seemed fixed. A windswept island lay in the middle of the river. A glow entered his eyes. It was clear that he loved the land. Born a city girl, she was a fool falling for him the way she was. Then again, lust didn't necessarily equate to love. She breathed in the river air.

"I've seen a ghost here on several occasions," Geoff said slowly. "A man in uniform."

"Civil War?"

He nodded. "I've seen him in a few other places around the estate, but I see him here most frequently. His uniform is faded blue or gray. I really can't tell which." Geoff led the way to a clump of bushes. "He vanishes over here."

Chris couldn't see anything unusual until Geoff parted the bushes to a door—an old cellar door. He withdrew the flashlight, fiddled with an old skeleton key in the lock, and opened the door to a black pit.

She swallowed hard. "Where does it lead?"

"Back to the house. It was made during Colonial times as a way to escape from Indians." He started down the steps.

"Geoff... I'm not certain about this."

"I've been down here a number of times. It's okay."

Chris took a deep breath and followed him down the six steps. The flashlight cut through the darkness, and she finally reached the brick floor. The tunnel was about three feet wide and six feet tall. In the tight quarters, Geoff had to duck to keep from hitting his head.

Their heels echoed against the bricks. After several feet, the tunnel still stretched in the darkness before them. They continued forward until entering the main section of the cellar. Honeysuckle descended upon Chris.

Missing both legs, the soldier with the reddish peach fuzz lay on a bed of straw. As Margaret drew a tattered blanket over him, his eyes fluttered open. "Mother . . ."

"I'm not . . ." She thought better of her words. What harm could come from giving a dying boy comfort? She grasped his hand. "I'm here."

Under the lantern's dim light, he gazed intently upon her face. "Thank you," he whispered. Then he closed his eyes and took his final breath.

* * *

"Chris?" Geoff grasped her hand.

She blinked, then glanced up. "Geoff?"

His headache was back. A groan escaped him, and a hand went to his temple. "Are you all right? I smelled honeysuckle. Did you? Sit down before . . ."

She threw her arms around his waist for support. "I didn't smell honeysuckle. And Saber will warn me." He liked having her arms around him. As the headache faded, he grew more aware of her pleasant embrace.

To his disappointment, when she realized that he wasn't having a seizure, she drew away. He didn't blame her for being cautious. Given a choice, he wouldn't deal with epilepsy either. "What just happened?"

"I'm not certain. I keep having visions. When I first arrived, they were mostly of a man who looks like you, but now they seem to be focused on the Civil War." As she glanced at him, a brisk wind swept through the tunnel from the river. "A soldier died here. She tried to give him comfort."

The chill vanished as quickly as the gust had blown in. "She?"

"Margaret."

Her visions kept pointing to his great-grandmother. There was something at the back of his mind, if only he could remember. "It's almost as if you're seeing into the past."

"I keep seeing Poplar Ridge during another time, but it's more than that. It's as if I've lived it."

"As Margaret? *Chris*," he scoffed.

"I know." Sparing herself a lecture, she held up a hand. "I'm not a believer in reincarnation any more than I am ghosts. Still, my visions and dreams must be leading somewhere. And Margaret is obviously the key."

Intrigued by her determination, Geoff said, "I've already told you what I know."

"Last night you called me Catherine. If Judith didn't tell you my middle name, how did you know what it was?"

"I often get confused before a seizure."

Skeptical, she said, "That's your explanation for what happened?"

"That's my explanation for calling you Catherine. Judith must have mentioned it, and I subconsciously remembered it." Her mouth quivered, and he resisted the temptation to kiss her. "I said that I'd help you find answers. I meant it."

Wind whistled through the tunnel again. Chris stepped closer, and he placed his arm over her shoulder. He liked the way she felt next to him. He moved to kiss her, but she drew away. "I don't know what you want from me, but I'm confused."

"That makes two of us."

Her back faced him.

"Is there someone else?" he asked.

With a sigh, she shook her head. "There's no one."

"Then I don't see the problem, unless . . ."

"Dammit, Geoff." She whirled around. "Don't you dare bring up the seizure. It's lack of time. In case you haven't guessed, I'm married to my career. Plus, there's the tiny problem of distance. Or were you thinking of nothing more than a wild time in bed?"

Delighted with the idea, he grinned. "I admit I've had the thought."

"You're incorrigible," she muttered. "I've had exactly two fumbling, postadolescent sexual experiences. I don't care to add another. What's more, the Southern gentleman whom I met when I had car trouble seems to have vanished completely."

"You said you wanted me to say what was on my mind. Besides, Southern men don't fumble. We prefer our women like our horses—spirited." Geoff aimed the flashlight around, searching for the light switch. "How about dinner this evening?"

"Dinner?"

"You know, a perfectly respectable activity for two people to engage in."

"Judith put you up to this. You needn't make me a charity case."

By the stairs, Geoff flicked on the switch. Wine bottles lined the far wall. "Judith didn't put me up to anything. I'm asking because I'd like you to accompany me to dinner."

She pointed to Saber. "Is he invited too?"

"Anyone who has lived here long enough knows what I was like before he came along. The locals allow him as much latitude as a guide dog."

"I think I'd enjoy having dinner with you." She glanced at Saber. "And you." Wagging his tail, the dog barked.

Returning to the reason that had brought them on the excursion, Geoff gestured to the cellar. "Here's another place that I've seen a ghost."

"Like the hospital scene I envisioned?"

"No, a single ghost—the one I mentioned earlier."

She shook her head. "Nothing. Whatever I saw here is gone now."

He grasped her hand and led her to the stairs. Pleased that she didn't withdraw from his grip, he showed her to the parlor.

Chris's hands went to her stomach, and she swayed on her feet. "I think I'm going to be sick."

Chapter Four

BLOOD FLOWED ACROSS THE WOOD FLOOR. *Margaret stepped carefully over the wounded lying in the hall. Agonized groans surrounded her. Even though the soldiers wore blue, she spoke words of comfort. Bending down, she placed a tin cup to a scruffy bearded man's lips and helped him drink.*

"Mrs. Cameron." A hand rested on her shoulder. The soldier finished drinking his fill, and she returned to her feet. Another soldier, using a crutch due to a missing leg, stood before her. "The doctor needs your help. A boy was brought in. He's wearing gray."

Her neatly pinned hair had long degenerated to stray locks, which she brushed away from her face. Without acknowledging the soldier, she gathered her blood-stained skirts together. In the parlor, windows were wide open to keep the doctor and his staff from being overcome by the chloroform. A table had been fashioned from a door. A man with a saw in his hand and wearing a bloody apron loomed over a soldier in gray. Clutching his arm, a freckle-faced boy rolled into a ball and sobbed.

Margaret gripped his hand and spoke in a soothing voice, assuring him that everything would be all right. He cried on her breast, and she held him tight. "I'll stay with you," she whispered.

Finally, his crying halted. With his face an emotionless mask, he lay back. A cone went over his mouth and nose. At first, he resisted the chloroform and struggled to rise. Then every muscle was still. The surgeon's saw cut through flesh like butter, then it made contact with bone.

* * *

Seated on a walnut-framed sofa in the parlor, Chris held her head between her hands. The queasiness in her stomach began to fade.

"I can't believe you took her to the cellar and told her ghost stories." Judith patted Chris's hand. "Chris? Are you all right?"

Chris glanced around the room. Beside the sofa stood a table with a silver teapot atop it, and a grand piano filled the center of the room. Relieved to see no doors propped up as makeshift operating tables or blood flowing across the floor, she took a deep breath. "I think so. Geoff?"

"He's here."

Geoff stepped in beside Judith. "Chris, I'm sorry."

She grasped his hand. "Don't be. I saw it."

"Saw what?" he asked in confusion.

"A Civil War hospital. A man wearing a bloody apron was amputating a boy's arm."

"Let's get her up to her room where she can rest," Judith suggested. With Judith on one side and Geoff on the other, they helped Chris up the stairs to her room. Judith thumbed at Geoff to leave. As soon as he closed the door behind him, she asked, "Why did Geoff take you to the cellar?"

"He wanted to show me where he had seen a ghost."

A worried frown crossed Judith's face. "I don't think that was a good idea for either of you."

Her friend must be concerned for her sanity again, but Geoff... "What did the neurologist say?"

Judith shook her head. "If Geoff wants you to know, he'll have to be the one to say something. But, Chris, if the seizures are back, you should be aware that stress can lower the seizure threshold."

"I see. I promise I won't involve him in any more ghost stories."

"Good," Judith said, smiling in relief. "Get some rest."

Chris watched Judith leave. *Rest?* After what she had witnessed, how was she going to rest? Or keep her promise? But if

telling Geoff about her visions affected his health, she'd find a
way to keep from sharing her experiences with him.

Dinner was a quiet affair at a Colonial tavern on a nearby
plantation. The seafood and wine were excellent, but Chris had
picked at the Chesapeake Bay crab, pretending to enjoy it. As
she went up the steps of Poplar Ridge, Geoff joined her. "Chris,
you've barely said more than a couple words the entire evening.
Is it because of what happened this morning?"

As he grasped her hand, she shivered and withdrew it from
his grip. Like in her dreams upon arriving, an overwhelming
sadness surfaced when he was near. Retaking his hand, she
stroked the rough calluses. "I was concerned about what the
doctor had said."

Geoff led the way to the drawing room, studying her a moment as if deciding whether to answer or not. He motioned for
her to make herself comfortable, poured a drink from a crystal
decanter, handed it to her, then poured a glass of mineral water for himself. "Not much. He doesn't consider one seizure in
two years much cause for concern, not with my history, which
is why I wouldn't have called him in the first place."

His annoyance at Judith for interfering was obvious. "It's my
fault. I'm sorry for telling her."

He sat beside her on the tapestry sofa and let out a weary
breath. "Don't worry. I've fared worse."

"Share with me."

His eyes narrowed in suspicion. "Trying to decide how involved to get?"

He *was* afraid because she had witnessed a seizure. "Geoff,
you needn't get defensive." She grasped his hand. "Not with
me. I think you already know that, but I'm concerned that my
ghostly tales may have caused you undue stress that you're not
telling me about."

He took a sip from his glass. "You've obviously been talking
to my sister, so she'll probably tell you what you want to know,

regardless of what I want. What's worse to me, though, is being treated as a curiosity."

"Curiosity?" Astonished by his accusation, she asked, "What would make you think such a thing?"

"You went to Judith rather than me, and you've already begun using kid gloves around me, like she does."

He didn't trust easily. Chris set her drink on the mahogany table. "Then tell me what I need to know, so I can stop making stupid mistakes."

His gaze softened, but he remained silent.

"Please..."

"What is it that you want to know?"

A giant step—she breathed out in relief. "Can't people die from seizures?"

"Not usually. It's not a disease."

Neat sidestepping. "Then they do die."

"Rarely," he finally admitted, "but people die from being hit by lightning too."

How could she keep him talking? She obviously had to go into her probing attorney mode. "You said that you take medication."

"Dilantin. I tried several other medications, but it was hit and miss until we found the best one and dosage." He held up his glass. "It's also why I tend not to drink much alcohol. Anticonvulsants and alcohol can cause a dangerous mix to the liver."

"I noticed that you only took a small glass of wine at dinner."

"When I've imbibed more than my usual amount, I've paid for it. It's difficult to keep seizures under control. But then the medical community regards control as no more than one seizure a month."

Frustration registered in his voice. Unable to fathom such a ludicrous definition, Chris understood his relief when he had gone two years without a seizure. She glanced at Saber curled by Geoff's feet. "How did you train Saber to detect seizures?"

"I didn't. He just knew. I had a couple of seizures before I realized that he was alerting me to them, but he sensed them right from the beginning." Geoff reached down and scratched Saber's head, and the dog gave a lazy stretch with a groan.

"Then you originally got him for the same reason anyone gets a dog?"

"I've always felt more comfortable around dogs and horses. My nickname in school was Spaz."

Horrified by how cruel kids could be, Chris felt his pain.

"Certainly when you grew up..."

"By the time I got to college, the name calling stopped, but when people found out, they gave me nervous stares and distanced themselves. I tried to fit into the social scene, but they eventually found out and withdrew. Finally, I stopped trying and immersed myself in my studies."

Notably absent from his discussion was the mention of his marriage and son, which led her to surmise why her questions had been regarded with suspicion. Upon her arrival, she had felt a familiar pitter-patter when he had stopped to help her on the lonely road to Poplar Ridge. Mature love went beyond simple desire, extending to caring for someone—unconditionally. Epilepsy was part of him. Was it love—or lust? Her head was spinning. Everything was happening too fast.

The clock in the hall chimed one time. "I hadn't realized that it was so late." As Chris rose to her feet, he stood. More than anything, she wanted to ignore the consequences. In his arms, she could forget the visions. But if she invited him to her room, there would be no turning back. "Geoff..." She swallowed hard. "...goodnight."

"Goodnight."

Before changing her mind, she hurried to her room. Against the wall, the mirror attracted her attention. In its reflection was a woman with black hair pinned at the nape of her neck. Chris touched the glass, and the image vanished. "Margaret?"

Had he said too much? Geoff retreated to the library to attend to some bookwork. The computer screen froze, and he cursed, rubbing tired eyes. A floorboard in the hall creaked. He glanced up. *Just the house settling.* Another creak. Alert, Saber pricked his ears in the direction of the sound. Someone was definitely there.

As he got to his feet to investigate, a knock came at the door. "Come in."

With a pale face and still attired in her V-necked dinner dress, Chris stepped into the room and closed the door behind her. "Geoff," she said, catching her breath, "I was hoping that you might still be awake."

Concerned that she might have had another vision, he moved closer. "Is something wrong?"

"No. I . . .," she stammered. "I had forgotten to thank you for the wonderful dinner."

He regretted filling her head full of ghost stories. "You didn't forget. What's happened?"

She shook her head. "Just talk to me."

He showed her to the sofa, then sat beside her. "If you don't want to tell me what's wrong, what should we talk about?"

Chris forced a laugh. "The weather?"

"A nice, safe topic. Are the big city lawyer types not supposed to admit when something is bothering them?"

She shrugged. "It's a defense mechanism. All the same, I promised Judith . . ."

Something *had* happened. "To hell with Judith."

"I'd really rather not talk about it."

"I see," Geoff replied in frustration. "It's a one-way street."

Calm now, she stood. "I didn't mean it that way. I'm sorry I bothered you."

When he grasped her hand and kissed it, she trembled. "And I didn't mean to send you running. Tomorrow is supposed to be in the seventies and sunny."

With a smile, Chris reseated herself. "Does that mean we can go riding?"

"If you wish," he whispered. He drew her close and kissed her full on the mouth.

"Geoff . . ."

"Did you also promise Judith that we wouldn't kiss?"

Another laugh. "No, but . . ."

He cut off her sentence by kissing her again, and she eagerly reciprocated. At least, she was sounding more like herself. He thought of the cottage and how that's where he'd like to be now. With her. No warning scent of honeysuckle this time. Just to be certain, he checked on Saber. Disregarding their presence, the dog rested on the rug beside the desk. Unable to let the moment pass, Geoff knelt before her and lifted her skirt.

His fingertips traced the length of her legs, then her inner thigh. She opened her legs for him to explore further, and he tugged off her panties. As she helped him with his zipper, his ache intensified. It was like discovering a lover from long ago. *Long ago.* They had been destined to meet here—like this.

After so much grief, they were finally together again. Clinging, almost desperately, they united in a rhythmic unison. His fingers dug into her so tightly as he frantically clutched her hips. *To touch and feel again, she was his lifeline, lifting him through the darkness of death and despair. Catherine.* He could no longer hold back and shuddered. She slumped against him.

Still caught in the sweet euphoria, he held her head and kissed her mouth. She blinked. "No. This wasn't supposed to happen."

"Of course it was."

She lowered her dress and scrambled to her feet. He kissed her again. At first, he felt resistance, but her lips parted. She gave him her tongue, then she abruptly shoved away from him and made a mad dash for the door.

The following afternoon was a sultry day, reminding Chris that summer this far south hadn't drawn its final breath. Even the light cotton shirt clung to her body. In the outdoor arena, Judith coached a riding student in the ballet-like movements of dressage, while Chris looked on from the bleachers. She felt like an absolute fool. After her tryst with Geoff, she had nearly packed her bags and left the estate. But such a drastic action in the middle of the night would have led to many embarrassing questions. With the excuse of a migraine, she had taken meals in her room. Taking no chances of bumping into Geoff accidentally, she had used Judith's bathroom, rather than traipsing down the hall in the west wing. Had she really drunk so much that she had even forgotten birth control? Or had the face in the mirror frightened her more than she had imagined?

"Chris . . ."

Damn, it was him. If she looked his way, the craving would return. "Go away." She heard his retreating footsteps. Chris jerked her head up. Saber trotted by Geoff's side as he returned to the barn. "Geoff, wait."

He shoved his hands in his pockets and faced her.

"What is it you wanted?" she asked.

"Judith has riding students all day today. I've finished the majority of my chores. I thought you might like to go for a ride." Shifting uneasily on his feet, he hadn't met her gaze. He must feel the same awkwardness. A casual affair wasn't her usual style. Was that why he scared her?

"I can't."

His gaze locked with hers, and he cracked a grin. "Or we could go back to the house."

"I don't think so," she said, a little louder than she had intended.

Judith cast a quick glance from the center of the arena, but quickly returned her attention to her student.

Oh, what the hell! She had to face him sometime. By the time Chris caught up with him, he had reached the barn. Two horses, a gray gelding and a brown mare, stood in the aisle—saddled and ready to go. "You're pretty sure of yourself, aren't you?"

"As a matter of fact, no. I'm not sure about anything. You've been going out of your way to avoid me. If a quick fuck is all you want, that's fine by me. You wouldn't be the first to wonder if I'll have a seizure while getting it on."

"Is that what you think? If that's the impression I gave, then I'm sorry. I'm confused and trying to make sense of what happened." Aware that she must be blushing, she felt her cheeks warm. "While I'm certainly no prude, I'm not usually so easily swept off my feet. Neither of us even bothered to think about the consequences."

His voice wavered slightly. "You're not on the . . ."

"I've already told you that I'm not in the habit of sleeping around."

"Then I apologize for not taking precautions. I was obviously not thinking with my head." After handing her a helmet, he led the horses to the outside courtyard. Hooves clattered against the stone surface. She slipped the helmet on her head, and he boosted her onto the back of the brown mare. "This is Tiffany, Her Royal Highness and queen bee of the stable. Chris, if you should find yourself . . ."

He cleared his throat, and she nodded that she understood. She leaned over in the saddle and kissed him on the forehead. "It should be okay this time, but let's not do anything so foolish again." She giggled. "You'd think we were a couple of teenagers. Where are you taking me?"

He nonchalantly adjusted her stirrups, then met her gaze in a teasing manner. "Worried that I have ulterior motives?"

Her heart beat so hard that it felt like it was pounding in her throat. "You do. I already know that. I wanted to make certain that you agree with what I've said."

"Don't worry. I understand that I'm dealing with a truly spirited woman now." He momentarily vanished into the tack room. When he returned, he carried a box of condoms.

Surprised, but amused, Chris asked, "You keep them in the stable?"

"T.J.'s assistant does. And if I don't remember to replace them, Ken will kill me."

She laughed.

Calm again, he shoved a helmet on his head and mounted the gray. The muscles in his arms commanded strength as he reined the gelding next to her, and his calloused hands—she recalled their coarse gentleness when he had touched her.

"Which way?" she asked, attempting to keep her voice even. In that same even composure, he pointed to a grove of oak and sycamore trees. She gave the mare a swift kick in the side. "Race you!"

The leather reins slid through her fingers, and the mare galloped off, leaving Geoff behind in the wake of her dust. Muscles strained beneath her and hooves pounded the path, leading to a grassy meadow. Exhilarated, Chris coaxed the mare for more speed as her hair whipped back. She breathed in the scent of lathered horse. In the clearing, she streaked across a carpet of chicory and black-eyed Susans. As the wind hit her face, tears filled her eyes. The rich green forest lay ahead.

Out of the corner of her eye, Chris caught a glimpse of a gray, steadily gaining on her. She clicked her tongue, but the mare had nothing left to give. They reached the grove, and the gray pulled even. She slowed the mare to a walk, and the gelding slid to a halt beside her.

"Where did you . . ." Geoff's chest heaved as he attempted to catch his breath. ". . . learn to ride like that?"

"Judith mostly." The gray continued to prance. She rubbed Tiffany's sweaty neck and dismounted under the oak trees. Her legs were like rubber, and she nearly fell.

Geoff vaulted from the gelding's back and threw an arm around her waist to steady her.

"Obviously," she said, "it's been a few years."

Fresh forest scent lingered everywhere, and a swift running stream hid among the trees. Rocks projected above the crystal clear water; silvery-scaled fish darted along the bottom. Her body molded to his, and when he pressed against her, he kissed her intimately. When their kiss ended, he pulled away slightly, caressing her hair between his fingers. He kissed her again, this time taking care to be gentle.

Chris grasped his hand and bent down. With a sharp wrist action, he hoisted her back to her feet before she reached the ground. "What's wrong?"

"Not here—not unless you want a nice case of poison ivy on your ass, city girl."

Familiar heat returned to her cheeks. Strangely cool and calm, Geoff folded his arms over his chest and laughed. Chris burned the three-leaf plant to memory. "I learn quickly. Besides, I'd like to see how you fare in the city."

His face twisted as he gathered up the horses' reins. "I don't do well in cities."

She had obviously drummed up another bad memory. What

a fool she was for accompanying him. If she had any sense, she'd take the mare and head back to the barn. Instead, she hooked her arm though his, and they led the horses through the forest with green leaves glistening against the sunshine in the wind. Saber snuffled ahead of them, and the path wound along an animal trail, becoming narrower and narrower as they walked. Finally, the forest opened to a clearing. A rustic log cottage stood nestled among the oaks.

Geoff tied the horses to a hitching post out front. "This place is only used occasionally anymore," he explained. Again his voice had been strangely collected, but a distinct bulge in his jeans revealed the truth.

Chris suppressed a snicker. "You've brought me to your secret, little hideaway."

His only response was a smirk. The wood creaked under their feet as they went up the steps. Hinges groaned when Geoff opened the door. Pegs lined the inside wall for colder days and hanging coats. Ashes remained in the fireplace, and a cupboard held tin plates. The cottage was at least as old as the main house—maybe older. Against the far wall was a bed with a patchwork quilt and plump feather pillows. And he had brought her here—to this special place. Suddenly regretting her decision, she wondered if he had brought others here.

As if reading her thoughts, he responded, "I don't bring every woman here."

"It doesn't matter," she lied.

He drew her into his arms. "Why do women always say the opposite of what they mean?"

"You're right," she said, taking a step back and breaking their embrace. "It does matter, but not in the way you might think. I'm not certain what's happening between us, but I can't promise anything beyond the week."

His gaze fixed on her. "So now you think the country boy can't handle the city girl?"

"Can you? Geoff, you're good at putting on a brave front, but I can easily guess how many women you've brought here. I can't be *her.*"

He exhaled slowly. "In all honesty, I haven't thought beyond the week myself. I only know that I enjoy your company." The edges of his mouth upturned in a slight grin. "Think of all the tending you would require now if you had gotten that nasty case of poison ivy."

"And you would have provided the tending?"

Bending slightly at the waist, he grasped her hand and kissed it. "Of course."

The sound of his baritone voice and Virginian accent made her breath quicken. Why did he arouse her so?

He drew her over to the bed, and they made their way through the other's clothing. The quilt was tossed to the floor. Naked on the bed, they touched, kissed, and caressed. Out here where no one could hear, she let her cries go unrestrained.

Geoff couldn't remember the last time he had felt this satiated. Chris lay in his arms with her head resting on his chest. He hovered between the worlds of sleeping and waking. Her fingertips traced along his midsection and down, attempting to fondle some life into him again. In that dreamy state, he laughed softly and kissed her on the mouth.

The door creaked, and a woman with black hair stood in its frame. Sunlight shimmered and flashed until the woman was absorbed by the bombarding light. Saber stood at the side of the bed and barked in a high-pitched warning. Geoff drew in a quick breath and closed his eyes.

"Geoff?"

"Get out."

"What?"

His forehead beaded with sweat and he reopened his eyes to Chris's bewildered expression. "You heard me. I said, 'Leave.' "

"But . . ."

He seized her wrist. "Get out before I throw you out."

"I see." Narrowing her eyes, Chris got up and dressed. "You fooled the city girl. Are you happy now?"

He hadn't meant to be harsh. *Tell her.* The words wouldn't come. Without looking back, she vanished through the door. More flashing light. "Chris . . ."

But he heard hoofbeats pounding away. He had let his guard down the other night. After two years without a seizure, he had grown complacent. He didn't want to repeat the spectacle he had made of himself.

In slow motion, Geoff retrieved some Dilantin from the pocket of his jeans. Over by the sink, he got a glass of water. After swallowing the anticonvulsant, he clutched the glass. If he seized now, he could fall on it. Shards would pierce his body, and there would be nothing he could do to prevent it. He tossed the glass across the room and heard the tinkling of shattering glass. Better over there than in him.

He gathered the quilt around him and sank to the floor. The cottage had been a sanctuary for as long as he could remember. Saber huddled next to him. Only one other woman had been here. The seizure was obviously near. He couldn't remember her name or what she looked like now. So why had he brought Chris? One more seizure, and she'd disappear. Hell, he'd probably never hear from her again after she returned to Boston.

Sometimes he wondered if women regarded him as nothing more than a curiosity. To his credit, he had never seized while having sex. If he could get stinking drunk without seizing, he'd toast to that small blessing.

The shimmering, flickering sunlight grew brighter, and the scent of honeysuckle surrounded him. He closed his eyes to her soft cries beneath him. *Catherine.* There was no sense in fighting it. The honeysuckle always won.

By the time Chris reached the barn, Judith had finished coaching her final student for the day. Judith called T.J. to see to the mare. "You went riding by yourself?" Judith asked in puzzlement.

To keep from blurting to Judith what a bastard her brother was, Chris bit her tongue. How could she have been so blind?

Christine Catherine! she heard her father's voice chastise. "Geoff was with me."

Judith scanned the grounds for another horse. "Where is he now?"

How much should she confide? Suddenly downright pissed, she nearly spit the words out. "He's at that little cottage you've got in the woods having a good laugh at my expense."

Judith blinked in confusion. "A good laugh?"

Curling her hands to fists, Chris paced back and forth along the dirt aisle. "I've met a lot of guys like him. I thought I was too smart to fall for lines, but I was so taken in that I failed to notice what he was really like."

"Chris..."

With a swift halt, Chris ran a hand through her hair. "Dammit, Judith, I didn't mean to involve you. This is exactly what I meant by leading to awkward situations."

"Then you and Geoff..." Looking a little pale, her friend pursed her lips.

Chris nodded. "I'll leave, rather than be the cause of disruption between family members."

"You'll do nothing of the kind! If my brother is behaving like a jerk, I'll skewer him personally. I was aware sparks were flying, but obviously didn't realize how far... uh... I don't wish to pry, but what was it that makes you think Geoff was insincere?"

"We were sharing the moment, when he suddenly got infuriated and told me to leave."

"Thank you for being discreet."

Calmer now, Chris took a deep breath. "Then you're not angry?"

Judith gave her a reassuring hug. "Why would I be angry? Whatever happens is between the two of you, but, Chris, you should know that his sudden mood swing sounds like a seizure might have been coming. Sometimes he just sort of loses it."

A seizure... She had been so absorbed in her hurt that she hadn't paid any attention to the signs. "How does Saber warn him?"

"With sort of a high-pitched bark."

Chris's eyes widened. "Then I need to get back to him."

"Leave him be. It may be one of the hardest things to accept, but he usually seeks solitude. Saber will let us know if he has any problems."

"What if Geoff hits his head, or stops breathing?" Chris asked in utter disbelief. "Saber is a dog. He can't call for medical help, if necessary."

"I'm well aware of that, but there's not much else we can do. There's no rhyme or reason to his moods before a seizure. He'll be fine in a few hours. Now you have some idea as to why Beth left."

Geoff's ex. Chris wondered when someone would get around to mentioning her. She sat on a bale of straw. "Why did she leave?"

Judith wrung her hands. "Geoff needs to tell you. I'll give him a reminder that you have a right to know."

Chris got to her feet. "I shouldn't have involved you. I'm sorry." Torn between rushing back to the cottage and jumping in the car to head for Boston, she hesitated. "Are you certain he prefers being alone?"

"I'm afraid so."

T.J. finished brushing the mare and led her to a stall. No wonder the help always seemed to know what went on in a household. He had tended his duties and blended right in without her noticing. Chris sprinted to the house. Once in the mansion, she scurried up the stairs to her room. She stood in front of the mirror, and the reflection of another woman stared back again. Her complexion was fair and her hair longer, and much darker than Chris's. Black, like Raven's. And her violet eyes—full of rage. "What do you want, Margaret?"

As if being struck by an object, the length of the mirror cracked, and the woman's image vanished.

* * *

The Yankees had agreed to let her stay if she tended their wounded. They finally retreated from the James River after she had spent endless hours bandaging wounds, holding hands, and whispering words of comfort. Margaret prayed for her husband's safety. Not long afterward, she toiled fields like a common field hand, all the while hoping for his eventual return.

Then, late one night, she heard his voice whisper his love for her. With each passing day, she hoped and prayed. She regretted answering the door that morning. Before that moment, she could pretend he would return. When she saw the gray uniform, she thought he had.

But it was none other than General J.E.B. Stuart himself. In a proper stance of duty, he told her about the heavy fighting. Many Confederates had died as well. At the bottom of the steps, a coal-black horse waited. His last wish was to have the stallion returned to her. The general explained that normally such a request wouldn't be honored, but the horse had been wounded in the fighting as well.

The voice had been his goodbye. With a throaty sob, she collapsed to the lane and cried.

In the clear night sky outside the cottage, stars sparkled. When Chris had accompanied him, it had been daylight. Wondering what time it was, Geoff tapped his watch. It had quit running sometime during the seizure. Perhaps that was significant—as when watches stopped after a person had died. Maybe a piece of him died with each seizure. Without conscious memories, he might have reached the plane of death, never realizing it. He laughed aloud. Technology could chart exactly which neurons misfired, but none of the drugs kept them from going haywire. What good was one without the other?

He mounted the gray gelding and rode back to the stable. After hitching the gelding in a crosstie, he uncinched the girth.

"Geoff, let me see ta the horse."

"T.J." Geoff glanced around, but continued unsaddling. "What are you doing here this late?"

"Waitin' fer ye. I saw the lass when she returned. Are ye all right?"

Geoff pulled the saddle from the gray's back. "I'm fine. How was Chris?"

"I told ye that I'd see ta the horse." T.J. snatched the saddle from Geoff's arms. "Mighty angry. If ye know what's good fer ye, ye'll march up ta the house an' explain things ta her right now."

"She already knows about the seizures. She saw me have one."

"All the more reason ta explain ta her." T.J. headed in the direction of the tack room with the saddle. "An' I better warn ye. Yer sister knows aboot ye an' the lass."

Judith would likely be furious. "Thanks for the warning." Geoff strode toward the house. His throat was parched, and he went into the drawing room and poured himself a glass of water.

"Geoff..."

He had hoped that he would be able to delay a confrontation with Judith until after speaking with Chris. "Yes."

"You've had another seizure, haven't you?"

Not only did his throat scratch, but his head pounded. He took a sip of water and faced her. "Is this another inquisition so you can run and phone the neurologist again?"

"You can be dense at times. I'm wondering if you're all right." He nodded, and she lowered her voice. "I know about you and Chris."

What a stupid ass—screwing his sister's best friend. He eased himself into the wing chair. "And?"

"It's none of my business what happens between the two of you, but like it or not, I'm caught in the middle. Just tell me that it's not like when Beth left."

He raised the glass. "It's water."

Frustrated, Judith flipped her hair across her shoulders. "That's not what I meant, and you know it. Dinner I can understand, but why in hell did you have to go and sleep with her?"

Even now, he thought of her intoxicating scent and the taste of her skin. "It just happened."

Judith grew red faced. "Goddammit, Geoff! She's my friend, and here you are treating her like a two-bit whore!"

"It's not like that."

"Then why haven't you told her about Beth? So help me, if you don't, I will."

Beth. What was he going to tell Chris about Beth? "I'll tell her. That is, if she's willing to listen after what happened this afternoon."

"I think she will." Calmer now, Judith sent him a knowing smile. "Remember, we've been friends for a lot of years. Trust her. She doesn't ruffle easily."

"If you say so." After setting the glass on the table, he went up to Chris's room and hesitated. He stared at the door for a couple of minutes, then got the nerve to knock. The door cracked open. "I'm sorry if I upset you. Sometimes, I need to be alone."

"Does the doctor think you should be alone?"

No.

He nudged the door slightly with his foot, but she kept it from swinging open. "Obviously not," she answered for him. "Why couldn't you tell me?"

"I don't always think rationally."

Her resistance faded. Chris stood aside, allowing him to enter. Her bag was on the bed and clothes were strewn about as if she had been packing. "I know you said people rarely die of seizures, but it can happen, can't it?"

"Most injuries are from falls. Because of Saber, I usually have enough warning to prevent that. Before he came along, which was close to seven years ago, I did break a couple of bones."

"That doesn't really answer the question. We once had a dog with seizures, and the vet warned us about *status epilepticus.*"

Being an attorney, she could detect a run-around, and he anticipated her next question. God, he hated spilling his guts this way. "I went into status once—five years ago. Beth left before I was out of the hospital."

Her arms went around his neck, and she kissed him on the mouth. "No wonder you don't trust easily."

With her body pressed against him, his resolve was weakening. Geoff thought of the afternoon at the cottage. "There's more."

She lowered her arms and straightened her blouse, inadvertently outlining the curve of her breasts. Her lip quivered. "More?" Chris sat on the bed and patted the spot beside her for him to join her.

"Not a good idea. I'll only think of you." The room suddenly seemed small. With all of the Dilantin in his bloodstream he should feel drowsy. Like a caged animal, he paced. "Beth was the first woman to accept my problem, or so I thought."

Chris pulled her legs up on the bed. As she crossed them, he thought of the cottage. Her cries—and the look of satisfaction.

"I assume there was more that you wanted to tell me."

He stopped pacing. Leaving a gap between them, he sat on the edge of the bed. "We went together in college. I noticed something wrong after we spent a weekend here. She had some strange dreams."

"Are you making a comparison between Beth and what's been happening to me?"

Swallowing hard, he wished he could forget Beth and make love to Chris now. "No. After college, we got married, and she would sleepwalk—sometimes for the entire night. The doctors could find nothing physically wrong."

Chris scooted next to him and squeezed his hand.

"We lived in Richmond for a while. I've already told you that I don't do well in cities. It was difficult to keep the seizures under control. When we returned here, Beth was pregnant. I didn't want kids. If I passed this on . . ." A lump rose in his throat as he gestured to his head. "I'd never forgive myself."

Chris began massaging his shoulders. "But you said it was after the accident that the seizures began. How would they be genetic?"

He clenched a hand, then opened it again. *Why was he telling her all of this?* "That's everyone's best guess, since no one can really determine the cause. The seizures began four months after the accident. To me, it wasn't worth the risk. Neal is six, and so far, he's had no seizures. Before I got out of the hospital after going into status, I was served with divorce papers." He got to his feet and noticed a crack in the mirror.

Without having to ask the question, she responded, "I was angry with you and threw my brush."

Geoff checked the wood-handle brush resting on the dresser. It would have taken more force to have caused that deep of a crack. Chris moved in next to him, distracting him. He breathed in her scent. Thank goodness, it wasn't honeysuckle. But something at the back of his mind filtered like wisps of light. Not the stray thoughts before a seizure, but the memory of a woman in his arms. Not Beth, but . . .

"I want you to promise me one thing," Chris said.

The image faded. "And that is?"

"If you know a seizure is coming, tell me. Once I learn everything I can, I promise not to be overprotective. If at all possible, I'd rather you weren't alone." Her hand slipped in his, intertwining their fingers.

"I'll try, but I need to be leaving."

"Leaving? I thought you'd stay the night."

"We ran out of—protection, earlier in the day."

She blushed slightly. "Then I trust you know where to get more."

"There is a drugstore, but with all of the Dilantin in my system, I think you should do the driving."

"Gladly."

His hands went under her blouse and along her back down across her hips with uncanny familiarity. *Where did these thoughts keep coming from*—the feeling like he had known her for years, then craving her all the more when she was in his arms? Separation had ended. She was the essence of life itself.

Chapter Five

WHEN CHRIS WOKE, SUN BEAMED through a narrow gap in the drapes. With Geoff's arm protectively around her, she forgot about any threat of seizures—or the image of Margaret in the mirror. She reached for Geoff's face, tracing a finger through his goatee. His nose twitched and eyelids fluttered open. "Didn't mean to wake you, but I wondered what you would look like if you only had a moustache," she whispered.

He rubbed his eyes. "Forget it, I'm not shaving to satisfy your curiosity." With a growing smile, he tugged the sheet off her and scanned the length of her unclad body. "Good morning... and what a sight to wake up to."

"We have a few left," she laughed. While she twisted reaching for a foil package on the nightstand, he kissed her back. The brush of his tongue tickled her spine. When a rap came to the door, Saber barked but wagged his tail.

"Chris..." *Judith.*

"Go away," Geoff grumbled, over his shoulder.

Chris clamped a hand over his mouth. "We're supposed to go horseback riding," she whispered. In frustration, he rolled to the side. She tossed the bedclothes over him. The last thing she needed was to have Judith discover Geoff naked in her bed. He yanked the blanket from his face and sat up. She waggled her finger. "Don't say anything and don't come out from under there. Be right there, Judith." She slipped from under the covers, grabbing a robe on her way to the door.

Geoff's eyes danced, and he suddenly seemed amused by the predicament.

"It would serve you right if I invited her in."

"You wouldn't."

"Don't tempt me," she responded with a smirk. Wiping the grin from her face, Chris cracked the door slightly.

Attired in tan breeches and knee-high boots, Judith was dressed for a morning ride. "I fear that I'm interrupting," she said, clearing her throat.

"Not at all." Chris heard Geoff laugh and she waved at him to keep quiet.

Shifting on her feet, Judith blushed. "Perhaps it's best if I meet you downstairs." She turned. "By the way, I'm pleased the two of you have talked things over."

As Chris closed the door, Geoff only laughed harder.

"You didn't make that easy," she said.

He shrugged. "Sorry."

"You're not."

He searched through the clothing scattered across the floor. Unconcerned that she watched, he pulled on his briefs over his nicely muscled butt. Then came his jeans. Still shirtless, he reached inside her robe and drew her next to him. "I don't know how—or why—but it seems like I've known you all my life. Chris..."

Her fingers went to his lips. "Don't say anymore. I need time to think."

Already familiar with where she liked being touched, he lightly traced over her bare skin. "This isn't the same room that you shared with Beth?"

He shook his head, then anticipated her next question. "Across the hall from Judith. Do you feel better now?"

The same room she had been drawn to upon her arrival.

"I won't lie that I wasn't hurt," he continued, "which is why I relocated to the room I have now, but I'm not making comparisons."

Then why had he taken her to the cottage? "I believe you."

Oblivious to her lingering doubts, he cupped her breast and kissed it, then his arms dropped to his side. "Reality calls," he sighed. "If I don't get my daily dose of Dilantin, I could wind up having another seizure." As he leaned over to locate his shirt, she wished she could do something to make the seizures go away. "No sad faces. It's something I've learned to deal with." "Are . . . " Hesitating, she hoped he wouldn't think she was asking for selfish reasons. ". . . two in one week common?" Finished dressing, he stroked the side of her face. "No. I'm sure it's because of the reduced medication." She opened her mouth to question further, but he continued, "And don't worry. I will call the neurologist for all the good it'll do. They'll run more tests, tell me what I already know, then increase the dosage."

"You're going to the doctor? Let me go with you."

"There's no sense in you wasting your day too. You did come to visit my sister," he reminded her.

He was right. "Will I see you later?"

After a nod, he gave her an intimate goodbye kiss.

When Geoff opened the door, Saber bounded into the hall. Geoff closed the door behind him, and Chris dressed in a pair of jeans and a T-shirt. She threw a light jacket over her shoulders to break the morning chill and met Judith at the bottom of the stairs.

They went outside to the pillared steps. "You don't look very well rested," Judith remarked, attempting to sound casual, "but you certainly have a glow about you that wasn't there earlier in the week."

"Judith . . ."

Her friend's response was a giggle, and Chris suddenly felt like she was in college again.

"I truly hope you don't mind what's happened; after all, he is your brother."

"I'm happy if you're happy," Judith said. They crossed the neatly mowed grounds. The red-brick stable had arches facing the stone courtyard and a cupola topped by an elaborate trotting-horse weather vane on the roof. "But I worry that one of you or the both of you are going to wind up getting hurt. You're so very different."

In the courtyard, Chris halted. "I haven't felt this way in a long time. I'm out of control, yet it's wondrous."

"You're falling for him, and that's what worries me. Geoff won't ever leave here, and I don't see you giving up your career in Boston. Look how long it took me to get you down here for a visit."

"And now I wish I had made the effort sooner."

They laughed.

"Just be careful, Chris."

Inside the stable, Judith enlisted T.J.'s aid to help with the horses. They gave Chris a dark bay gelding by the name of Ebony. Like the brown mare the previous day, the gelding was gentle.

Judith guided her chestnut mare from the courtyard to a dirt path leading away from the barn, and Chris brought Ebony in line behind her. Unlike the oak woods, the meadows opened up to dying summer grasses that would have been hip deep on a person. The trail curved around a sharp bend. With surefooted agility, the horses made their way along the path. "I've been meaning to ask if you can get time off next month."

"I doubt it," Chris responded with a shake of her head. "I have an upcoming trial and will probably be in court. Why?"

"There's a Halloween costume ball at one of the nearby plantations. It's one of our big social events. David will be there, and I'd like for you to meet him."

Chris thought of the blue silk dress hanging in the wardrobe. *A costume?*

"I bet Geoff would be happier about attending if he knew you were coming from Boston."

She attempted to sound casual. "With an event this important, I'm sure he has a date already."

Judith laughed. "I honestly don't know what his plans are, but after this week, I have a feeling he won't be thinking of anyone else." She sent the red mare forward.

The meadow led to the river. Chris halted Ebony alongside the edge of the James. To get a closer look, she dismounted. Waves rippled against rocks, lapping at an old tree standing near the bank. Many branches were leafless from the brackish water, but the tree clung tenaciously to life.

Breathing in the river air, Chris leaned forward. *He was gone. He had promised to return. One step forward. The river would carry her away, and she would join him.*

Breathe. Her heart fluttered. With a gasp, Chris choked back a breath. Dizzy, she blinked. Another vision.

As she caught her breath, Chris stepped away from the bank and looked to the river. Margaret had come here to think. Among black thoughts after George's death, she had nearly taken her own life. *George?* His name had been George. He had been killed during the war, and Margaret was devastated.

"Chris, are you all right?" She focused on Judith's pale face. "You were staring into empty space. If I didn't know better, I'd swear you had some sort of winking out like my brother."

Like Geoff. Didn't he say he often became confused before a seizure? With a twinge of guilt, she realized she was comparing a medical condition to spirits. "I'm fine." A new thought occurred to her, but she hesitated asking. Judith would think she had gone totally mad. "Judith, tell me about the Civil War."

"What about it?"

"Geoff said that your Great-Grandmother Margaret stayed behind and nursed the wounded."

"She cared for the wounded to keep the Yankees from burning the house."

Poplar Ridge. With a shudder Chris envisioned the house in ashes. "And your grandfather?"

"He served in the Confederate cavalry."

"Did he survive the war?"

"I'm not certain. I'd need to look at the genealogical records. Why?"

"Do you mind if I have a look? I have the strangest feeling that he died and your grandmother never recovered." As she mounted Ebony, he tossed his head. The dark bay gelding trotted along the trail, and she reined him to a walk.

On the return trip, scenery passed without notice. At the sharp bend the gelding's ears pricked forward as if listening to something on the trail ahead. Hooves drumming... She had heard them too. Ebony's neck lathered, and his muscles strained. Chris tightened the reins. Without warning, the dark bay lurched sideways, hurling her from the saddle.

She smacked to the ground, and pain shot through her hip. *A horse and rider came to a sliding halt in front of her. The rider hurdled from the horse's back and seized her wrists, wrenching her to her feet. A uniform—he wore Union blue. But his face—a cavernous hole gaped where his left eye should have been.*

With a scream, she struggled against his grip. Intense pain—she thought her bones might snap under his hold. Even when she tripped, he forged forward and dragged her to the nearest tree. Two faceless soldiers in blue lashed her wrists to a branch overhead. The ropes bit into her skin, but she continued fighting them.

The red-haired man with the missing eye withdrew a knife from his boot. She felt the cold blade against her neck. Thinking of George, she said a prayer. The soldier bellowed a laugh as the knife sliced through her bodice. He unhooked her corset and ripped through her chemise. The others gathered around, tearing and shredding her dress until she was bare to the waist. Too exhausted to fight. *Blood trickled down her arms from struggling against the ropes, and she ceased her futile resistance.*

The soldier's good eye was the color of smoke. It kept peering at her until he finally nodded in approval. He leaned into her, and to her horror, she could feel his erection pressed against her person. His left hand pinched her nipple, while the right one snapped her head back by her hair. His tongue explored her mouth. Unable to breathe, she gagged.

He finally let go, and she gasped to catch her breath. His bellowing laugh returned, and he paced around her. She twisted just enough to see him take a horsewhip from one of the faceless soldiers. She howled when it made contact with her bare skin.

* * *

"Chris?"

Staring at the tree in front of her, Chris blinked, realizing that it was Judith's voice. Her hands went to her mouth, and her voice trembled. "Judith?"

"What just happened?"

Chris fought the tears. "An eye—he was missing an eye."

"Are you certain?"

"Judith, surely you saw him." She gripped Judith's blouse. "Tell me that you saw him."

"I saw him."

Chris's mouth dropped open. "Really?"

"If you remember, he's the one that I told you about. A Yankee soldier. He must have been wounded in battle."

Still trembling, Chris brushed back her stray hair. "And you have no idea who he was?"

Judith shook her head. "There were a lot of Yankees through here during the war. He probably died when the house was used as a field hospital."

That would explain the missing eye, but why was he horsewhipping Margaret?

"I usually see him near the river," Judith continued, "by the tunnel entrance to the cellar."

The same place Geoff had shown her the other day. Chris began to tell Judith all that had happened. When she finished, her friend's face remained unchanged. "Well, say something."

"If it ever happened, it was over 140 years ago."

"There must be a reason why I'm seeing these events."

"A reason, yes. Discovering what that may be might be a difficult task."

Frustrated, Chris placed a hand to her chest.

"Chris . . ." Judith pointed.

Before she saw what Judith was gesturing at, she felt the pain. On her wrists were red welts from rope burns.

* * *

In the library, Judith brought Chris ledgers with the genealogical data that her family had gathered over the years. "Great-Aunt Greta has documentation going back to the Scottish Camerons. She had to piece details together from public records during and before the war, because as I already told you, most of our private ones were lost."

Seated at the desk, Chris pored over dusty volumes. She grew fascinated by the numerous names and dates—Cameron after Cameron with their children and children's children listed. She found entries for Geoff and Judith. Their mother's name had been Sarah MacGillivrey. *MacGillivrey?* Wasn't that the stable hand's last name? If they were indeed related, that could easily explain why T.J. remained on a first-name basis with the family.

A picture of the house at the turn of the twentieth century caught Chris's attention. Shutters were falling off or missing. Bricks tumbled from the chimneys, and the columns were smaller, making the appearance of the house look less grand. Three buildings stood in the place of one sweeping mansion. She pointed to the picture. "Judith?"

"The war and Reconstruction were difficult times for the family. We nearly lost the house and land, but as time went on, the economy improved. The wings were added in the 1920s."

"So, where I'm sitting . . ."

"Was originally in a separate building from the main house." Judith blew dust off another ledger and set it on the oak surface in front of Chris. "I think this one has the details from the mid-nineteenth century."

Chris opened the heavy leather cover. The volume began with 1850. She searched through pages of meticulous entries. Judith pointed to one. *Margaret.* Hopefully, now she would find some answers. Margaret Harrison had married George Cameron in 1861. They had one son by the name of Jason in April 1866.

"That's a full year after the war," Judith said, pointing to Jason's birthdate. "George had to have survived."

"Unless there's a skeleton in the Cameron closet," Chris muttered.

Judith laughed. "There are plenty of those, but Aunt Greta wouldn't have made the entries unless she had been able to verify them."

"Short of a time machine and a DNA test, I don't know how anyone can prove paternity from so long ago."

"Didn't you say the man in your vision looked like Geoff?" Her own conclusion, but not something Chris was ready to admit. "Circumstantial evidence, especially since there are no pictures of him."

Judith gestured to the entry. "Look at the dates. George died in 1867."

"It doesn't make sense. In my vision, Margaret thought George was dead." Chris flipped the yellowed page to more entries in a woman's handwriting.

As told to me by my grandmother Margaret Cameron,
Greta Cameron Williams

Chris read the entry with interest. It verified that Margaret had remained at Poplar Ridge to nurse wounded soldiers and had received a visit from General Stuart. Taking in a deep breath, Chris halted a moment. *Her visions were real.* For some reason, she was seeing past events through Margaret's eyes. She continued reading. Margaret had rejoiced when George suddenly returned to her—very much alive. Her joy had been short lived because he had been captured and taken to Fort Delaware as a prisoner of war.

Odd, but that was the last mention of George. In fact, the rest of the entry was rather sparse, including barely a reference to the birth of her son. According to the previous page, Margaret had died in 1924. Such a long life, and nothing significant happened after the war?

"Well..."

Chris glanced over at Judith. "George did survive the war, but it's puzzling."

"How's that?"

"If I were handling such a case, I'd try to uncover evidence that the entry had been scripted. Something happened to Margaret, and she's trying to let us know what." Less puffy, the welts on her wrists remained painful red rings. Was that why she was experiencing the visions? Margaret must realize that Chris would eventually be able to uncover the truth.

God, he hated the drugs. Between the mental dullness and nervousness, Geoff sometimes found them worse than the seizures. Ironic, others took mind-altering drugs to get high, but he would cherish life if he could live without them. As Geoff eased into the wing chair in the drawing room, he wondered how long it would take to adjust to the new dosage.

"What did you find out?"

Judith. Had she had been in the room for a while or had she just entered? "The seizures are back. I didn't need to go to Richmond to learn that."

"Geoff, I'm worried." Judith sat across from him on the tapestry sofa. "I nearly told Chris what it was like after Beth left."

When he had woken in the hospital and discovered that Beth and Neal were gone, he hadn't cared much about living. "What held you back?"

"I wanted to give you the chance." She fidgeted in the seat. "I'm trying not to intrude."

"I know, you're worried about your friend."

"And you." She reached over and patted the back of his hand. "Now go see her. She's still very disturbed from her experience this afternoon."

Had he missed part of the conversation? Geoff waved for her to back up. "Experience? Did you tell me about an experience?"

"When I came into the room." She blew out a breath. "I forgot how the drugs can wipe your memory. She saw *him.*"

Beth had seen the ghost too. He jumped up from the chair and swayed. The side effects made his head spin.

Judith grasped his forearm. "Wait, that's not all . . ."

He gripped the chair to help steady himself.

"She keeps talking about the War Between the States. She was curious about our great grandmother. Then she went on to name our grandfather. Did you remember that his name was George?"

Groggy, Geoff shook his head.

"That's probably not too surprising because Aunt Greta never knew him, but Chris went on to say that he had died during the war."

"And?"

"He was captured, but he did return. If he hadn't, none of us would be here. But when we were riding back . . ."

Geoff listened as Judith relayed Chris's encounter with the ghost and her search through Greta's genealogical ledgers. "I'll talk to her. Where is she?"

Judith frowned in concern. "In her room. I trust you know the way."

Rushing to Chris's room, he rapped on the door. No answer. He knocked louder. When she failed to respond, he became worried and burst inside. In deep thought, Chris stood beside the canopied bed. The blue dress from the third floor lay spread over the quilt, and she held the fabric up, studying it. "I knocked . . ."

Blinking, she looked over her shoulder. "Geoff, you're back." She rushed into his arms. "What did you find out?"

"Nothing new." He stepped back. The rings on Chris's wrists had faded to pink, but they remained distinct. "Judith told me what happened today."

"She shouldn't have."

His rush of adrenaline had lowered the medication's side effects. "She's worried about you. Quite frankly, so am I. Nothing like this . . ." He extended her arm to reveal the rings around her wrists. ". . . has happened before."

Chris withdrew her arm from his grip. "She needs my help."

"Margaret? She's been dead for a very long time."

"You promised that you'd help me find out what is going on."

"That was before anyone got hurt. Besides, you're returning to Boston tomorrow." Why did the thought of her leaving suddenly make him feel like he had been wounded?

A small smile formed on her face. "Judith invited me to the costume ball next month. I thought I might return for it. That is, if you want me to."

His sadness gave way to hope. "Want you to? Of course, I want to see you again."

She wrapped her arms around his neck and kissed him. "Then I'll come. I've never been to a costume ball before."

She amazed him. Even after all she had been through, she rebounded. It must be that stubborn city-girl attitude. "I'm glad." He gestured to the cracked mirror. "Now if you want my help, you can start by explaining what happened to the mirror."

"I told you . . ."

"The truth."

"The truth?" She settled into the rocking chair beside the bed. "Margaret. She's appeared to me twice in the mirror, and the last time, it cracked. She's upset about something that happened. I think I may be close to discovering what it was."

He bent down and touched the fading ring on one of her wrists. "And what if something like this happens again?"

She exhaled slowly. "I once had clients whom I discovered were embezzling. During the trial, I had to testify against them, and as you might imagine, my life was threatened. Do you think a ghost or two can unnerve me?"

Her words were brave, but he detected a tremor in her voice. He took her hand and gripped it in his.

A smile appeared on her face, and she squeezed his hand. "You're going to have me believing in knights in shining armor too."

"Sorry to disappoint you, ma'am." He kissed her hand. "I'm nothing but a simple country boy."

She laughed. "There's nothing simple about you."

"In that case, I'm hungry. Should we go down to dinner? I'm sure the family is waiting by now."

Her eyes widened slightly. "Does your father know about us?"

"Only if Judith has told him."

She waved at him to continue. "Well, how is he going to take the news?"

How could he explain what his father was really like? *You see, Chris, the old man turned the farm over when he did to keep me out of the public eye as much as possible. Heaven forbid, what would the neighbors think if I had a seizure in front of someone?* "He likes you, so don't worry."

She took his hand, and Geoff helped her to her feet. The rings around her wrists had vanished.

After dinner, the family retired to the parlor, where Judith played Chopin on the piano. Plagued by visions of the surgeon amputating the boy's arm, Chris shuddered. Seated next to Geoff on the walnut-framed sofa, she inched closer. With a gleam in his eyes, he grasped her hand. Civil War hospitals were obviously the furthest thing from his mind. The elder Cameron sat in an adjacent chair. If he hadn't known about her affair with Geoff, he certainly did now. She could care less. He was bound to find out sooner or later anyway.

The maid, Laura, entered and whispered in Geoff's ear. He nodded, then leaned in Chris's direction, so the others wouldn't overhear. "Phone call. I'll be in the library should you desire my company later." He gave her a wink and strode for the door with Saber in line behind him. Geoff's gait wobbled slightly, and she worried that he hadn't revealed everything about his visit to the doctor. No wonder—she had been so wrapped up in the one-eyed ghost and Margaret that she hadn't given him much of a chance to say anything.

Judith finished the final note, and silence descended throughout the room. Chris stood and applauded. "I never knew you could play like that, Judith."

Her friend smiled her dimpled grin, and Winston Cameron beamed with pride. "Let's adjourn to the drawing room for some brandy," he said, bowing slightly and motioning for them to proceed. "Ladies."

Chris gave Judith a congratulatory squeeze to her arm for a

job well done. "Thank you, Chris, but if you'd rather join Geoff, I understand."

"I'll see him later."

As they made their way from the parlor and down the hall lined with portraits to the drawing room, Judith's father's expression remained stoic. If he held reservations or disapproved of her relationship with Geoff, he failed to show it. Chris almost wished he would say something to gain an inkling as to what he was thinking. Once in the drawing room, he poured brandies from the crystal decanter. "Should we have a toast?" Chris raised her glass, and he directed his gaze at Judith. "To your mother, who would be especially proud at this moment."

Glasses clinked, then he glanced in Chris's direction with a nod of approval. She breathed out in relief and finished her brandy before excusing herself. Polished brass sconces in the shape of candles lit the way down a wood-paneled hall. From the end of the hall came a whimper—a woman crying. She followed the sound to the library.

Tessa spread cool salve across the swollen welts on Margaret's back. "You gots to stop fightin' dem, Miss Margaret. Men like dese only gets angrier da more you resist. Dey ain't goin' to quit just cause you white."

A nut-brown face came into focus. "Tessa." Brushing back the tears, she grasped the servant's wrist. "If you can fetch George's gun from the main house . . ."

Tessa placed two fingers to her lips. "Dey hears you," she whispered. The servant continued spreading salve and lowered a shawl over Margaret's back.

The threadbare fabric rubbed her tender lacerations. After whipping her, the Yankee scouts had left her bound to the tree for several hours. Only at Tessa's insistence that she nurse her had Margaret been allowed to return to the library.

Margaret heard nasal voices singing an off-key song outside. They sounded drunk. Expecting any one of them to burst through the door, she huddled next to Tessa. Two women—alone. Her only solace was thinking of other days, dancing in her blue silk dress with George. She choked back a sob.

"Miss Margaret, dey comin'."

She had heard it too. Boots on the steps outside. The door creaked, and Margaret said a silent prayer that it might be George. But the men wore Yankee blue. The one-eyed scout seized Tessa's arm. "Take the wench."

A faceless soldier obeyed, and she heard Tessa's screams as they retreated out the door.

"Now Miss High-and-Mighty . . ." As the scout moved toward her, Margaret took a step back. "I'll be gentle if you do as I say."

Her chance. *She nodded that she would do as he instructed.*

His smoke-colored eye stared at her in eagerness. He pressed next to her and stroked her cheek. "I don't like hurtin' you, but you Rebel women are just so goddamned feisty that you need to be taught to keep your place."

Keep calm. *If she could gain his trust, she would recognize her chance to confiscate his pistol, but her heart pounded so hard that it felt like a beating drum in her throat. When he kissed her, as much as the action revolted her, she reciprocated.*

He shoved the shawl from her shoulders to reveal her bare breasts. "Finish undressing."

She froze. "What?"

"You heard me." He withdrew his pistol from its holster. "I said I want to see the rest of you."

Biting her lip to keep from crying, Margaret silently obeyed.

The single piercing eye ogled her. "On the sofa."

Oh, God. Could George ever forgive her? *When she didn't move fast enough to suit him, he motioned with the gun. She sat on the sofa.*

"Now you just stay right there, lookin' so purty." He lowered his trousers and drawers to reveal his erect male member.

Keep focused on the pistol. *But he placed the gun in the desk drawer, then moved toward her. Unable to restrain herself any longer, Margaret bolted. Beside the desk, she had the pistol in her hands. She aimed.*

* * *

"Chris?"

A dog barked, and Chris blinked, staring into Geoff's bewildered face. "A gun. She was ready to shoot him—in here."

His arms went around her. "Who was going to shoot whom?"

"Margaret... she was going to shoot *him*." Distraught, she spilled the tale on his shoulder. He showed her to the sofa, then poured her a drink from the liquor cabinet before sitting beside her. She took a sip and wrinkled her nose. Whiskey. Trembling from the vision, she gulped the rest. "Maybe the gun is still in here."

"I don't keep any guns in the house."

His response had been harsher and more abrupt than she would have anticipated. "I wasn't accusing you..."

"I know. There are some other things that I should tell you. Not here. I'd only think of you." He grasped her hand and guided her from the library.

Outside the door, a staircase led to the second floor and the floral-designed wallpaper. His room lay directly above the library. She had only seen the room from the adjoining bathroom. Another time, she would have reveled in the antique furniture—leather and aged wood that signified quiet, gentle masculinity. "What's wrong?" she asked.

Regret appeared on his face.

"Geoff?"

"Not yet," he replied in a shaky voice. He showed her to an oversized leather wing chair beside the fireplace. "I should have told you before, but Beth saw the same ghost."

So, there was a connection between her and Beth. Her arms went around him. His muscles remained tense, and he resisted the embrace. Finally, he relaxed and joined her in the chair. Content just holding him, she nestled in his arms. "If it's not intruding, would you mind if I speak to Beth?"

His muscles tensed again.

"Forget that I asked. I only thought it might lend some insight as to what's been happening."

He let out a weary breath. "I'll ask her, but don't count on her cooperation. She only speaks to me when it's necessary for Neal's sake. There's more you should know. I didn't cope with Beth's leaving very well. I turned to alcohol and—shit, I might as well say it, or my sister will likely tell you—women. With that kind of abuse, I couldn't keep the seizures under control. Ironic, but the seizures may have saved my life."

"Saved your life?"

"The reason why I don't keep a gun in the house is because I used to own a Civil War pistol. I thought about using it—on myself."

Biting her lip, she withheld a gasp.

"If it hadn't been for a seizure, I might have succeeded. The incident woke me up. I straightened out my life, but because of it, I failed to petition the court for joint custody. Neal's been through enough. I didn't want to drag him through a court battle as well."

Another hug—she didn't want to let go. "I'm so sorry."

"Just be glad you've learned all of the dirty, little secrets around Poplar Ridge while there's still a chance for you to get out without be hauled off to the funny farm."

He was trying to make light of the situation. "Do you mind if I stay the night?"

"I can't imagine why you'd want to after everything that's happened."

"Because I love you." There—she had said it, with conviction.

"Chris . . ." His voice broke.

She placed a finger to his lips. "Don't feel obligated to repeat it."

"I think I felt it when I met you on the road and helped you with the tire." He kissed her, and she tightened her embrace.

Grateful for their time together, Chris woke to the sound of rain drumming against the window pane. Geoff's arm was around her, and he slept soundly beside her. The clock on the night-stand read 6:45. She kissed him on the cheek. "I'm going to return to my room," she whispered in his ear.

He muttered an acknowledgment, and she slipped from beneath the covers. Beside the bed, Saber raised his head from the rug as she dressed. Chris made a quick stop to the bathroom, then shuffled sleepily down the hall of the west wing to her room in the main section of the house.

Before reaching her room, she felt a distinct chill. Notes from the piano sounded from downstairs. Odd that Judith would be playing so early in the morning. Without closing the door behind her, she entered the bedroom. Drapes swirled in blowing gusts. She rushed over to close the window. The silk dress lay undisturbed on the bed where she had left it. She turned. The mirror had another crack running through it. "Margaret, I know you're angry, but I need more clues before I can fit the pieces together." Had Margaret killed the one-eyed ghost?

"Chris?" Judith stood in the open doorway, hesitant to come inside.

"Come in."

Judith stepped in but kept staring in Chris's direction as if she were afraid to look about the room.

"Don't worry, Judith. Geoff's not here."

Judith glanced at the mirror. "Then who were you talking to?"

"Myself. And before you ask, I have no idea what happened to the mirror! It was that way when I returned to my room this morning." A partial truth—but Chris felt it was unimportant to go into all of the details.

"I wasn't going to say anything," Judith said, shaking her head. "It is old. Maybe there was a stress fracture when I had the men move it in here."

A logical explanation, but she had experienced too much to explain everything away to rational reasons. Perhaps she was overlooking the obvious. "Judith, is there anyone still alive who would have known Margaret?"

"Aunt Greta."

"You're aunt is alive? Why didn't you tell me?"

Her friend shrugged. "You won't be able to speak to her
if that's what you're thinking. She's visiting a sick friend in
Florida." A thoughtful grin appeared on Judith's face. "But if
you come back for the costume ball, she should be here then."

"I've already decided that I will."

Judith clapped her hands in delight. "Wonderful! And I have
the perfect idea." She went over to the bed, picked up the gown,
and pressed it against Chris. "You can wear this."

Her own thoughts, but something held her back. "Margaret's
dress?"

"Take it with you. That way if it needs any alterations, you
can see to them."

Chris glanced at her reflection in the mirror. Should she? By
wearing the dress, she might gain further insight into what was
troubling Margaret. "I'll do it."

"Good, then it's settled. I only wish you could stay longer
this time." Judith's eyes danced slyly. "I bet Geoff does too."

"I hope . . ." Chris shook her head.

"Go ahead. You can say it."

"I fear that it's been nothing more than a wild vacation ro-
mance. You were right to warn me because I can't think of a
way in hell that we could actually make it work."

Judith hugged her. "Perhaps in the coming month you'll be
able to think of something."

A little uncomfortable by the embrace, Chris stepped back.
"Thanks, Judith. I should have known you would have something positive to say."

"And if things don't work out, don't be afraid to confide in
me. We're still friends."

Judith hugged her again, and Chris instantly regretted that
she hadn't told the entire truth about the mirror.

After breakfast, Chris set about packing her things. Geoff had
been called away during the meal, and she worried that he
wouldn't return by the time she was ready to leave. She took

great care packing Margaret's gown, then gathered her clothes from the drawer. As she closed the suitcase, a black dog hopped onto the bed and licked her in the face. "Saber." Relieved to see him, she snuggled next to him. Entering through the open door, Geoff strode over to her. "As I suspected, it's really my dog that you're after." She laughed. "You've found me out. I have this thing for guys with pointy ears, but Mr. Spock has an annoying tendency to sound like a lawyer."

"And if Judith discovers Saber on the bed..." He gave the dog a hand signal, and Saber bounded off the bed. He sat in the spot that Saber had vacated. "How about showing me some of the same attention that you were giving Saber?"

"I don't know." With soulful, dark-brown eyes, Saber stared up at her, and she scratched him under the chin. "Saber swears that he's given up drinking from the toilet bowl. Can you make the same claim?"

"You drive a hard bargain, but if it's the only way..." He kissed her on the mouth.

"If you say so." She smiled. "I had heard that Southern men were half-mad."

"Only half?" A glimmer entered his eyes. "By now, you should be convinced that we're totally crazy."

Becoming serious again, Chris said, "I was afraid that you wouldn't make it back before I left."

"Nothing would keep me away." He kissed her once more. "The mare that had put her leg through the fence on your arrival split her stitches. T.J. has everything under control until the vet arrives."

"T.J.?" She recalled the entry in Greta's ledger. "MacGill-ivrey? Isn't that the same as your mother's maiden name?"

"T.J. is her brother."

As his gaze met hers, she missed him already. She ached for the horseback ride to the woods and making love in the cottage. She touched his cheek and kissed him. "Geoff?"

"Don't say it, or I will too."

"You'll call me?" He nodded, and she stood. "It's time."

"I was afraid you were going to say that." Geoff carried her suitcase into the hall. Judith met them, casting nervous glances from her brother to Chris. "I'll take this to the car," he said and disappeared down the staircase.

A hint of a smile appeared on Judith's lips. "I'm looking forward to next month."

Chris touched Judith lightly on the arm. "Would you keep an eye on Geoff for me?"

"He's going to miss you. I haven't seen him this twitterpated in a long time."

They went down the stairs. "Will he be all right?" Chris asked.

At the bottom of the stairway, Judith replied, "I'll let you know if he's not."

Chris took one last look around the hall at the Persian rug, the vase, and the Colonial table. Only a few days before, she had been overwhelmed by the grandeur. Magnificent material items didn't matter. She went outside. Geoff waited at the bottom of the steps, beside her car parked in the circular drive. Judith gave her a hug and a kiss, then rushed back toward the house. "Bye, Chris. I'll give you a call."

Chris unlocked the trunk. "Now what?"

Geoff placed her suitcase in the trunk and slammed it shut. He drew her in his arms. "I'll see you in a month's time."

"Then what?" she whispered.

"I wish I had the answer."

A lump formed in her throat. "Then I guess it's goodbye."

"For now." Geoff bent down to kiss her in a way that was more like an exchange between two friends. In a daze, she got in the car and put the key into the ignition. She lowered the window. "Geoff . . ." She had nearly said *I love you* again. "I'll see you next month."

He nodded. "I'll be waiting."

She started the car and shifted it into drive. Tears filled her eyes as she released the brake and drove down the lane. She couldn't look back. If she had, she would have said, *To hell with Boston*, and turned right around.

Chapter Six

MORE THAN TWO YEARS HAD PASSED since Geoff had last visited the seedy bar on the outskirts of Richmond. He couldn't face going home—not yet—and glanced around the smoke-filled room. The jukebox echoed an ear-shattering rendition of Bruce Springsteen's "Born in the USA." Times had changed—it had been considered an honor to serve in the Civil War. Being wealthy, his father had weaseled out of the draft during Nam, and he was exempt from the military due to the seizures. He drained the remaining beer from his mug.

"Ye're still mopin' fer the lass. It's only been a couple o' days. Give yerself some time."

In this rundown place, few knew or cared that he was the son of a rich bastard. "I know, T.J."

"Ye can call her," replied the gray-bearded Scotsman.

"It's not as simple as that."

T.J. waved to a waitress. "What ye need is ano'er pint."

Right—another drink. He was drifting into the same routine that he had fallen into after Beth had left. *Why?* Chris had promised that she would return. *For a dance, and then what?*

T.J.'s scrawny stable assistant with a cleft chin, Ken, slid into an empty chair, setting a frothy mug in front of him. "The waitress was busy. Told her I'd bring it over."

Geoff dug into his pocket for the change. "What do I owe you?"

"Forget it. I'll let you buy the next round." Ken took a gulp from his mug, then pointed to Geoff. "Is he still drowning his sorrows for the highfalutin lawyer from Boston, T.J.?"

"Aye."

Ken snorted a laugh. "Maybe the old man thought Geoff's relationship was too much like when he fraternized with the working class."

T.J. raised a finger. "I warn ye. There wasna a finer woman than Sarah. Even after she became the lady o' the house, she ne'er fergot her humble Scottish roots. Rather fittin', don' ye think? The Camerons came from Scotland ta seek their fortune in the new land, an' Sarah MacGillivrey did the same."

"Yeah, yeah, T.J.," Ken said with a sarcastic laugh, "we've heard that story a thousand times."

Geoff stood, but swayed, so he decided to reseat himself before he fell. "And what good is a fortune when she's dead?"

Both Ken and T.J. looked in his direction.

"Her bairns aren' grubbin' fer handouts on the streets o' Glasgow," T.J. replied. "That's how."

And the moral of the story was to marry rich. Geoff wondered if T.J. really believed his implication. "So why was she leaving my father at the time of the accident?" He raised his mug and took a gulp. "Or is it that all of the Cameron males are impossible to live with? Heaven knows we have a long history of failed marriages. No wonder the goddamned place is haunted. All of the women have returned from the dead to get even."

"Would the two of you quit being so serious? We're supposed to be cheering you up, Geoff, not making things worse. Here," Ken said, waving for a couple of women to join them at the table, "I've got the perfect solution."

Careful not to stagger, Geoff stood. The women snickered at his manners. Their low-cut blouses, short skirts, and heavy makeup hinted they were for hire. "Ken, I don't need . . ."

Ken raised a hand. "I know exactly what you're going to say, but before you say no, have you ever been with a working girl?"

"As a matter of fact, my old man worried that I'd never get

laid because of the seizures and hired one for my seventeenth birthday. Scared me shitless." The women giggled once more, and Geoff threw some change on the table for a tip. "If you don't mind, I'll be leaving now. Come along, Saber." He collected the leash, and the dog hopped to his feet, ready to go.

Once outside, Geoff breathed in the night air. Relieved to be away from the smoky atmosphere, he felt the dizzying effects of alcohol. Unused to more than a couple of drinks at a time, he wondered how many beers he had drunk. He remembered nursing only one.

As he zipped his jacket, T.J. joined him. "They weren' quite what ye had in mind, were they?"

"No."

"I tried ta tell Ken ahead of time, but he wouldna listen. Women like that can only give so much. When it's time ta get up an' go home, it sorta leaves a man feelin' empty." T.J. held up several wadded bills and grinned. "At least, I won the bet."

Geoff's eyes widened in surprise. "You bet on whether I'd leave with one of them?"

"Aye, an easy one it was at that. Now go call Chris."

"Not yet." A car's headlights sent a beam like a tunnel of light piercing through the night, not unlike what he witnessed before a seizure. Geoff watched curiously.

"I detect more ta the story than ye're tellin'."

The sound of waves from the James lapped against the bank, and he turned to T.J. "I wonder if she can really accept the seizures."

"Ach, is that the problem? If she canna live wi' it, then yer better off makin' yer bed wi' one o' the whores."

Even the seizures couldn't explain Chris's visions—or how Beth was connected. "I thought Beth had accepted them."

"Is that what this is all aboot? Chris isna Beth." T.J. slapped him on the shoulder. "Now go call her if fer no o'er reason than ta ease yer mind. Afterwards, ye come back ta me place, an' I'll make ye a nice pot o' coffee an' whiskey."

The thought of more alcohol made his stomach churn.

T.J. laughed. "Ye're lookin' a mite green. I only meant a wee bit o' whiskey ta help ye sleep."

"Thanks, T.J. I'll pass on the whiskey, but since neither of us is in any condition to drive..." Geoff took out his cell phone and dialed home.

"Are ye calling the lass?"

"I'm calling for a ride." A sleepy Judith answered. He might as well suffer his sister's wrath. Sometimes, she was more like a doting mother hen, but unlike his father, she had always accepted T.J. Surprisingly, she remained calm when he explained the situation. "She'll be here in a few minutes."

"I'll wait inside."

Thinking about Chris, Geoff nodded as he dialed again. A woman answered the other end. "Beth..."

Chris's days had returned to normal, and she buried herself in work. The job helped her concentrate on something besides Geoff. She glanced over the cases that had piled on her desk during her absence. Fidgeting with a pen, she opened a book on epilepsy that she had borrowed from the library. No wonder Geoff was frustrated. Medical treatment had improved only by margins over the years, and the cause typically remained unknown.

"Chris." Her boss poked his bald head through the doorway to her office. "I need the briefs on the Cottler case."

"Right away." Shoving the book aside, she checked if the papers she had drawn up before her vacation to Poplar Ridge were in order—Cottler Inc. vs. a list of names. Nothing unusual, but she started counting—forty-two names. Forty-two innocent families were at potential risk of losing their homes to development.

The legal pages blurred. She'd rather see deer leaping in the forest instead of concrete walls or a heron fishing along the James River unmarred by condos. *City girl, indeed.* Jumping up, Chris stormed to her boss's office and tossed the manila folder on his desk with a resounding crack. "I can't take the Cottler case."

His bushy eyebrows knitted together in a line, taking on the appearance of a goofy-looking caterpillar, adding an unintended comical edge to the fact that he was growing annoyed. "Chris, several others were fighting for it. It could lead to that senior associate position."

Her hands curled to fists. "I don't care. I can't throw forty-two innocent families out of their homes."

Unsympathetic to the families, he shrugged. "They were offered fair market value and refused."

"Did you ever stop to think they might not want to move? We don't need more shopping malls." Furious that he refused to bend, she rushed to the lady's room and splashed cold water on her face.

"Chris." She jumped at the sound of her secretary's voice. "I didn't mean to startle you."

"Nancy." Chris pressed a hand to her chest. "I'm a little frustrated. I had a run-in with you-know-who."

The silver-haired woman shook her head. "No, it's more than that. You've had run-ins before. They never fazed you. Something has been bothering you since returning from vacation. I thought you went to visit a college friend."

"I did."

"Too much change after all these years? I know the feeling. It's a big letdown when it happens."

"It's nothing like that. Judith is the same as always."

"Then it must have been a man," Nancy concluded.

"Judith's brother," Chris admitted.

Nancy sipped from her coffee mug. "I see."

Chris forced a smile. "I think I'm in love."

"I detect something amiss." Nancy took another sip, then her eyes widened. "Good heavens, he's not married?"

"No, he's not married, but he'd never leave Virginia."

A grin spread across Nancy's face, and she gestured to the walls. "And you think this place is the universe? "

Chris laughed. "I'm seriously beginning to have doubts."

"Then unless there are no attorneys in Virginia, I don't see the problem."

Move to Virginia? Apprehensive about the idea, Chris sucked in a sharp breath. "I'm not quite ready to take a plunge like that, but I'll keep your suggestion in mind. Thanks, Nancy."

"Glad that I could help."

Calm now, Chris returned to her office. Just because Geoff hadn't called her, didn't mean that she couldn't call him. She picked up the phone and dialed. Laura relayed that he had an appointment in Williamsburg and didn't know when he'd return. Chris left a message and thanked her.

Her boss stepped into the office, holding up a manila folder. "Chris, are you positive about the Cottler case?"

When his eyebrow wiggled like a dancing caterpillar, she struggled to suppress a grin. "I can't take it."

Shaking his head, he disappeared from the doorway.

The intercom buzzed. "Yes, Nancy."

"There's a Geoff Cameron on line four."

"Thanks, Nancy." Chris took a deep breath. She hadn't expected him to return her call so quickly. Her hand trembled with excitement as she picked up the receiver and pressed the button for line four. "Geoff."

"Chris, I received a message that you called."

There was a slight metallic hum as if he were calling from a cell phone, but it was wonderful hearing his voice again. He seemed so near. "I just love hearing your sexy accent again."

"Warn me if you're going to talk dirty so I can pull over."

She laughed. As she suspected, he was using his cell phone. "You're not going to lay blame on me for causing any accidents. How have you been?"

"Fine. No more seizures if that's what you mean."

"I meant in general, but I'm looking forward to seeing you later this month."

"I've been meaning to call. I checked the death records. My grandfather did survive the war and died in 1867."

Her palms grew sweaty. "What about Margaret?"

"She died in 1924."

She hadn't meant to talk about the ghostly happenings, but Greta's entries in the ledger were now corroborated by public records. What could Margaret have been trying to convey to her? When Geoff spoke again, he lowered his voice. *"I also talked to Beth."* She swallowed hard. "And?" *"She's agreed to talk to you."* As Chris scribbled down the details, her mind rushed. "I've been thinking." *"About what?"* "Us." Silence. "Before I return, let's think of a way that we can make it work." *"Talk to Beth first. If you feel the same after that, we'll definitely discuss it."* That hadn't been the answer she was expecting, and she was uncertain whether it gave her hope or not. "All right. Bye." She hung up the phone and stared at the number Geoff had given her. For over six years, Beth had been his wife. They had a son. And she had left him after a seizure. Despicable—serving a divorce summons before he was discharged from the hospital. Gritting her teeth, she picked up the receiver and started dialing. When a woman came on the line, Chris said in a business-like manner, "I'd like to speak to Elizabeth Carter."

Beth had refused to speak with her over the phone. After a quick flight to Richmond, Chris rented a car to the city. Countryside dotted with swamps gave way to gleaming high-rises. Instead of taking the interstate, Chris decided to travel through the city. A wide two-lane cobblestone boulevard had monuments of the Confederacy—Jefferson Davis, Stonewall Jackson, Robert E. Lee—in the median. One statue in a circle caught her eye—a man with a plumed hat and cloak on a fiery horse, General J.E.B. Stuart. The same general that had paid a visit to Margaret.

After driving the length of Monument Avenue, Chris turned off to an older section of the city. The sun was setting on refurbished, gabled Victorian houses, making an old neighborhood appear new again. She parked on the street, and a young boy approximately six years old answered the door. His tow hair and blue eyes reminded her of Geoff. "You must be Neal," she said, bending to his level.

The door widened. "And you must be Chris Olson. Neal, why don't you go up to your room and play?" The boy scampered up the stairs.

Taking a deep breath, Chris stepped into the darkened foyer. "That's correct, Ms. Carter. I'm Chris Olson." She held out a hand.

"It's you."

"I beg your pardon?"

"Never mind. It wasn't important. Please, call me Beth." Beth switched on a light, and a breath caught in Chris's throat. Suddenly overheating, she fanned herself. Long black hair and thoughtful violet eyes—she was staring at the reflection in the heavy-bodied mirror at Poplar Ridge. *Margaret.* "Are you all right? Come in and sit down, if you're not well." Beth indicated to a room on her right.

"Thank you." Catching her breath, Chris entered the parlor and sat on a Bentwood rocker, while Beth settled on the sofa across from her.

"Can I get you some lemonade?"

"I'm fine. Thank..." Chris swallowed. "...you."

"You said on the phone that you know Geoff."

She couldn't start by blurting out they were lovers. "I do. Judith..." She wished she could stop stuttering. "...is a good friend... of mine."

"I see," Beth said, leaning back. "Then I presume you and Geoff are more than friends."

She couldn't damn Beth for her directness.

"If you're here because of the way I left, it's none of your..."

Chris shook her head. "I'm not."

The fire in Beth's eyes faded. "Then what? Is it Geoff? Is he all right?"

Surprised by Beth's concern, Chris answered, "After two years without a seizure, he's had a couple, but, otherwise, he's fine."

Beth closed her eyes as if shutting out a nightmare. When her lashes flickered open, she said, "He hadn't told me they had returned, but then, I'm probably the last one he'd say anything to."

The woman she had wanted to despise, she couldn't. Instead, for some odd reason, she felt compassion. After all these years, Beth still must care a great deal. There had to be more to Geoff's version of the story. "I doubt that."

Beth laughed. "Chris, I hope you don't mind me calling you that." Chris shook her head. "I see we have something in common, so how frank do you wish me to be?"

"I don't wish to pry, but I prefer honesty."

Beth nodded in understanding. "Then let's start with why you're here."

Chris clasped her hands. If Beth wasn't the image of Margaret, she might feel friendship. "When I visited Judith, the last thing I expected was to find myself caring for someone. Up until now, my career has been the most important thing in my life, but as you've already guessed, I care—a lot."

Beth smiled in a bittersweet way. "I know the feeling, all too well."

Almost comfortable, Chris unclasped her hands and swallowed her pride. "During my visit, I had some dreams. There's no easy way of explaining them without sounding crazy." Beth stared thoughtfully, forcing Chris to look away from Margaret's image. "Geoff said you used to sleepwalk and have sighted the one-eyed ghost." As Beth continued staring, Chris shifted uneasily in the rocking chair.

"Yes," Beth admitted with a waver, "to both of your inquiries."

How much should she take Beth into her confidence? "In some of my dreams, I saw a man who looked like Geoff." After meeting Beth, the whole mystery made sense. Judith must have shown her a picture of Beth during college. She had transplanted that subconscious image into her visit to Poplar Ridge. A logical explanation. Chris got to her feet. "I shouldn't have come. I'm sorry to have wasted your time."

"Please—sit down." Beth waved at her to stay. "Something's bothering you and if it concerns Geoff . . . "

Beth's voice choked. After all these years, she still loved Geoff. There was definitely more involved than his side to the story. Chris reseated herself. "When I looked in a mirror—the one with the hand-carved horse heads . . ."

"I know the mirror," Beth admitted.

"In it, I saw another woman's face—yours."

Beth paled. "I saw my face, but it wasn't. There were subtle differences between us, and she wore her hair this way." She demonstrated by gathering her long black hair together and knotted it at the nape of her neck. *Margaret.* "And she had a beautiful ball gown."

"Made of blue silk," Chris finished. With Beth's revelation, her stomach felt ill. The events hadn't been her imagination. "Did you learn her name?"

Chris's heart pounded before Beth finally responded, "Margaret. I thought it was a silly dream. It was almost as if I were living someone else's life." She frowned. "But it wasn't all dances and pretty ball gowns."

"The one-eyed ghost."

The muscles around Beth's mouth twitched nervously. "Don't go back there, Chris. He's dangerous."

Curious. Why would Beth say that? "Margaret had the gun in her hand."

"I know," Beth said, her voice wavering, "but . . ."

"But what?"

Beth lowered her face to her hands with her sides heaving. "I can't . . . talk about it."

Something had unnerved Beth. Was that why she had left? "Because of the ghost?" Chris asked, pressing for more information.

When Beth looked up, tears streaked her cheeks. "I said that I can't talk about it. I think it's time for you to leave."

"Very well." Disappointed that she had gained little information, Chris dug through her purse for a business card. Beth refused to take it, and Chris slipped it on the coffee table in front of her. "If you should change your mind, don't hesitate to call me." Chris got to her feet. "One more thing before I leave..." Beth opened her mouth to protest, but Chris held up a hand that she wouldn't continue with the same line of questioning. "When I first got here, you said, 'It's you.' What did you mean?"

Beth immediately averted her eyes. "Nothing. At first, I thought you were someone I had met in college."

And Beth was a lousy liar. Tempted to pursue the matter, Chris decided against it. She had already overstayed her welcome. Anything else she said would be taken in contempt. For that matter, why had Beth even agreed to see her? It almost seemed that she had been equally curious.

While in Richmond, Chris had nearly turned onto the road along the James River leading to Poplar Ridge, but instead she returned to the airport. She needed time to think, and in the evening following her return to Boston, she picked up the phone. "I'd like to speak with Geoff," she said when Laura answered.

"May I ask who's calling?"

"Tell him, 'Chris.' "

"One moment, please."

Geoff was in. Her hands trembled, and she watched the clock. A minute passed, then two. She envisioned him in the library, seated in the leather chair at the desk with acorn carvings.

"Chris..."

She breathed out. "Geoff, I paid a visit to Beth."

"And?"

"Why didn't you tell me that she looks like Margaret?" she asked, shuddering at the memory.

"Beth looks like Margaret? I didn't know that she does."

How could he not know? But he had sounded genuinely surprised. "All of that doesn't matter, but she did say the most peculiar thing when I got there, 'It's you.' Do you have any idea what she could have meant by that?"

"Judith has pictures of the two of you from college. I suspect she saw one."

If that were the case, then why wouldn't Beth simply have said so? Convinced that Geoff was telling her all that he knew, she decided to drop the subject until seeing him in person. "I'm counting the days until I see you again." Silence. "Geoff?"

"Why didn't you stop by when you were in Richmond?"

"I almost did. I'm still a little confused about everything that's been happening, but I'm genuinely looking forward to seeing you." This response seemed to satisfy him. They talked a few more minutes before finally saying goodbye.

Chris retrieved Margaret's gown from the closet and pressed the dress against her. A costume ball . . . They'd dance and make polite conversation. She relished the thought of being in Geoff's arms. After the dance, they would retire to his room.

In the library, the one-eyed soldier shoved Margaret's hand aside, and the pistol went flying. He leaned into her with the brunt of his weight, forcing her to the wooden floor. "You're goin' to be sorry you did that, Mrs. Reb."

A scream caught in her throat as his mouth met hers, his tongue forcing its way in. She flailed her hands and broke his grip. With her hands, fists, and fingernails, she continued fighting. His fist connected with her cheek, but she staggered to get away. He caught her legs and tackled her to the floor, face first.

He flipped her onto her back and pinned her hands to the floor. His leg was firmly across her thighs. Unable to move, she smelled his grimy sweat—felt it dripping against her body. Brutal fumbling, and he thrust himself inside her. Pain. She screamed.

"Shut up," he snarled. He smacked her on the side of the head.

No use. She bit her lip to keep from crying out and stopped fighting. At that same moment, a part of her died inside.

Margaret had been raped. Stunned, Chris sank to the floor with the dress still in her arms. Tears entered her eyes. She tried blinking back the vision, but she kept seeing his cruel face with red hair and the gaping hole where an eye should have been. A link to Margaret—she clutched the sky-blue gown next to her. "Is that what you wanted me to know, Margaret?" Who else knew? Beth—she was aware of much more than she let on. "If it's justice that you want, there's little I can do for something that happened so long ago." Or was Margaret attempting to warn her away from Poplar Ridge? Beth had said the ghost was dangerous. Suddenly more determined, Chris vowed that she would discover the truth.

An official-looking envelope from the Department of Motor Vehicles lay on the desk. Before even opening it, Geoff surmised that his license had been suspended. He tore open the envelope and cursed.

"Bad news?" came his father's voice.

Geoff held out the letter, and his father's expression changed from one of concern to stoic. For as long as Geoff could remember, any subject relating to his seizures had the same effect. "Sorry, I forgot I wasn't supposed to even hint at my..." He lowered his voice to a whisper, as his father often had in the past. "...affliction." Geoff chucked the letter into the wastebasket.

"Geoff, I..." The old man cleared his throat. "It's probably for the best."

"For the best?" Geoff narrowed his eyes. "I'm no more likely to have a seizure while driving than anyone else, and you know it—not with Saber along."

"But the dog won't be around forever."

"That's right, focus on the negative." Geoff headed for the door. "I don't have time for this. I promised Neal that I'd take him to see *Shrek*." Without waiting for a response, he went out to the garage. He'd have the neurologist issue a report and hope that DMV would reconsider on a provisional basis. In the meantime, he opened the door, and Saber hopped onto the back seat of the Mustang. After placing the car in gear, Geoff drove the

winding river road to Richmond. He parked on the street outside Beth's house.

As he got out of the car, he heard voices, many of them, whispering. Glancing to the street, he saw no one. The leaves were
changing to muted fall reds. He grasped Saber's leather leash,
and they walked up the brick walk to the yellow Victorian. Daffodils lined the walk. *In October?* How was that possible? He
knocked.

The door opened, and Beth gave him a welcoming smile.
"Neal's ready. Let me call him. Geoff, are you all right? You're
looking a little pale."

Disoriented, he blinked. The voices—he couldn't locate the
voices. Saber gave a high-pitched bark, and Geoff closed his
eyes, wishing he could block out the sound. *That's why.* Saber
barked again and seized his wrist. "I'm going to have a seizure.
I'll leave if you want, but I'd really rather not seize on the
street."

With a quiet calm, she drew him inside. "How callous do
you think I am?"

"I don't know."

She blew out a breath in frustration. "Let's not argue about
it now. I'll take you to the room in back."

In passing, he smelled her perfume. No, it was honeysuckle.
The scent grew stronger. "I'd appreciate that."

More potent than before, honeysuckle drifted over him. The
seizure was near. His senses were heightened, and it felt as if
Beth and he crept down the hall to the guest room.

"Do you want me to stay with you?" Beth asked.

Almost smothering him, the scent grew stronger. "You don't
need to."

"I know I don't need to, but do you want me to?"

Answer. With the honeysuckle near but not quite as
strong, he couldn't concentrate. He could no longer ignore the
fragrance—or her. "Beth . . ."

"Geoff, lie down or you're going to hurt yourself."

When she helped him to bed, he thought of her standing in
front of the full-length mirror beside their bed at Poplar Ridge—
naked, and her long black hair ruffling gently in the breeze.

"Mom," came a voice from the hallway.

"I'll tell Neal that you're not well and will see him in the morning," Beth whispered. She left his side and rushed into the hall. Her voice drifted. "Your dad can't see you right now." Neal protested with several "whys."

Geoff heard their footsteps retreat up the stairs. As he got to his feet, Saber barked frantically, but he stumbled over to the dresser. In the foggy world before a seizure, none of his senses remained the same. Drawn to the top drawer, he searched it, locating an antique pistol. He remembered. That's why he no longer kept the gun at Poplar Ridge.

"Geoff?"

Beth stood in the doorway, and he withdrew the gun from the drawer. "Why did you take it?"

"For your own good. You were obsessed with it." Edging toward him, she held out a hand. "If you're thinking of using it, I don't keep any bullets in the house."

"Use it?" Why couldn't he recall the details? "On the night you left, but I ..." He placed a hand to his head. "... don't remember."

Trembling, Beth inched next to him. Tears streaked her cheeks. "Right now, it's best if you don't remember. Now—give me the gun."

"It's a Colt .44. Civil War era." Something niggled him at the back of his mind. He had thought about killing himself, but there was more. He handed her the pistol, and she breathed out in relief. "Beth, did I try to use it on you or Neal?"

"No, you wouldn't hurt us." She returned the gun to the dresser drawer. "We'll talk about it when you're coherent. Let me take care of everything," she whispered in his ear. "You'll feel better soon."

"I didn't come here ..." His thoughts jumbled. The Colt .44 had been in his hand. Stray images. Flickering light, and a woman's scream. Pain. Honeysuckle smothered him. He threw his hands to his head. No more pain. Quivering, then nothing.

* * *

By the time Geoff returned with Neal the following afternoon, most of the day had passed. Fall flowers were fading, and Geoff found Beth around back in the garden, planting bulbs for spring. Her long black hair was tied away from her face. He remembered it hanging loose, draped across his chest. Forbidden thoughts. He had to put them out of his head.

As Beth brushed the dirt from her hands, Neal saved them from the initial awkwardness by rattling on about his day, then charging off to his room. She laughed. "He gets so excited when you've been here."

Beth fidgeted with her gardening spade, and Geoff shifted uneasily on his feet. "I want to thank you for your help last night."

Her smile faded. "Why didn't you tell me the seizures had returned?"

In the hospital, he remembered calling her name—only to discover that she had left him. "So you can disappear farther away this time?"

"That isn't fair."

His irritation heightened. "It worked when we were married."

She let out a breath. "You've refused to listen to what I went through."

So, Margaret looked like Beth—long black hair and puppy-dog eyes that she batted soulfully to get her way. He wondered if Margaret had the same bitchy temper to match. "Forgive me if I don't sympathize." He turned to leave.

"Geoff, I kept seeing *him*."

The word drew him back. *The ghost?* "Everyone has seen *him* at some point."

"Not like I did. You admitted last night that you don't remember what happened that night."

That was true, and he had no desire to dredge up old wounds. "Let's forget it. We can speak civilly for Neal's sake. What more do we need?"

"Blame me if you must, but know the *real* reason why I left." She sat on the wrought-iron bench along the garden path and motioned for him to sit beside her. With stubborn determination, he remained standing. "I planned a romantic dinner. It was the cook's day off and I burned it. But you weren't concerned—we were together."

Relieved the memory was gone, he wanted nothing reminding him how much he had loved her. But he had loved her. With some reluctance, he sat on the bench next to her. "You never were a cook—at least not in the kitchen."

She laughed. "You said something similar then. We went to the cottage . . ."

Beth had been the other woman he had taken to the cottage. He held up a hand. "I've heard enough."

"You haven't. You had never taken me to the cottage before. It was quite obvious that you wanted to be with someone else."

Someone else? "Beth, I never cheated on you."

Her eyes widened in disbelief. "Don't lie to me. You called me Catherine."

The same name that he had called Chris. *Coincidence?*

"I see that you recognize her name."

"It's not what you think," he replied weakly.

She sighed. "It doesn't really matter anymore."

"If you left because you thought I was having an affair, then it does matter."

"No, if that had been the only reason, I would have waited until you were home from the hospital." Tears formed in her eyes. "I left the cottage hurt and angry. When I got back to the house, I packed Neal's things together. After that, I had calmed down, so I went to the library to see if you had returned. That's when I saw *him*." She choked back a sob. "He raped your grandmother. I left before the same thing happened to me."

Margaret had been raped? "Why are you suddenly telling me this after all these years?"

She wiped the tears from her face. "Because you wouldn't listen before, and I fear history may repeat itself if you're not careful."

Jealousy? He hadn't expected Beth to resort to pettiness. He stood. "That's what all of this is about. You don't want me seeing Chris. I think you gave up any say in the matter when you left me for dead in the hospital."

"Geoff, for once in your life, stop being so stubborn. Chris has the dreams. She saw *my* face in the mirror, and she's seen *him*. I didn't even know that you had gone into status until after the papers had been served."

She hadn't known. After waking in the hospital and learning she was gone, he'd spent the next year in a daze. He shook his head. "I need to be leaving."

"Be careful," she whispered.

As Geoff turned, he caught a glimpse of tears streaking her cheeks. He had always hated to see her cry. If they were married, he would have taken her into his arms and comforted her. He couldn't allow himself to think about that now. It would remind him that he had never stopped loving her.

"Geoff..."

He resisted the temptation to look, but she called, over and over again. He halted and studied her a moment. Memories from that night formed in his head—the cottage and Beth. "I remember, at least some of it."

"Don't, not if it'll make things worse." Beth stepped nearer. Tears filled her eyes once more, but she quickly brushed them away. "Your father called me and let me know that you were in the hospital. He also asked me to reconsider my decision."

His father coming to his aid? "That's odd. He never bothered to visit me in the hospital."

"And you're just like him. I was too frightened to return. I don't expect forgiveness, but at least try to understand what I went through."

His head swam. "I'm listening now, but I don't think I've absorbed everything."

"It'll take time," she agreed. "Would you like to stay for supper? I promise not to burn things this time."

Geoff nodded that he'd stay.

And true to her word, Beth fixed fried chicken without the use of a mix for the batter. One of Neal's favorites, the meal included mashed potatoes, but his son scrunched his face, uttering a loud "yuck" at the lumpy gravy. Throughout the evening, Beth cast glances in his direction, then quickly reverted her gaze, pretending that she hadn't been looking. At Neal's bedtime, Geoff read their son a story set in a medieval castle. For a change, he felt like a real father, rather than a "weekend dad." Closing Neal's bedroom door behind him, Geoff stepped into the hall and withdrew his keys from his pocket.

"Should you be driving?" Concern registered in Beth's voice.

"Saber will warn me."

"That really doesn't answer my question." Beth playfully snatched his keys from his hand. "I'll drive you home." Before he could ask who would watch over Neal, she finished, "In the morning, after Neal goes to school."

He hadn't misinterpreted her signals. Geoff reached for his keys, but she tossed them down the darkened hallway.

"Not a good idea," he said. "We'd both regret it if I stayed."

She giggled. "Then let's regret it in the morning. You were thinking it too."

Her twitters and appraising looks reminded him of the college girl she'd been when they had first met. With a wink, Beth turned away, but left the door to her room open. *Search for the keys, dammit.* Over thirteen years of common history wasn't so easily denied.

By the time he reached the door, Beth stood beside the bed and had begun to unbutton her blouse.

"We *will* regret this," he repeated.

"You're free to leave."

"You know that I'm not. I never was."

Chapter Seven

STRAIGHTENING A STRAY LOCK OF HAIR, Chris looked at herself critically in the mirror. The cracks were an ominous reminder of her previous visit to Poplar Ridge, but since her arrival in the late afternoon, there had been no visions. *The calm before the storm?* Squelching the disquieting thought before it got a firm grip in her mind, she returned her attention to her reflection. Margaret had been trimmer, or had more likely worn a tightly-laced corset. The dead woman's black hair would have accented the sky-blue gown more than her mousy-looking, cinnamon-colored hair, but she had taken the time to curl it in ringlets. A pearl necklace adorned her throat. To complete the period effect, she had gone to the bother of borrowing a hoop skirt. Margaret would have been proud.

Satisfied with her costume, Chris picked up her mask and turned away from the mirror. Eager to see Geoff, she glanced in the direction of the bed. Would he be joining her here after the dance, or would they retire to his room? She hadn't talked to him in a few days. What if he had changed his mind about their relationship? *Stop worrying.* A man didn't share his innermost thoughts without caring.

Her dress rustled as she went into the hall. At the bottom of the stairs, Judith, with her hair piled high in a lavish coiffure, greeted her. Dressed for the occasion in a jade-green Colonial-period gown with frilly lace sleeves, her friend blinked. "Chris, you look lovely wearing the dress."

The silk was so soft that she had difficulty believing the dress was over a hundred years old. "It's such an elegant dress. Thanks for letting me wear it for the occasion. It would be shameful to keep it stuffed away in a wardrobe."

Judith smiled warmly. "It would be at that. Geoff will need his eyes examined if he doesn't notice." Her smile faded. "He promised to be here on time, but as you can plainly see . . ." He was nowhere in sight. "I can't imagine what's keeping him. He went into Richmond this afternoon, but he hasn't called to say that he was running late."

"He probably lost track of the time."

Judith agreed, and a beaming smile appeared on her face. "I have someone that I'd like you to meet." She led the way to the drawing room, where a nearly six-foot-tall man costumed as a red devil waited. She hooked her arm through his. "Chris, I'd like you to meet David Markey. David, my college friend Chris Olson."

Ever gallant, he bowed. "Pleased to meet you."

His horns were distracting, but she managed to make small talk without giggling. "Judith tells me that you're from northern Virginia, Leesburg, if I remember correctly. I've never been there myself."

"I have a 200-acre horse farm two miles outside of Leesburg."

No wonder her friend loved him. Just then, attired as an admiral, Winston Cameron entered the drawing room. Judith went over, and they whispered among themselves. Judith's head started shaking and her hands waving. Chris detected an argument brewing.

"It's getting late," Winston Cameron said in an overly loud voice, then it turned gentle. "If she wishes, I'll be happy to escort Chris."

All eyes focused on Chris. Damn Geoff for being so late without calling, but she was tickled by the elder Cameron's Southern charm. "Thank you. I'd like that."

Before Chris could take his arm, Laura entered the room and whispered in Judith's ear. "Chris, a phone call—my *beloved* brother." She passed the cordless receiver to Chris. "If you'd like some privacy, just step into the hall."

Chris took Judith's suggestion. What if Geoff wasn't going to be in time to attend the dance? She switched on the receiver. "Hello."

"*Chris...*"

"Geoff, where are you?"

"*Richmond.*" His voice sounded apologetic. "*I've had an unexpected delay.*"

"Not a seizure?"

"*Not everything I do is seizure related.*"

"I know, but I can't help but worry."

"*I'm sorry. I'll be there as soon as I can.*"

No details—should she be concerned? "Everyone's ready to go. How long do you think you'll be?"

"*About an hour, maybe two. Why don't you go ahead without me?*"

Attend the dance without Geoff? Just a minor delay, Chris reminded herself. Slightly disappointed but not undaunted, she hung up the phone and joined the others.

As Geoff lowered the receiver, he faced Beth. "Thanks Beth."

Pale and trembling, she placed a hand to her throat. "You're leaving?" He nodded. "But Neal..."

After receiving Beth's panicky call earlier in the day informing him that Neal had taken a tumble down the stairs, he had rushed to Richmond. "He'll be fine. The doctor said it was only a bump on the head. If you need me, I'll have my cell phone."

"Geoff..." She threw her arms around his neck, and her mouth met his. Dammit, he wanted to be rid of the past. But then, he wasn't the first man to have slept with his ex. He drew away. "I told you that we'd regret the other night."

"I don't regret anything."

"I do, and I don't plan on letting it happen again. Beth, our lives went in separate directions three years ago."

Tears entered her eyes. "Then you still blame me."

"It's not about blame," he said, touching her lightly on the cheek. "I think I understand what you must have gone through, but we can't just pick up the pieces pretending nothing has ever happened."

Beth dried her tears and forced a smile. "She told me this day would come."

"She?"

She shook her head that it wasn't important. "I'm taking Neal to Williamsburg for the day tomorrow."

"Is that wise?"

Her eyes seethed. "You said yourself that he only got a mere bump on the head. Oh, but then I forgot, you won't be calling about him anyway. You'll be preoccupied with your girlfriend."

They had quickly returned to petty jabs. "Beth . . ."

She pressed herself against him in a provocative manner. "Do you plan on telling Chris about the other night?" The flat of her hand struck his face. "You two-timing bastard."

Saber rose from his resting spot on the floor. Geoff gave the dog a hand signal to stay, then rubbed his stinging cheek. "I'll call you later to see how Neal is." He grabbed Saber's leash, and they slipped into the night.

The ballroom extended to half the length of a football field. All sorts of wild and wonderful costumes abounded, from pirates and wizards to princesses and witches. Chris even spotted a skunk with a musky odor. She overheard one woman speaking French and realized some guests had traveled from abroad. These people were the type she expected to meet as clients, not socialize with.

Couples floated across the dance floor in an assortment of colors—a rainbow butterfly to vampires in black. A server offered her a glass of champagne. Gladly accepting, she located a table away from the dancers.

Judith sat beside her. "Chris, you're shaking like a leaf. Relax, for heaven's sake. You said he'd be here, so he will be."

"Did he tell you what he'd be wearing?"

"No," Judith answered with a laugh, "but if I know my brother, it'll be sporting."

"Has he been distracted lately? He seemed distant on the phone."

Her friend swallowed noticeably.

"So, he has been."

"He disappeared last weekend. I suspect that he's had another seizure but doesn't want to tell anyone." Judith leaned across the table and squeezed her hand. "Don't worry. He'll likely tell you. Now, what do you think of David?"

"A man with a 200-acre horse farm. That sounds like your kind of guy. Does he like kids too?"

A growing smile spread across Judith's face. "Loves them."

"Then what more do you need? Unlike me and . . ." Bubbles tickled her nose as she sipped champagne, and the music for the next dance began to play. "In fact, you should be with David, instead of entertaining me."

Straightening her shoulders, Judith crossed her arms. "I'll wait until Geoff arrives."

"Don't be silly. I'll be fine. He'll be here any minute."

Judith glanced to the dance floor.

"Go on." Chris waved at her to leave.

Judith got to her feet. After a few steps, she glanced back over her shoulder.

"I said, 'Go on.' " As Judith vanished among the dancing couples, Chris swirled champagne around in her glass. Where was Geoff? Would a gentleman keep a lady waiting? But the silk dress had been fashioned during a bygone era, and the champagne must be going to her head. Snickering to herself, she finished the bubbly drink. Barely was the glass empty, when a server replaced it with another.

"Chris?"

To her disappointment, it was the elder Cameron, not Geoff. He checked his watch. "Geoff hasn't arrived yet?"

"No." For a minute, he stared. Discomforted by his steady gaze, she looked away.

"Forgive me for staring. I've seen that dress before—in a photograph somewhere." He shook his head. "Never mind, I apologize for my son's rudeness. I assure you he wasn't raised this way. Perhaps you won't mind dancing with the old man. Lack of manners doesn't run in the family."

Lack of manners—yet when she had first met Geoff, he had been the perfect Southern gentleman. "I'd like that, thank you." She hooked her arm through Winston Cameron's as the orchestra began to play the next dance. As if they had been born to the dance floor, they flowed across it together. The music stopped playing all too soon. As they glided across the floor one last time, she thanked him for the dance and returned to her private area. Without her noticing, a man in a gray uniform with gold embroidery on the sleeves and a yellow sash tied about his waist had slipped in behind them. The mask couldn't hide his blue eyes as they peered over the rim of a glass. *Geoff.*

Their gazes met. With his goatee, he looked as if he could have stepped right out of the pages of a Civil War history book.

"Do you think we're tempting fate with what we're wearing?"

"If you can't beat them . . ." Geoff set his empty glass on the table and put a hand to his temple as if in pain.

"Geoff, you're not . . ."

"It's not a seizure. Sometimes, you worry too much."

"I can't help it. I love you." There—she had said the words again—rather easily, in fact.

"I'm sorry for being late. Neal fell down a flight of stairs and hit his head, then when I got home, Saber cut his paw on a piece of glass."

She had noticed the dog was missing. "Are they all right?"

"They're fine."

Fahn. Chris was definitely growing to love the Southern accent.

With a broad smile, Geoff presented his left hand from behind his back, bearing a single red rose. "I hope this helps make up for my extreme tardiness."

Accepting the flower, she inhaled its sweet scent. His eyes

were laughing, yet somehow remained sad. She thought of Margaret's heartbreaking story and had to find some way to tell him about what had happened to his great-grandmother.

"Would you care to dance?" Taking her hand, he led her to the dance floor.

Thankfully, the dance was slow, and they drew close. Under the dim lighting, he kissed her, and she responded enthusiastically. In his arms, everything seemed right. She could almost forget Margaret's tragedy. He pressed nearer, and they kissed again. Following the dance, they would return to her room, undress, and his hands would caress her bare skin. She had difficulty concentrating when they stayed on the dance floor for several more numbers.

"Geoff, I'm having a wonderful time, but we need to talk. Do you mind leaving?"

"Because of Saber's injury, I walked over."

"I like the idea of an evening stroll."

"Stroll? It's a good three miles, city girl."

His words sounded like a challenge. "I don't mind. Now, are you going to escort me, or do I have to hike it by myself?"

His eyes danced, and with a charming smile, Geoff bowed. Pretending to be the perfect gentleman of another time, he held out his arm, and she laced hers through it. *Another time . . .* She glanced over her shoulder. Judith winked with a knowing grin. In the hall, Chris collected her cloak, and they stepped into the night. In Boston, the evenings had grown brisk, but Virginia still felt like fall. Geoff showed her along the cobblestone path, and she grasped his hand.

Comforted by his protective grip, she followed the winding path to the edge of the river. Although she felt awkward in her dress, Geoff helped her across the uneven ground. Along a narrow section of the bank, she turned her attention to a view of the James. Under the soft glow of moonlight, waves lapped against the bank. "Geoff," she said, turning to him. He studied her, but there was a distinct sadness about him. "What's wrong?"

He shoved his hands in his pockets like an embarrassed child. "I've had another seizure."

Judith's suspicion had been correct. "Are you all right?"
He blew out a breath. "I'm fine, but my license got suspended. I've sort of been driving without one."
Since he had left Saber at home, that explained why he had
walked to the party. "Sort of? How does one sort of drive without a license?"
Geoff laughed slightly. "I think you have a fair idea how. I
will get my license back."
"Not if you're caught driving with an invalid one."
"Legal advice?"
"Friendly." When he made no further response, she realized
that his subdued mood had become apparent since leaving the
party. "I accept the epilepsy. It's part of you. I've read up on it. I
know the different types of seizures, even that grand mal is no
longer considered politically correct, and that stress can lower
the seizure threshold. There are other common factors, but you
haven't told me if they're relevant in your case. I know the side
effects of Dilantin, and what to do, so I'll know how to react
when you have a seizure. It will play havoc with our lives, but
it can't keep us from being happy, unless we let it."
"Chris, there's more." He fell silent a minute. "I love you. For
some reason, I knew as much when I first met you."
How long had she waited for him to say the words? Her
heart pounded. "I was hoping you might say that. So what do
we do to make things right?"
He closed his eyes and placed a hand to his temple.
"Are you all right?"
Forcing a smile, he looked over at her. "I thought you said
you knew the side effects of Dilantin. The doctors have been
messing with the dosage. If it doesn't wipe me out, it gives me
a headache. Second thoughts? I understand if you change your
mind."
"You can't get rid of me that easily. Do we steal weekends
back and forth until I can take the Virginia bar?" The proposi-
tion was out of her mouth before Chris had the chance to think
it through.
"That should work," Geoff agreed with a growing smile.

He drew her in his arms and kissed her—gently at first, then with the burning, tempered force that she had come to crave. He grasped her hand, and they continued along the path to the mansion. His firm grip gave her leverage as they negotiated a slight hill over exposed roots. Chris stumbled. Nearly twisting an ankle, she let out a cry. Geoff's grip tightened. She latched onto his free hand, but her feet slipped from underneath her, bringing him down with her. Calling his name, she swung her arms wildly. Brambles near the path sliced into her bare skin.

Familiar blue eyes focused on her. "Chris . . . "

Scratched and bruised, she drifted through a daze. The one-eyed ghost loomed over her. Her fingernails were torn and bleeding, and she threw her hands to her head and screamed.

"Chris, you're fine. Relax . . ." Geoff took her into his arms and held her.

There was that soothing Southern drawl again. Her trembling hand touched his face to make certain that it was really him and not the one-eyed ghost. "He raped her."

"If you're talking about Margaret, I recently discovered that myself."

"I saw it in a vision. And I think the other soldiers may have done the same to a woman named Tessa."

Geoff clenched his hand, then released it. "Tessa was a house servant during the time. I found a copy of her emancipation papers several years ago, but it wasn't uncommon for soldiers to rape black women."

"And Margaret?"

"If it's underreported now, you can imagine what it must have been like then."

That made sense during an era when a woman's reputation was regarded as all important. "How did you find out?"

He hesitated a moment before responding, "Beth."

The rose and his withdrawn behavior suddenly made sense. "I see."

"I meant everything I've said."

"That doesn't change the fact that you have never stopped loving *her*." Chris struggled to her feet. When she nearly slipped again, Geoff grasped her arm to keep her from falling. She shook free of his grip and climbed the hill.

"Let me explain."

"Don't bother. So much for her barely talking to you." Lifting her skirt, she crossed an extensive grassy section.

"Chris..."

Without turning, Chris forged ahead.

"Chris, the house is over here."

Feeling foolish, she halted but refused to face him.

"Stop being so headstrong, and let me show you to the house."

Relenting, she accompanied him but kept a respectable distance between them. Finally, they arrived at Poplar Ridge. Inside the door, Saber met them with his tail wagging. Chris caught a glimpse of her scratched face and cracked lip in the hall's mirror. "I'll be going to bed now—alone."

He grasped her lightly on the arm. "At least let me make certain that you're all right."

She twisted free of his grip. "It won't get you any brownie points."

"I don't expect any." With a wrapped right front paw, Saber limped alongside them as Geoff guided her to the drawing room. "Let's get you in here where there's more light."

She eased into the wing chair, and he lifted the hem of her dress slightly. "You've got a couple of nasty-looking cuts. I'll get something to clean them with."

Geoff vanished from the drawing room, but Saber remained dutifully by her side. When Geoff returned, he carried a first-aid kit under his arm. Kneeling on the floor, he wrung a cloth in a bowl of water and dabbed at the cuts on her leg. Pain. She jerked her leg away from the cloth.

"I know it hurts," he said, "but you need to hold still."

She planted her feet firmly on the floor to keep from moving as he cleaned the cuts. "Where did you learn first aid?"

"Horses, dog, kid—take your pick. One or the other is always gashing or breaking something. I'm only too happy to help others, rather than others..."

He didn't need to finish. She was well aware of what he had been about to say. "Geoff..."

"I know what you must be thinking..."

"Do you? The fact that you haven't denied anything speaks volumes." She raised her voice. "Then you have the gall to give me a stupid flower, hoping to absolve your guilt, and tell me how much you love me."

"What would you have me do?" He tossed the cloth to the bowl with a splash.

She met his gaze. "Tell me the truth. I'm a big girl. I can handle it."

"I *have* told you the truth. I meant everything I said." Pretending that he was unfazed by her line of questioning, Geoff continued his task but fumbled with a bandage.

Chris held up two fingers. "You left out two significant details—that you've been sleeping with your ex and have never stopped loving her."

After a couple of false tries, he managed to bandage her leg. He stood. "I will admit to making a mistake, and I can't give you any reason why it happened that would likely make sense. Hell, I don't understand it myself other than I've had difficulty letting go of the past. But I *have* let Beth go. I realize that I don't love her anymore because I love you." He collected the first-aid kit and bowl of water. "Sorry for disillusioning you about knights in shining armor, but I thought a city girl wouldn't be so easily swept up by fairy tales."

His accusation stung. As Geoff left the room, Saber waited a moment before hobbling after him. Why hadn't she listened to her inner voice? Her rational side had warned her that things were progressing way too quickly between them. Chalking the entire experience to life, she trudged up to her room. The mirror reflected her bruised face. And the house was... *peaceful.* Ever since her return, there had been no visions. "Have I discovered what you wanted, Margaret?"

There had to be more. And Geoff? Dammit anyway—her heart ached. She *did* love him. Hadn't he called her headstrong? Blind was more like it. She quickly changed out of the gown and into a comfortable pair of jeans and a T-shirt, then headed down the hall. First, she checked Geoff's room. Empty. The library was also empty, but she thought of Margaret and the pain inflicted on her by the one-eyed scout.

"Chris?" Geoff's voice came from behind her.

"It happened in here," she said.

"What did?" His voice was closer now.

She faced him. He still wore the Confederate uniform— *George*. "Margaret."

His face wrinkled as if imagining the long-dead woman's pain. He hadn't known the details.

"Can we talk?"

He nodded. "I was just about to feed Saber and check his paw."

"I'll join you." They walked the length of the wood-paneled hallway until reaching the main section of the house. Another hall went into the east wing and led to the kitchen. "I've been unfair to you."

He bent down to Saber's level and unwrapped the bandage on the dog's paw. "In what way?" he asked calmly.

His tending to Saber reminded her of the way he had cared for her earlier, and she hadn't even thanked him. "I asked for you to tell me the truth, and when you did, I didn't respect it. The truth is something I've always held dear. Besides, you hadn't made any promises to me."

"Maybe not, but that doesn't make me proud of what happened." He checked Saber's paw. After letting the dog's foot go, he glanced up. "What now?"

"I'd like to continue with *our* plans. I love you." Geoff stood, and Saber bounded to his feet, jumping up on Chris and wagging his black feathery tail. "What happened to your hurt foot?"

"You can't keep a Belgian down for long." Chris laughed, and Geoff put his arms around her.

After the brutal attack, Margaret felt nothing—no shame, no grief, only emptiness. The faceless Yankee scouts sat around the breakfast table, laughing and boasting about their exploits, while she and Tessa obediently served what little food they had to them.

Readying to leave, the scouts stood. When the one-eyed soldier stroked her cheek, she didn't flinch. He kissed her harshly on the mouth. "Why don't you boys go ahead? I'll catch up."

The other scouts hooted at his insinuation but left the kitchen. When he grasped Margaret's elbow, Tessa protested. He drew his pistol and aimed at her dutiful servant.

"That's all right, Tessa. I'll accompany him," Margaret responded. He shoved the pistol in its holster and escorted her from the kitchen. Around to the other side of the house, she heard the hoofbeats of the other scouts riding away. Bypassing the main house, he half-dragged her the length of the grounds until they reached the river's edge. He began unbuttoning her bodice. "You're so purty that I had to give you a proper farewell."

So little fight left. *She closed her eyes as his hands groped her breasts. She took a deep breath and touched his hard form through his trousers. To keep from retching, she bit her lip. While her right hand stroked him, her left reached for his pistol. With the gun in hand, Margaret backed away and stumbled, falling into the mud. Finally realizing what had happened, he hurtled after her. She fired. Hit in his left eye, he tumbled backward until his head struck the mucky river ground.*

"She killed him." Chris withdrew from Geoff's embrace and tugged on his hand, leading him from the kitchen. "He's missing an eye because Margaret shot him." Outside, a light, but cold, autumn rain had begun to fall. Through the darkness, she followed a path across the grounds to the river. "Here—he tried to rape her again, but she managed to confiscate his gun and shoot him."

Near the cellar door—it explained why family members had often spotted the ghost in that particular location. "It serves the Yankee bastard right," Geoff said. Dim lighting filtered from the house—enough to see by, but not for carrying out a major search. "Let me get a flashlight."

"I'll wait here."

"Chris?"

"I'll be fine," she assured him.

"Saber, stay." He threw his wool jacket over Chris's shoulders. Against his better judgment of leaving Chris alone, Geoff went back to the kitchen to retrieve a flashlight. The rain had grown heavier, and as he returned to the spot on the river bank, he heard Saber barking. He followed the sound. To his relief, Chris stood beside the cellar door. "What was Saber barking about?"

"I saw one-eye. Saber went after him, but he vanished."

Geoff called Saber, and the dog hobbled back on three legs. He bent down and inspected Saber's paw with the flashlight. At least it hadn't begun bleeding again.

In the growing cold, she clutched his jacket around her. "Is he all right?"

"I think he's okay, but I'll have the vet check him over in the morning." He straightened.

"What would Margaret have done with one-eye after she had killed him?"

He shrugged. "Buried him most likely. The Yankees would have made things worse for her if they had found out."

"Exactly, so she would have buried him right where he lay?"

Geoff shook his head. "The river floods here. He would have been washed up again with the first flood. She wouldn't have taken that chance."

"So where would a lone woman have buried him?"

In the growing cold and rain, his headache was back. He rubbed his temple. At least Saber hadn't barked.

"The medication?" Chris inquired.

He nodded, but the pain became a sharp stab. "Tessa would have helped her. Two women could have dragged him..." He pointed the flashlight in the direction of the cellar. The door stuck when he attempted to open it. He handed the flashlight to Chris and applied pressure to the door with his weight. The heavy wood door finally budged. Six steps led to the tunnel. He closed the door behind them and grasped Chris's hand.

In the tight quarters of the tunnel, he was relieved to be out of the rain. Chris radiated warmth, making him realize how numb his fingers had gotten. As they walked the brick path to the cellar, he thought he saw a woman kneeling and crying at the end of the tunnel. "Chris?"

"What?"

Geoff took the flashlight from her and waved it, but the woman had vanished. His head pounded. "I think I'm being drawn into this ghost story. I saw a woman in the cellar."

"What did she look like?"

He scanned the area with the flashlight one more time. "It was too dark to make out any features." Saber sniffed the air, then put his nose to the ground. The dog knew something was amiss. A feminine voice whispered. Geoff quickened his pace to reach the cellar. Chris latched onto his arm and followed along.

They entered the cellar, and Geoff fumbled around for the light switch near the stairs. He flipped the switch. The lights flickered but went off again. Except for the flashlight beam, everything remained dark. He laughed slightly. "I guess this makes for a real Halloween. It's probably a fuse."

With the flashlight guiding the way, he went into the adjacent room and opened the fuse box. None of the switches had tripped. The woman's crying returned. He glanced over his shoulder.

"Geoff, are you all right?"

The sobbing grew louder. "You don't hear her?"

"Hear who?"

Was this what Chris experienced when she had the visions? He returned to the main section of the cellar. With her back to him, the woman knelt on the floor, her sides heaving. Geoff extended an arm, when Saber gave a high-pitched bark.

"Was his bark a warning?" Chris asked.

He nodded.

"How much time?"

"It varies."

"Then we had better not risk going upstairs."

A steadying arm went around his waist. His vision was foggy, but the black-haired woman wailed. *Margaret.* Except for skin as pale as porcelain, she did look similar to Beth. She was more beautiful than he had imagined.

"Geoff—lie down."

Focusing on Chris, he did as she ordered. *Why was Margaret crying?* His mind was sluggish, and he smelled the honeysuckle. Chris placed something soft beneath his head. He lost sense of time and huddled in Chris's arms. Margaret's crying grew louder. His hands went to his head to block out the sound. "She buried him here." He recognized the random images bombarding his consciousness. "When George returned . . ."

Chris squeezed his hand, and honeysuckle enveloped him.

Chapter Eight

WHEN GEOFF WOKE, A TUBE TRAILED from his forearm to a clear plastic bag hanging beside the bed. Drab white walls, subdued lighting—a hospital... *Not again.* He reached for the IV.

"Geoff, no!"

A hand clamped onto his before he could pull the needle out. He blinked. *Chris was here.*

Her brows knitted together, and she gripped his hand. "Are you in pain?"

Groggy, but he had no pain, except for his swollen tongue. He must have bitten it during the seizure. He licked his lips and rasped, "I could use ... a drink."

"The nurse says, 'No.' You've had several seizures in a row."

Several? "A cluster? Never ... done that before. Always ... something new."

Her face was etched in fear. "Be serious. The doctors don't know whether they have them under control yet."

"How many ... have I had?"

She looked like she might cry, but no tears filled her eyes. "I've lost count."

Chris would leave just as Beth had. When he woke in the same hospital, Beth had been gone. He smelled honeysuckle. He *was* going to have another seizure. "Chris, she buried him ..."

"You said in the cellar where we were looking."

Geoff tried to nod but wasn't sure if he had succeeded.

"You also mentioned something about when George returned."

He had? He couldn't recall. "You were right. She looked like Beth." Another face joined Chris above him. He blinked, taking a moment to recognize Judith.

"He's getting disoriented again," he overheard Chris say. "The doctor's coming."

"Thanks, Judith," Chris replied, "for everything."

"It's nothing." Judith shrugged. "My brother may be crazy, but I'd kind of like to keep him around for a while." Then she added under her breath, "Although I'm not sure why."

"I'll remember that, especially . . . if you keep talking about me . . . as if I'm not here."

Judith moved closer. "Geoff . . ."

Her lips continued moving. Like a silent movie, no words came out. Was it the drugs being pumped into his system or the impending seizure causing the effect? The hospital—when he woke *she* hadn't been there. To keep Chris from leaving, he tightened his grip on her hand. "I don't think he wants me to leave," she said.

Who was she talking to? A nurse looked up from a chart. How long had she been there? "All right, you can stay a while longer. You . . ." She motioned to Judith. ". . . out." As she checked the IV, she added, "Remain calm. Everything will be fine." Had she been speaking to Chris or him?

"Chris . . ."

"I'm here."

The scent of honeysuckle grew stronger, and his throat constricted. He licked his lips and swallowed. It hadn't helped much. "If anything should happen . . ."

"Don't think like that."

"It *was* Margaret. She wants . . . " That wasn't right. Uncertain what he had been about to say, he shook his head. "Forgiveness."

"For killing that horrible man?"

He placed a hand to his head. "I'm not sure."

"We'll discover the reason when you're feeling better. You'll come to visit me in Boston."

That sounded nice. *So tired.* He laid his head against the pillow and closed his eyes.

"It's time to leave," the nurse said.

He reopened his eyes to discover Chris staring at him. Unable to hide the worry lines along her brow, she clenched her jaw.

"He'll be fine, Ms. Olson, but he needs rest."

Chris looked over at the nurse, then back again. When he let go of her hand, she smiled. She leaned over and kissed him on the cheek, squeezing his hand before turning. As he watched her go through the door, iciness enveloped him. Vague images took shape. Not the ones he normally experienced before a seizure, but faces . . . Blurred outlines—crying and shouting.

"Chris . . ." He snapped his eyes shut. He should have told her that he loved her.

Whirring machines and people talking surrounded him. Woozy, he found himself in a dark world. Geoff commanded his eyes to open, but nothing happened. Darkness remained. Was he in the same hospital room? Feeling incredibly light, he floated to the ceiling. With no conscious sensation of turning his head, he looked back. Suddenly, he could see. His body was on a table in the full throes of a seizure. Strange—he felt nothing seeing himself like that.

Someone shouted. "Blood pressure dropping!" A scurry of personnel and emergency equipment went into place. At peace, he turned away from the scene. Cannon roared, and a flash from a gun muzzle sparked. Men charged over a hill, firing muskets. From the hill, the shape of Poplar Ridge formed, and a woman with open arms greeted him at the door. Separated from her for too long, he buried his face in her hair. A dream? Or was it death? He had been in a hospital with a face beaming over him.

No longer in his arms, the woman stood a few feet from him with a soft glow behind her. Long black hair cascaded down her back. *Margaret.* The scent of honeysuckle was soft and feminine. Her perfume. Her presence brought mixed thoughts. Dances and parties, but that way of life could never return. She reached out and whispered his name. "Geo..." Ignoring shouts in the emergency room, he stepped toward her. "Respiratory arrest!" A loud buzz came from a machine.

"Geoff!" In the waiting room, Chris jumped to her feet and raced for the door. Judith seized her right arm before Chris reached it. She struggled to break Judith's grip, but it tightened. "You don't understand. Margaret's in there."

"Somebody, help me!" cried Judith.

"He'll die!" A security guard stood on Chris's left side and his grip was stronger than Judith's. "I have to go to him. Please—let me go." She tugged and wrenched to free her arms. They escorted her down the corridor to another room. She kicked, just missing Judith. Her right arm broke free, but the guard caught it and pinned both arms behind her back. A nurse joined them and called for a doctor. A man with a syringe shoved in next to her. The needle pricked her arm, and she cursed at them. With a tight hold on her arms and legs, the two men carried her to the bed. Straps went across her wrists. Held fast, she gave up the struggle. "But you don't understand. Margaret's in there."

With a pinched face, Judith returned to her side. "The sedative will help you relax."

As Chris grew drowsy, Judith's voice brought comfort. She laid back and closed her eyes. With darkness came a dream world—the only place she could see Geoff. He was moving away from her toward a swirling vortex. The light was so bright, she could barely see. Shielding her eyes, she saw Margaret at the center. "Geoff!" He glanced in her direction. Chris reached out, urging him to return. Inside the vortex, men—hundreds in gray uniforms, some in blue—waited. Geoff disappeared. Only the dark dream world remained.

When Chris opened her eyes to the bare white walls, she wanted to cry but couldn't. Geoff was gone. Beside her Judith was slumped over on the bed. "Judith?"

Raising her head with a start, Judith blinked and rubbed her eyes. "Chris, don't ever do that again. I thought for sure we were going to lose both of you."

"Then Geoff?"

"He's fine."

Lying back, Chris finally allowed herself to breathe.

"He's in intensive care. He stopped breathing when they were trying to break the seizure cycle. How could you have known?"

"I felt him die. But it had nothing to do with the seizures. Margaret was there."

Judith squeezed her arm. "You rest. You'll feel better once you do. After that, I'll take you to see him." Relaxing, Chris allowed the sedative to do its job. Another squeeze of reassurance, and then Judith went into the corridor. At the intensive care unit, the nurse nodded for Judith to pass. In Geoff's room, tubes led from his arm, and a heart monitor gave a steady beep. Hearing her enter, Geoff opened his eyes. "I didn't mean to disturb you," she apologized, "but you gave us quite a scare."

Still groggy, he muttered, "The last thing I remember— feeling a seizure coming. And someone crying, then waking up here."

"All in good time, big brother. We almost lost you."

His eyes darted back and forth, searching the room. "Where's Chris?"

The only other time she could recall him looking as frightened was when she had broken the news of Beth's leaving. "She needed rest. She'll be by later."

Fear changed to suspicion. "Then she hasn't returned to Boston?"

"No, she's here resting. I didn't lie to you before. I wouldn't now. You had several seizures in a row. The doctor thinks they're under control, but Chris waited with you through hours of not knowing." She breathed in deeply. "Geoff, you need to get away from here for a while."

Geoff raised his arm with the tube attached. "I don't think that's too likely right now, but Chris made me an offer that may be difficult to refuse."

"Be serious," Judith hissed.

"I am, presuming she doesn't perform a disappearing act like Beth."

For as long as she could remember, seizures had been a dominating factor in his life. Over the years, in spite of taunts and teasing from other children, he never wavered and faced them with courage. Circumstances didn't automatically change for the better once they had grown up. Always holding a secret admiration for his bravery, she now realized it for what it truly was—a cover for frustration and anguish. "She won't. Chris is tougher than Beth."

He arched a brow. "Then you approve?"

"I do," she said with a laugh. "Before you went to the emergency room, Chris says you mentioned that Margaret had buried *him* in the cellar."

He placed a hand to his head. "I did?"

She was afraid that he might forget. The nurse stepped between them, breaking off further questions. "It's time to leave."

Letting out a frustrated breath, Judith bid Geoff goodbye. She'd just have to find out for herself.

Seeming lost with Geoff away, Saber trailed after Chris and Judith down to the cellar. Wine bottles lined the wall. With shovels in hand, they trod across the thick stone floor. "Geoff said that she had buried him here," Chris said, "but I suspect he meant in the cellar somewhere, rather than literally." She pounded the shovel against the heavy rock. "It would take several men to lift this."

"How would Margaret have moved a man's body in the first place? You said that she killed him near the river?"

"That's right." Chris relayed her experience with Geoff the other night. At least this time her venture to the cellar was during daylight. Not that it really made that much difference. The tiny windows in the thick cellar walls let in very little light. Fortunately, the lights were staying on.

"Over by the tunnel," Judith suggested. "If Margaret and Tessa dragged him from the river, they would have buried him..." She ran to the section beside the tunnel and showed Chris the dirt floor. "... here."

"He wouldn't be deep."

Both of them began to dig. After half an hour of fruitless shoveling, they grew exhausted. Judith shoved the hair away from her face and panted, "This is useless."

With stubborn determination, Chris continued to dig. "He's got to be here somewhere."

"If he were here, we would have found him by now. No, we're looking in the wrong place." Judith tapped her shovel.

Finally relenting, Chris stopped digging. Over by the wine bottles, Saber lifted his leg and urinated on a rotting panel beneath the staircase.

"Saber!" Judith shouted. "You know better than that."

The black dog wagged his tail.

Judith raised a finger at him. "You're shameless too. I swear," she continued, directing at Chris, "that sometimes words go into one of his pointy ears and right out the other."

Chris merely laughed. "I've grown rather fond of him." Taking a break, she dropped her shovel. She went over to the dog and scratched behind his ears.

Judith joined them and petted Saber on the back. "And he's enjoying all of this extra attention."

Chris only laughed harder until it dawned on her. Margaret hadn't buried the scout. "Judith..." She pointed to the panel that Saber had urinated on. "What's behind there?"

Her friend shrugged. "Nothing that I know of." She exchanged a look with Chris, finally realizing what she was suggesting.

Together, they tugged on a rotting board. It crumbled beneath their grip. The next board broke away with ease, but the one nearest to the stairs resisted. Chris struggled with it. Judith added her strength, and it finally gave way. A trunk rested in the recess behind the stairwell.

Her palms grew sweaty as Chris dragged the trunk from beneath the stairs. Although it was heavy, she had no doubt two determined women could have placed a body inside and hidden it. She barely had the trunk on the cellar floor before Judith opened the wooden lid. Chris had mentally prepared herself for what they might find, but Judith screamed. A complete skeleton with bits of faded blue fabric lay inside the trunk. Reddish tufts of hair clung to a grinning skull with a bullet hole where his left eye should have been.

The police had yet to verify the age of the skeleton in the cellar, but the wool fabric suggested that it was indeed from the Civil War era. The door to the third floor creaked on ancient hinges. In an attempt to forget all that had happened, Judith grasped David's hand and led the way. "The view is magnificent. Just look."

She pointed to the round, multipaned window, and he crossed his arms with a smile. "I'm sure it is."

"David..." She playfully tapped his arm, but dropped her hand to her side with a frown. "So much has happened."

He wrapped his arms around her. "Your brother is getting better."

Normally, she'd relax when he was near. "Geoff isn't the only one I've been worried about." She ran a finger along his cheek, tracing the outline of his firm jaw.

His eyes were the color of acorns, and they flickered in empathy. He kissed her neck. "Why don't we elope—tonight?"

"I can't do that. My riding students would never forgive me."

With a smile, David kissed her gently. "Then a June wedding?"

Wedding? At any other time, she would have been thrilled with the proposal. Breaking the embrace, Judith went over to the wardrobe and touched the horse etchings with flowing manes in the smooth, old wood. Here Chris had found the silk dress, Margaret's dress. She opened the wardrobe to the old clothes.

"Judith, what are you thinking? You keep tuning me out."

Puzzled, she looked up and spotted the stack of crates in the corner. "I'm trying to make sense of things. I want to say yes, but there's just so much going on." She glanced back to the clothes in the wardrobe and started sifting through them. One of the capes had a chain clasp attached. As Judith unfastened it, the old metal crumbled between her fingers with the pieces falling to the bottom of the wardrobe. She bent down to clean up the debris. "David?"

He moved in behind her.

Judith ran her hand along a section of wood at the bottom. The right side wasn't as finely finished as the left, and the wood grain was a mismatch. A square section of approximately a foot had been noticeably removed and substituted. *A false bottom.* "Do you see this?"

"Someone replaced it," he acknowledged.

"But why would anyone replace the bottom of a wardrobe unless they had something to hide?" She felt along the edge and added a little pressure. With some resistance, the piece moved.

David knelt beside her and helped. He exerted more force, and the section gave way.

Judith lifted the wood square out.

"Just a few old letters," David said. He gave her the letters, bundled with a faded velvet ribbon. A portrait was underneath. His eyes widened.

"Something wrong?"

"Doesn't the man in the picture look like your brother?"

Breathing in sharply, Judith lifted the tintype from the box. The man in the uniform had an upswept moustache, but, otherwise, he looked like Geoff. The date on the back read—1864. She flipped through the letters. They were addressed to Margaret Cameron. Fumbling with the ribbon, she opened the first letter. Dated 1864, the yellow paper crinkled and nearly crumbled between her fingers. She began to read:

My dearest Margaret,
*   I must apologize for such a lengthy absence. The news of my death was premature. Soon after leaving your loving arms, I was wounded. The surgeon sincerely believed the wound was mortal, and my comrades left me for the enemy. Yankee infantry overran our lines. Do not fear. They saw to it that I should die with grace. When they discovered that I might survive my wound, I was sent to a hospital where a kindly nurse tended me and gave me comfort. After a month, I was sent to Fort Delaware.*
*   Conditions here are almost as harsh as the field. There is too little food, clothing, and medicine. Some Yankees believe it is just punishment for the South starting the Rebellion, and they may confiscate this letter for my saying so. None of the other letters I have written have made it outside these prison walls. I can only hope this one will be the exception because not all Northerners agree. Like the nurse in the hospital, some are kindly and will slip us extra morsels to abate starvation. Even then, it is never enough.*
*   To ease my hunger, I lie awake at night and reflect upon the moments we have shared. Those memories are as precious to me as life itself. I cling to each one until dawn reminds me of where I am. It has been so long that I literally ache to hold you in my arms. If that shall never be possible, I hope you will find comfort in these words expressing my love. My last thoughts will be of you, and if you hear a whisper on the breeze calling your name, you know it will be me in my final breath.*
*   You need not remind me of my solemn oath to return to you. I will do my utmost to honor it, for nothing in this life could make me happier than returning home and one day having children to carry on the family name. I often think of what our future will be like together and the many happy years ahead. Hopefully, these are not simple dreams merely*

passing like ships in the night. Death surrounds me. I hear its cry and wonder if I too will soon join it. My love for you is timeless and cannot die, but more importantly, I feel the power of your love. In the end, it is what binds us, and if I am fortunate, that alone shall be the reason I have been spared.

I must stop here, Margaret, but I will not say goodbye. To do so would be an admission I am not quite ready to make. The thought of you at home waiting for me is what gives me strength to face each day.

All of my love,
George

"1864. We thought everything had been burned with the Yankee occupation." She swallowed hard.

"Judith, what's wrong? You look pale."

"This is his last letter." Judith searched through the stack—definitely the most recent date. "There are no more after this one. He obviously wrote this one from prison, Fort Delaware."

"Why the concern over someone who probably died over a hundred years ago?" David asked pragmatically.

"Chris told me about a man who looked like Geoff." She held up the tintype. "As we had suspected, he was my own great-grandfather, George Cameron." Without bothering to offer an explanation to David, Judith charged down the stairs to the second floor. "Chris!" When she pounded on the door to the guest room, Saber barked. "Chris!"

The door opened to a befuddled looking Chris with Saber at her side. "Judith?"

Judith burst through the door and held out the box. "Letters from George and more importantly . . ."

"A picture?" Chris's hands shook as she grasped the tintype. She stared at the photograph and studied it.

"I'd say this is evidence that there may be skeletons in the Cameron's cellar, but not in their closet. George was most definitely our grandfather." Judith blew out a breath. "I'll admit that even I was a bit worried after you had told me that Margaret had been raped."

Chris held up the tintype. "Do you mind if I show this to Geoff?"

"Go ahead, and while we're at it, I think it's time that I arrange for that visit to see Aunt Greta. She may be able to shed further light on everything that's been happening."

"Thanks."

"For what?"

"For not dismissing me when I told you what sounded like a preposterous story."

"I knew *you*." Judith squeezed Chris's hand. Without voicing her concerns, Judith still worried. Geoff looked so much like George that Margaret might be searching for him more than resolving what had happened to her during the Civil War.

The wrinkled, bone-thin woman poured tea from a silver pot. On a chilly morning, the hot drink was a welcome relief. Chris cast a glance about the room. Among antique tinware, the interior of the Victorian house brimmed with brightly colored glass and china knickknacks. She moved closer to the crackling fire, where Judith already huddled.

Judith had relayed the fact that Greta Cameron Williams had been born in the turn of the century at Poplar Ridge. She was a connecting force to Margaret. As the silver-haired woman sat, the rocking chair creaked. Judith handed her the letters bound by the faded velvet ribbon.

A twinkle entered the old woman's pale eyes.

"Do you recognize them?" Chris asked.

"Where on earth did you find them?" Greta glanced from Chris to Judith in anticipation. "They're from my grandfather."

"Hidden beneath a false bottom in the wardrobe on the third floor," Judith explained. "From his letters, we've learned that he was captured during the war, but little else."

Greta unfolded the yellow pages. "He was severely wounded before he was captured by the Yankees."

"Can you tell us what happened?" Judith inquired further. The old woman's brow furrowed. "I'm not really sure. He only lived for a short time following the war. My father never knew him."

Judith's line of questioning wasn't giving them the answers they needed. Chris jumped in. "What do you know, Greta?"

Knobby fingers tapped the chair's arm. "Pa said the family thought he was dead, but my grandmother refused to leave Poplar Ridge. She had fared worse when the Yankees occupied it. Her faith paid off because my grandfather did return. Apparently, the wound gave him great pain up until the day he died."

"How did he die?" Chris continued.

A frown crossed the old woman's face. "My grandmother only talked about my grandfather when she was prodded. Even after all those years, she always spoke about him in the present tense."

Present tense? If Margaret hadn't let George go, then why hadn't he been included in more of her visions? "Go on."

"She said he was never quite the same after the war. He went on a rampage." Swallowing hard, Greta hesitated. "He shot himself. My grandmother found him with the gun in his hand."

Judith paled, and Chris grasped her arm, making certain that she was steady. Poor Margaret. First, what had happened to her during the war, then George in its aftermath. Yet several pieces to the jigsaw didn't quite fit.

"Oh, Judith, I'm sorry for telling you about such unpleasant family history." Greta crossed her arms. "Shall I continue?"

"Yes," Chris said without hesitation.

Greta glanced to Judith and received a nod of approval. "Some spiteful people say a rift had grown between my grandparents, and that before he died, he had taken up with another woman. I don't know what to believe. My grandmother was too proper to speak about such things, but whatever happened on that night, he snapped and could no longer bear living."

A similarity to Geoff after Beth had left? Another woman certainly added a twist. *Catherine.* Her middle name had been a coincidence. Geoff must have been having visions of the past as well, but the seizures kept him from seeing them clearly. After blowing on the steaming cup, Chris took a sip of tea. "Greta, are you aware that Geoff looks similar to your grandfather?" "Geoff?" Greta shook her head. "I never met my grandfather, but I suppose there could be a family resemblance." Judith handed her the tintype of George, and Greta adjusted her glasses. She smiled fondly. "They do look alike. Imagine that."

When Greta returned the picture, Chris checked her watch. "I need to be heading into Richmond, or Geoff is going to be upset with me for being late. He's being released from the hospital today."

"That is good news." Breathing heavily, the old woman pushed her thin frame from the chair. "If there's anything else I can do . . ."

They thanked Greta for the tea, and as they stepped onto the porch, Chris pondered the puzzle pieces. She wished she had several days to talk to Greta, but she'd be heading back to Boston soon after picking up Geoff. She only hoped the situation hadn't intensified with their recent findings.

On such a fine Indian summer day, Geoff had asked Chris to stop the Mustang along the banks of the James. After being cooped up in a hospital room for four days, he had gone stir crazy and relished the thought of walking in the sunshine. Taking in a deep breath, he realized how much he had missed the outdoors. Saber loped ahead of them along the sandy edge.

Chris joined him and clasped his hand. "I thought you might be in a hurry to return to Poplar Ridge."

Her tone had been suggestive. He held her and kissed her. "If you put it that way." The hospital stay had made him aware of how much he hated to be apart from her. He kissed her once more. "Don't go back to Boston."

"I can't stay until after I take the bar." She drew away from his embrace. "I've already checked. If I file within the next month, I can take the February exam."

Her response gave him some hope. "How long after that before you get the results?"

"A few weeks."

At least five months, maybe longer, where they'd be forced to live apart. "I'll do my best to visit you, but I'm not comfortable traveling without Saber. And I refuse to put him in the cargo hold of any plane. Too many dogs die that way."

"I understand. I'll visit you too. The time will go by faster than either of us can imagine." She frowned. "Geoff, I'm worried about you."

He pointed to himself. "Me? I'm fine now."

Chris shook her head. "I don't mean the seizures. There's more going on than the one-eyed ghost." She reached into her purse and handed him the tintype. "This is your great-grandfather—George."

His eyes widened as he fingered the rough edge. "It could be me."

"Exactly my point, and after all Margaret went through, she never got over George's death."

Confused, he said, "Never got over . . . What are you trying to say?" He cast his gaze to the calm waters of the James as she relayed what she had learned from Greta. The images that he often saw before a seizure must be some sort of clue. But to what? "Has Margaret been mistaking me for George?"

Chris shrugged. "I'm not certain, but I think the visions could be a warning. Remember Margaret cautioned both Beth and me about the one-eyed ghost."

A warning from Margaret? Geoff pondered the information and grew increasingly unsettled by the fact that George had taken his life.

Chapter Nine

BETWEEN STUDYING FOR THE BAR EXAM and her regular work schedule, Chris found visiting Poplar Ridge on the weekends an impossibility. Fortunately, Geoff had managed to set aside his fear of traveling without Saber and came to Boston at least once a month. On a snowy weekend in early January, he agreed to meet her at the theater. Although venturing outside her apartment was uncharacteristic for him, she was delighted to see him interested in doing so. As the snowfall grew heavier, Chris checked her watch. His plane had been due several hours before, and he always traveled light to make it unnecessary to check baggage. "I'm going to check his flight," she said to her parents.

"It's a few minutes yet," her mother replied. "I'm sure the cab probably got caught in traffic."

"Most likely," Chris agreed and left her real worries unsaid. As she cracked the lobby door open, an arctic blast cut through the warm haven. She bundled her coat around her. Cars honked wildly on the icy streets. No Geoff appeared among the faces waiting to enter the theater. She tried his cell phone. No one answered, so she left a message on his voice mail. Next, she dialed the airline. The flight had only been delayed by thirty minutes. *Where was he?*

Snow danced through street-lamp beams. Cascading flurries hypnotized her as squealing tires and screeching brakes changed to hooves clip-clopping against cobblestone. A horse-drawn carriage halted in front of the theater. Two men in top hats and capes helped women in long sequined gowns from the carriage. The group laughed heartily and entered the lobby.

She drew in a sharp breath. "It can't be." Turning from the scene, Chris ran into a man, almost knocking both of them over. "Sorry," she quickly apologized.

With a nod he tipped his hat. "Are you all right, ma'am?"

He offered a steadying hand. His black cape made of the finest wool was fashioned from a bygone style. Suddenly queasy, Chris backed away. "I was looking for someone."

A tap came to her shoulder. "Chris?"

She wheeled around and blinked. Geoff. Delighted to see him, she threw her arms around his neck and kissed him. "You're finally here."

"With a greeting like this, I may decide to come to the theater more often."

Forcing a laugh, she decided not to add to any stress by telling him about what she had seen. "I was worried. I tried your cell phone but got your voice mail."

He flipped open his phone. "I guess I forgot to turn it on after the flight."

"As long as you're all right. Between the weather and . . ."

He breathed out in exasperation. "I haven't had any since Halloween."

"Thank goodness." With the vision subsiding, she grasped his hand. "My parents are already inside."

His grip tightened on her hand. "Maybe this wasn't such a good idea."

Was his apprehension due to the theater or her parents? They had met briefly on one of his previous visits and seemed to get along fine. "Don't worry. I haven't told them about the epilepsy, but they'll handle it just fine when I do. They're not shallow thinkers. Besides, they know that I love you."

He relaxed his grip. "Very well."

As they entered the theater, Chris waved to her parents and rejoined them. Her mother greeted Geoff enthusiastically, but her dad inspected him. She worried that he might say something to upset Geoff. "Jeans," he breathed out in disgust. "You didn't have a clean suit?"

"Dad," Chris grumbled.

"Sorry," Geoff responded dryly. "My tux was out being dry cleaned. After all, what else would a gentleman wear during dinner on a plantation?"

To Chris's relief, her father laughed. "No wonder the South lost."

She felt Geoff's muscles tense, ready to continue sparring, but she poked him in the ribs.

"Chris," her father said, "I like this one. He isn't dull like that other one you went with." He snapped his fingers. "What was his name?"

So much for her dad not being shallow-minded. At least the tension between him and Geoff had melted. "I don't think his name is important right now, *Dad*."

As they entered the theater, her father grasped her mother's hand. "Christine Catherine," he said like a priest giving a blessing, "my own daughter, can't even take a joke."

"I wasn't sure that it was," she responded in annoyance.

"Honestly, Chris, sometimes you take me too seriously. Do you really think Geoff feels threatened by someone whose name I can't even remember?"

Far from threatened, Geoff seemed amused, and his blue eyes lit up.

"He might." Suddenly ill to her stomach, Chris plodded up the steps to the balcony. Finding her seat, she eased in. "I've been looking forward to this."

Geoff sat next to her and whispered in her ear, "I presume what's-his-name is one of your fumbling postadolescent encounters?"

"And to think," she responded in a mocking tone, "I never realized that I led a deprived life until my experience with a Virginian."

A grin formed on Geoff's mouth. "That's as it should be."

She elbowed him in the ribs once more. Her dad would be appalled. Like fathers most everywhere, he pretended she kept a separate room when Geoff visited. With her two favorite men near, Chris put her arm through Geoff's.

The theater darkened, and buzzing voices hushed. As the actors came on stage, she smelled honeysuckle. Hoping it would go away, she closed her eyes. The fragrance grew stronger. "Geoff," she whispered with a tug on his arm. "I want to go home."

He tilted his head to hear her better. "What?"

"I want to go home."

"But the play just started."

"I'm not feeling well." A sharp "shhh" came from the next booth, and she lowered her voice. "Geoff, please..."

With a nod, he regained his feet. After quick apologies to her parents, she rushed to the lobby. Geoff had a difficult time keeping up. "Chris, what's wrong?"

She stopped at the checkroom for her coat. "I don't feel well."

"You must be feeling rotten. You've been looking forward to this for over a month."

"Are you saying I'm lying?"

He stared at her in confusion. "Of course not. It's just that you've only acted strange when you've had a vision."

She headed for the door. "I haven't had any visions."

"Then what's wrong?"

A hand went to her head. "A migraine. I feel a migraine coming on." With a dubious expression, he crossed his arms. The lie hadn't set well. She turned back. "What does she want? I smelled honeysuckle."

"Just now?"

"Yes, and outside the theater, I saw carriages. I bumped into a man wearing a wool cape."

"But nothing else before tonight?"

She shook her head. "No."

"Take a look around."

A crystal chandelier hung in the lobby's center, and an arched stairway led to the balcony. The flooring had been restored to a fine polish of black-and-white marble, and the draperies were a satin brocade edged in a gold cord. "She's been here."

"What would a Southern lady have been doing here? But it definitely looks like the nineteenth century."

Nasal voices laughed. A crash of shattering glass came from the parlor. In the dining room came more laughing. The Yankees were stealing the silverware and lowering the chandelier.

Chris forced the horrifying vision away and focused on the lead crystal. "The chandelier. It's from Poplar Ridge."

Confusion crossed his face. "How could you know such a thing?"

The honeysuckle had faded, and she clasped Geoff's hand. "Margaret saw the soldiers steal it."

He nodded, then grinned. "Do you think there's a way to charge them for it with interest?"

His humor was exactly what she needed, and she breathed easier. "Shall we go to dinner instead?"

"It sounds like a splendid idea. Since my plane was late, I didn't have time to grab a bite before dropping my bag off at your apartment." He held out his arm. "Ma'am..."

Still unaccustomed to his manners, Chris laced her arm through his. She showed him to the parking garage. Beside the Integra, he kissed her and opened the door for her. "I'm perfectly capable..."

He pressed his fingers to her lips. "I know you're a liberated woman, but indulge me."

She laughed as she climbed in behind the wheel and waited for him to reach the passenger side. The snow had covered portions of the road, making it slick and slow going in places, but Chris stopped at an Italian restaurant not far from her apartment on the Back Bay.

Over lasagne and Chianti, they brought each other up to date since Geoff's last visit. "How's the studying going?" he finally asked.

Chris set her wine glass on the checkered tablecloth. "That was one thing I wanted to talk to you about and not on the phone."

"I detect this is something I'd rather not hear." He took a sip of wine, then set his glass down.

Chris took a deep breath. "I'm not going to take the bar in February."

Disappointment spread across Geoff's features. "Why?"

"There's no way that I can be ready. I've been cramming during every spare minute, but that's just it, I have very little free time. The July exam would give me the time I need to make certain that I pass." She reached across the table and grasped his hand.

"You could give up the job and have plenty of time to study."

She shook her head. "I won't sponge off you."

He withdrew his hand from her grip. "Then pay me back. Why do you have to be so goddamned stubborn? It's only temporary, and it's not like I can't afford to support the two of us. You should see how much I shell out to Beth each month."

"That's not the same, and you know it. I appreciate the fact that you want to help, but it's something that I have to do on my own."

He let out a weary breath. "I suppose I knew as much when I made the suggestion. Do you think we'll always have such conflicting viewpoints?"

"Probably. At least we won't complain about life being dull." Chris laughed and squeezed his hand once more. "July will be here before you know it, and I'll move to Richmond after taking the exam. And I'll definitely be in Virginia in June for Judith's wedding."

"All right," he responded somewhat reluctantly. He reached into his jacket and withdrew a jewelry box wrapped in gold paper. "I was saving this for the right moment."

Nervous that he suddenly might be thinking of marriage, she felt her stomach constrict. "The right moment?"

He fidgeted with the box, then set it on the table. "It belonged to my mother."

His mother? He never spoke of Sarah, but what would he say about her if he had no memories? At least the box looked a bit too large for an engagement ring.

"Well, aren't you going to open it?"

"Of course." Except for the rose, Geoff had never really been the romantic type when it came to gift giving. Forcing a smile, she undid the bow and peeled away gold paper. Inside was a crystal pendant on a fine gold chain. She held the necklace up to the light. A rainbow of colors appeared on the wall. "It's beautiful. Would you help me with the clasp?" As he came around to her side of the table, she lifted her hair from her neck. He clasped the necklace, then she felt his lips on her neck. Her skin tingled. Had her lack of preparation for the bar been an excuse to postpone moving to Virginia, or had she suddenly become unnerved with her vision in the theater?

With winter breaking, robins sang and buds were sprouting on the trees. Positive she had caught wind of daffodils, Chris dropped her briefcase on her desk. Her session in court had taken longer than anticipated. It was nearly five, and she had a brief to prepare for Monday morning. She had warned Geoff that she would be unable to meet him at the airport, but she checked to see if his flight was in—on time. She dialed his cell phone. Voice mail. He had likely forgotten to turn the phone on again after the flight. She dialed home, only to hear her own voice answer. Fidgeting with a pen, she waited for the beep. "Geoff, give me a call as soon as you get in. I've got a couple of things to look up before I leave, but I hope to be out of here in half an hour."

Nancy stepped into her office as she replaced the receiver. "Chris, if you don't mind, I'll be leaving."

Glad for a chance to get off her feet, Chris sank into the chair behind her desk. "Have a good weekend."

Her secretary gave her a knowing smile. "Isn't Geoff here this weekend?"

"He is."

"Then what are you doing hanging around here? I'd think with a handsome, sexy-sounding man like him, anything he has to offer would be more pleasurable than a tort book."

Chris felt her face warm slightly. "I'll be leaving in a few minutes. The last time I was late, he ordered a romantic dinner."

"Sounds delightful." Waving on her way out, Nancy bid her goodnight.

After researching a few facts for her brief, Chris checked the time. Seven. It had taken longer than she anticipated. She quickly packed her papers together, stuffing them in her briefcase. She dialed Geoff's cell number again. Still no answer. She checked the answering machine at home—no messages from Geoff. Suddenly worried, she grabbed her briefcase and headed home. As she approached the apartment, the Integra's headlights landed on Geoff, sitting on the steps.

Breathing out in relief, she slammed the car door. "I was worried sick when you didn't answer my calls."

He stood to greet her. "I lost your key," he responded in a monotone voice.

No kiss. Was something wrong? No, like the time she had been late before, he was planning something. "Did you lose your cell phone too?" She went up the steps and unlocked the door. To her surprise, there was no late dinner waiting. "Geoff, what's going on?"

Like a shy boy, he shoved his hands in his pockets and looked to the floor.

"What's wrong?"

"I had a seizure."

After six months without a seizure, she now understood what he had meant by how they always returned. "It didn't happen on the flight?"

"No, but I would have been better off if it had."

Suddenly confused, she asked, "What do you mean?"

"After I got off the plane, I felt it. Didn't want to make a grand spectacle of myself, so I ducked into the men's room. The next thing I knew, I was on the floor. When I came to, your key and my wallet were gone."

With the news, she swallowed hard. *Why hadn't she taken the time to meet him?* "You were robbed?"

"Don't look so surprised. A twitching fit becomes an easy target."

Ashamed that others could be so cruel, she put her arms around him. "I can't believe no one came to your aid."

He disengaged from her embrace and slumped to the sofa. "They did, but by that time it was already too late."

"Why didn't you call me?"

"There was nothing you could have done."

And if he would have had Saber along, the robbery would have been prevented. What if the thug had done more than steal his wallet? Terrified by what could have happened, she sat beside him and grasped his arm. "Are you all right, physically?"

"I think so." Blowing out a breath, he clasped his hands together. "I warned you it wouldn't be easy. The neurologist already wanted to add carbamazepine. I can imagine what he'll say after this episode."

Definitely not easy—more drugs would risk his health further. Chris hooked her arm through his. "Let's just relax, enjoy the weekend, and each other."

He closed his eyes and trembled under her touch. "Chris, I can't do this anymore."

"That's an understandable reaction. You've had a frightening experience."

"So, we're back to pretending the problem doesn't exist." His gaze finally fell upon her.

"No, I didn't mean that at all. I only know that when I'm with you, I'm happier than I could have ever imagined. Call us a mismatch if you like, but it doesn't seem that way to me."

His eyes flickered thoughtfully. "Then why don't we do something about it? Let's stop playing this long-distance nonsense."

"We've already been over this. I'll move to Richmond in July."

"I'm not talking about Richmond."

Her heart pounded. *Damn, damn, damn.* After what he had been through, she should have seen his change of heart coming. "Did you report the incident to airport security?"

"Airport security, the credit card company, and anyone else I could think of. I notice that you've conveniently changed the subject. Don't worry, I get the hint. I won't ask if you're that afraid."

"Afraid?"

"Yes, city girl—fear. You hide beneath that tough exterior, but you're afraid to return to Poplar Ridge. Why do you think you hightailed it back to Boston after seeing Beth, and now you've delayed the date for taking the bar?"

"I'll have you know I'm not afraid of ghosts," Chris insisted.

"Who said anything about ghosts?" Geoff laughed. "That little mystery is right up your alley. Weren't you the one professing to holding the truth dear? Truth is something you respect as long as it's someone else's."

He had been more affected by the robbery than he had initially shown. "What *are* you talking about?"

"Never mind." He rubbed his forehead. "I seem to have misplaced my wallet. You can buy dinner this evening."

Chris detected his sense of humor returning, but his accusations troubled her. She had purposely deflected a proposal, and Geoff had seen right through her. She twisted the chain of the crystal pendant between her fingers. Exactly what was she frightened of?

In the heat of a fever, Margaret tossed and turned for three days. Covered in sweat, she struggled to sit up. Tessa spooned her some broth. "You needs to regain your stren'th, Miss Margaret."

"My baby?"

"She be fine," Tessa responded in a flat voice.

"What's wrong?"

"Ain't nothin' wrong, ma'am. You bin mighty sick since birthin'. Barely had da stren'th to even speak a few words afore now."

Her breasts felt engorged. "Bring her to me, and I shall nurse her."

"Yes'm." Tessa stood and left the room.

Why did the servant continue to use such a dull voice? After the Union occupation, the baby was the only reason she had survived. Tessa returned, carrying bundled blankets over to the bed. Margaret lowered her gown and offered the baby a nipple. The blanket fell away from the baby's head and revealed red hair. "Tessa?"

"Yes'm."

Margaret swallowed. "This can't be my baby."

"She da one I helps deliver."

Clutching the baby to her breast, Margaret gripped the blanket. "But George has . . ."

"Mr. George gone, ma'am. You know dat."

Margaret's grip grew tighter. "How . . . how can that be? George is the only one . . ."

"Miss Margaret—you be forgettin' again. Da Yankee scouts . . ."

Yankee scouts? *She recalled the missing eye and pool of blood. She had shot him with his own gun.* Why? *Her mind was a fog, and she drifted through the layers. "He . . ."*

She closed her eyes and began to cry. "Nooo!"

"Let me take da baby." Tessa gathered the baby in her arms.

Margaret reached for the baby. "Tessa, no. She's all I have left of George. Give her back to me."

"But she ain't Mr. George's."

"She is." Margaret cradled the infant in her arms and hummed a lullaby. "I need a name for you, little girl." Red hair. What was it Tessa had said? *"Tessa, it might be best if you put her down for her nap. I'm still feeling weak."*

"Yes'm." Tessa took the baby once more.

As the servant left the room with the baby bundled in her arms, Margaret laid back. Unable to sleep, she thought of George. Dead? *Tears slipped unashamedly down her cheeks. He couldn't be dead. She made a fist and struck her pillow. "Dammit, George. You promised to return." She laid her head on the pillow, crying herself softly to sleep.*

When she woke, she heard the baby cry from the next room.

"Tessa . . ." No response. Still wobbly on her feet, Margaret got out of bed and negotiated her way to the nursery. With her fists bunched, the infant continued to cry from the cradle. Red hair. *"Tessa," she tried again. "This can't be my baby. George doesn't have red . . ."*

The scout. The Yankee scout had red hair. She had blotted out the memory.

She reached for the baby. "Georgianna," she whispered. Instead of taking the baby into her arms, her hands went around the infant's throat. The child gasped. No screams. The veins in her tiny neck bulged, and Margaret's grip grew tighter. Her face and lips turned blue. "You're part of that Yankee monster." A bloody froth appeared on the baby's mouth, and then she lay still. "Tessa!"

"Oh, God! She killed the baby." Gasping for breath, Chris sat up in bed. A light went on, and strong arms went around her, while she cried on Geoff's shoulder. "She killed the baby."

"What baby?" He brushed the tears from her cheek.

Either Beth hadn't known that portion of Margaret's story, or she hadn't relayed it to Geoff. Calmer now, Chris took a deep breath, but her words came out in a rush. "After she was raped, Margaret had a baby. She strangled her. Geoff, you were right. I *am* frightened."

He held her and whispered that things would be all right.

She clung to him. "I've only had visions when I've been in contact with something of *hers*. How is she still reaching me?"

Geoff touched the crystal pendant around her neck. "It was passed down to my mother."

"Of course, that must be the reason. It once belonged to Margaret." She resisted the temptation to remove the necklace. She *wasn't* afraid of Margaret, but... During the entire weekend, she had avoided her true fear by taking charge in helping Geoff overcome his ordeal. "I'm sorry. I never let you ask your question."

"It doesn't matter anymore," he responded dully.

"But it does," she insisted.

He shook his head. "You saved me from hearing no."

"No? Give me a chance to explain."

He placed his fingers to her lips. "The past few months have been great, but I accept the fact that we're too different to make anything as serious as marriage work."

Tears rolled down her cheeks. "But I love you."

He wiped her tears away with his thumb. "It seems in our case that love is not enough."

Forced laugh—and more tears. "I don't believe it. There has to be a way that we can make it work."

His eyes grew moist. "If you won't come back to Virginia with me, I don't see how."

"Geoff..."

"Don't say anymore." He cleared his throat. "Let's just savor the moment. After I get on the plane today, I'm not coming back."

He was leaving. Was this how Margaret had felt when George left for the war? No, unlike Margaret, she had a choice. All she had to do was agree to accompany Geoff to Virginia. Even now, her throat choked off her breath at the thought of consenting.

Confused by her mixed emotions, Chris clutched him tighter and felt the beating rhythm of his heart. She absorbed herself in his warmth and luxuriated in his coarse male skin. His fingertips stroked her cheek, and their mouths met. She loved him more than she could have ever imagined loving anyone. So why did she find it so difficult to commit to him?

Four weeks later, after taking Neal for a horseback ride, Geoff sat on Poplar Ridge's steps, watching his son throw a tennis ball for Saber. A child's laughter and the dog barking excitedly—without those sounds, the old house had grown so quiet of late that, like a sealed tomb, it smothered anyone who entered.

"Geoff..." Judith stood inside the door. "Beth's here."

His heart sank as he stood. Ever since leaving Boston, he had been living from one day to the next. He had hoped Chris might call with the news that she had changed her mind. Neal helped him focus on his responsibilities, rather than wallow in a cesspool of despair. As Beth started down the steps, Judith wisely vanished. She glanced at Neal with a frown. "I've come to take him home."

"I was hoping that he might stay the weekend."

Her features remained rigid. "You know that I don't want him staying here."

"Mom!" Neal charged toward them with Saber on his heels. "Look at what Saber can do." He waved the tennis ball over Saber's head. The black dog rose on his haunches and begged. Neal tossed the ball, and Saber caught it in his mouth, then bounded off. With a delirious laugh, the boy scampered after him.

"At least stay for supper. He's having fun."

Beth checked her wristwatch. "All right, but don't try to talk me out of taking him with me when I leave."

"Fine. I guess things have gotten bad if we can't even talk about Neal."

Her stern expression softened, and she shivered. "Over here." She started in the direction of the gazebo. Once seated in a wicker chair, she said, "I'm glad you have Saber."

Neal chased after Saber's tail with the dog remaining barely out of reach. "So am I," he replied, seating himself across from her with the luncheon table between them, "but I doubt that you brought me over here to discuss my dog."

"When was the last time you had a seizure?"

He hadn't told her about the airport incident. "I fail to understand what that has to do with Neal."

She held up a hand in a truce. "How far away can Saber be from you and still detect them?"

Further annoyed with her questions, Geoff narrowed his eyes. "I don't know, why?" She glanced over at Neal. "If that's what you're worrying about, he'd detect it from there. I'd be able to call Judith in time so Neal needn't witness dear, old dad having a spastic fit."

"Geoff, please, there's no need to be sarcastic. In a clumsy way, I'm trying to point out that a person, or dog, in this case, can be so attuned to another they know when something is wrong."

What did she know? "Please enlighten me. What's wrong?"

As if suddenly cold, she hunched her shoulders and rubbed her arms. She looked him straight in the eye. "You. I've noticed it the past few weeks when you've picked up Neal. Judith says she has too."

Chris must not have said anything to his sister.

As if reading his thoughts, Beth asked, "Are you still seeing Chris?"

Knowing that he could never hide anything from Beth, he bit his tongue on the angry retort that popped into his head. "No," he finally admitted.

She averted her gaze. "That explains things. I'm sorry."

"Right."

She looked in his direction once more. "We've both said and done things that we shouldn't have. I regret my mistakes, but there's no way I can undo them. I still don't want Neal staying. This house is . . . unsettled."

"Ghosts and goblins? There hasn't been a sighting of any apparitions since the skeleton was found. Some re-enactors even gave him a proper nineteenth-century burial as a military hero in one of the Union cemeteries."

"He was no hero," Beth snapped. "For God's sake, he raped your grandmother!"

"I didn't say he *was* a hero. I only said he hasn't made an appearance since the re-enactors buried him."

"Doesn't it bother you that your own grandmother was raped?"

"I would like to have taken care of the Yankee bastard myself," he responded, raising his voice, "but that was over 140 years ago. What can I do about it now?"

Beth calmed slightly, but continued rubbing her arms. "Did the gun belong to him?"

Suddenly annoyed, Geoff stood. "That's what this interrogation is about. Just because I've split with Chris doesn't mean I intend on using any goddamned gun on myself. You're holding it for safekeeping anyway."

Her brows knitted together. "I didn't mean to upset you."

Composed again, he reseated himself. "You may have difficulty believing this, but I *never* tried to kill myself. I admit, I thought about it. I even got the gun out, but before I could put it away, I had the seizure, so everyone concluded that I was suicidal. I wasn't."

Her gaze met his. "I thought..."

"I know what you thought, and if you had taken the time to ask me, I would have told you what had happened. We used to talk our problems through."

With a pensive expression, she frowned. "I seemed to have made a mess of things."

He reached across the table and clutched her hand. "Let's start over by being kind to each other."

She nodded. "If you insist the ghosts are gone, then Neal can stay the weekend."

"As far as I know, they are."

A smile crept to her face. "Then I'm looking forward to supper. It'll be nice not having to cook for a change."

During supper, Judith sent him scorching looks for inviting Beth. His father was more hospitable, and Neal was ecstatic. After the meal, when the others had retired to the drawing room, his sister drew him aside. "Geoff, what has gotten into you?"

"I'm not sure I know what you mean," he answered, pretending confusion.

"Why did you allow *her* to stay?"

"She's the mother of my son."

His response only made her angrier. "There's more going on, and you know it. What about Chris?"

"As best friends, I thought Chris would have informed you that we're no longer seeing each other."

Stunned by the news, Judith blinked in disbelief. "When did this happen?"

"After my last visit. In case you hadn't noticed, she never bothered to reciprocate any visits here."

Judith gestured in the direction of the drawing room. "So you invite *her* right back into this house like she never left? I can't believe you, after what she did."

"That was a misunderstanding."

Her voice climbed an octave. "Some misunderstanding. She left you for dead, taking Neal with her."

"Judith, calm down. I invited Beth to supper. It's not like she's staying the night, and even if she were, that would be *my* business—not yours. You can quietly butt out now." He strode down the hall, leaving Judith fuming behind him.

In the drawing room, Beth joked with his father. She had always possessed a special knack with him. Neal had found a rope toy and played tug-of-war with Saber. Throughout the evening, Judith avoided them. At Neal's bedtime, Beth joined him when he read their son a King Arthur story. Geoff got a sense of déjà vu, but before he completed the story, Beth vanished from the room. Finished with the story, Geoff closed the book and ruffled his son's hair. "I'll see you in the morning."

"Goodnight, Dad."

Whispering goodnight, Geoff tucked Neal into bed and closed the door behind him. In the hall, there was no sign of Beth, then he spotted the slightly ajar door to the room they had once shared. He swallowed hard. He hadn't entered the room since Beth had left the estate, yet something compelled him to move toward it.

The door creaked as he went inside. With only a small lamp to see by, Beth stared at him through the reflection of a full-length mirror. With her long black hair tumbling below her waist, she stood before the mirror—totally naked—the way he remembered her before that fateful night. He cleared his throat. "Beth..."

Nimble-footed, she moved with such grace that she appeared to float across the floor. His head spun, but there was no turning back. She possessed him—body and soul.

Chapter Ten

CHRIS STARED AT THE TEST STRIP in shock. Positive. *Pregnant?* She reread the instructions that came with the kit. Maybe she had performed something wrong. *How difficult is it to pee on a stick?* Bad dream—she couldn't be pregnant. True, there was some cramping in her abdomen, but she had dismissed the symptoms to PMS. She went into the kitchen to check the calendar and started counting—two weeks, four, six, eight. Had eight weeks really passed since her last period? That brought her to two weeks before Geoff's final visit.

No, there had to be another explanation. Her period was overdue because of the stress of breaking up with Geoff. Could a pregnancy kit give a false positive? Reality finally hit—she *was* pregnant. And once she informed Geoff, he'd likely want to take the chivalrous route and suggest marriage again. Couldn't they just live together before considering such a major step?

In a stupor, she dressed for work and drove to the office. Upon arriving, she dialed her gynecologist for an appointment.

As she hung up the receiver, her boss stood in the doorway. "Chris, I need the briefs on the Phillip's case today," he said curtly. She managed a weak nod, and he vanished from the doorway.

Nancy entered, carrying a stack of papers. "You're late this morning, but I've got the copies you wanted. Chris, you're looking pale. Are you all right?"

Her hand went to her head. "I'm late all right," she responded weakly.

Her secretary frowned. "Late? What's wrong?"

"Close the door."

Nancy obeyed. "Is there anything I can do?"

Shaking a fist, Chris laughed. "It's not going to work. I'm not going back!" With her jaw lowered, Nancy stared at her dumbfounded. "Sorry, Nancy. A tiny case of temporary insanity. This morning I discovered that I'm . . . pregnant."

"Are you sure?"

"As much as I'd like to deny it—yes, I'm sure."

Nancy sank into the chair across from her. "What are you going to do?"

"I don't know."

"Have you told Geoff?" When she didn't answer immediately, Nancy asked, "It is Geoff's?"

She forced a laugh. "Of course it's Geoff's, and no, I haven't told him. You're the first."

"That's where you begin," Nancy responded rationally. "Call him."

"If I tell him before I've made any sort of decision, he'll propose."

"That's a bad thing? Call him."

Chris waved that she wasn't ready.

"Then I'll dial." Nancy checked the file box near the phone and dialed. "I'd like to speak to Geoff Cameron. Tell him Chris Olson is calling." She placed her hand over the receiver. "He's there."

"It doesn't matter."

Nancy held out the receiver. Reluctantly, Chris took it. The line was on hold. Her palms were sweaty, and her heart pounded. What would she say? She hadn't totally absorbed the news herself. Another minute passed, and her shaking increased, then someone picked up the line.

"Chris?"

He was out of breath, but it was definitely Geoff. Say something—anything. No words came out, and she slammed down the receiver. "How can I tell him if I don't know what I intend on doing about it?" The phone rang. Only Geoff and her parents knew the number to her direct line. She was willing to bet that the caller wasn't her dad. Oh, what the hell—she had to tell him sometime. Nancy slipped out of her office as she switched on the receiver. "Geoff, are you sitting down?"

"*Sitting?*"

"Yes, I think it's best because I have something important to say."

"*Okay.*"

She took a deep breath. "This morning I discovered that I'm..." *Dammit, stop stuttering and just say it.* "I'm pregnant." Silence. "Geoff?"

"*I thought you had gone on the pill.*"

She fidgeted with a pen on her desk. "I had, but surprise... Believe me, it's as big of a shock to me as it is you."

There was a lengthy pause. He cleared his throat. "*What now?*"

She detected an edge in his voice. "I think it's something better discussed in person. Judith's wedding is only a couple of weeks away. I'll plan on arriving early to help her with the arrangements. We can talk then." To this, he agreed. "I won't cause any trouble. I'm not out for money."

"*I wasn't even thinking that. Hell, I don't know what I am thinking. Shit.*" He fell silent a minute before continuing, "*Do you want my input, or is this something city girl's decide on their own?*"

Chris held her tongue before saying something she regretted. "I think it's best to discuss it when we've both had a chance to absorb the news—in person."

His voice softened. "*You will let me know if you come to some sort of decision before I see you?*" She promised that she would. "*And, Chris, should you need anything, I'm only a phone call away.*"

"Thanks." With a quick goodbye, she hung up the receiver. A little surprised that Geoff hadn't proposed, she stared at the phone. Yet he had been supportive, so she guessed he was probably afraid that she would still say "no."

"Chris?"

She looked up to see Nancy standing across from her desk. "I saw the light to your line go out and wanted to make certain that you're all right."

"He was a bit surprised with the news but took everything in stride."

Nancy smiled. "That's good, isn't it?"

"Of course, and I'll be seeing him in another week, so we can discuss it at length."

Nancy's grin widened. "I just hope you like living in the South."

Chris laughed. "The South. Can you believe they're still fighting the Civil War down there?" For some reason, she suddenly realized how much she had missed Geoff. Would she say no if he proposed? Heck, she was an independent woman. What prevented her from asking him?

Chris's first visit to Poplar Ridge had been during the fall. The seasons had changed, and manicured boxwoods formed the perfect aisle. With the wedding barely a week away, Judith went through the motion of walking the brick path trimmed in daisies and black-eyed Susans. She halted in front of the trickling fountain carpeted with water-lilies where the ceremony would take place. "What do you think?" she asked.

Glancing in the direction of the brick mansion, Chris found it difficult to concentrate on preparations. She had yet to speak with Geoff.

"Chris . . ."

Determined not to let her distraction spoil Judith's happiest occasion, she forced a smile. "What were you saying?"

"The maid of honor usually stands next to the bride." Chris took her place by Judith's side and looked to the house one more time. "Talk about it . . . please."

"About what?"

"What happened between you and my brother. You're eventually going to run into each other. Even if you somehow manage to avoid him, he will be at the wedding."

Obviously Geoff hadn't told her about the baby, but then she would have been more surprised to learn that he had. "There's nothing to say, except..." Chris opened her mouth, but the confession failed to come out. "Another time."

"It's quite obvious that you still love him. Remember, it's me you're talking to, and I'll always listen."

Torn, she needed to speak with someone, but she thought it more appropriate to talk to Geoff first. "I came early to help you with the wedding, not talk about me—or Geoff."

Conceding, Judith raised her arms, pretending to hold a bouquet of flowers.

Another thought occurred to her. "Judith, is he seeing anyone?"

Judith raised a brow. "I thought you didn't want to talk about Geoff."

"You know I lied. Please, it's important. I need to know."

Her friend frowned. "Beth's been here a couple of times. Whether it means anything, I don't know. He's never been the sort to talk about such things."

Chris's heart sank. Judith wouldn't have said that much if she didn't suspect something going on between Geoff and Beth.

Judith glanced at her watch. "It's getting late. Why don't I have dinner served?"

Chris nodded weakly. In the drawing room, she made herself comfortable on the sofa, while Judith informed the cook of dinner plans. She sat back and touched the tapestry design. Here was where she had experienced her first vision. What did they all mean? So much had happened since then. Suddenly ill to her stomach, she clapped a hand over her mouth as Judith returned to the drawing room.

"Would you like a brandy?"

Morning sickness, afternoon, and evening—the thought of a brandy made her want to vomit. "No, thanks," Chris replied, hoping that she didn't need to make a sudden dash for a bathroom. "If it's not too much trouble, I'll take water."

"No bother at all." Judith poured a glass of mineral water, then a brandy for herself before easing into the wing chair.

"With all of the wedding talk, you haven't told me how the job is going."

Chris cast a quick glance to the entrance. As she sipped cool water, the nausea passed. "About the same. My boss complains about my hours. If I worked the entire twenty-four, he still wouldn't be happy. He's angry with me now for taking the week off."

"I'm glad that you did," Judith said with genuine warmth as she sipped from the brandy snifter. Chris rechecked the entrance. "Looking for Geoff?"

"It's important that I talk to him."

Judith's nose wrinkled, and a smile appeared on her lips. "He'll be along soon, but I'll warn you, I gave him the impression that you weren't arriving for another day or two, so he may be a little surprised with your *early* arrival. Chris . . ." Her grin vanished. "If you think I'm prying, tell me where to go, but what happened?"

Chris's hands trembled, and the ice clinked against the glass. A baby couldn't fix things—only make problems worse. "I thought love could solve everything, but it's the sort of thing that happens when a city girl collides with a country boy. We're just too different."

"I tried to warn you."

"You knew that I needed to find out the hard way."

Judith leaned closer. "The fact that he came to see you in Boston several times should tell you something. I don't know of anyone else that he would have risked traveling to see without Saber being along."

"But there's another problem . . ."

"I know. The seizures."

As she touched her abdomen, Chris swallowed hard. "Not the seizures." Her eyes widened. Geoff stood in the doorway. Wondering how much he had overheard, she straightened. His eyes darted back and forth as if he might shoot back into the hall. Then his gaze settled on her, and he continued in their direction. Saber raced ahead of him and greeted her with a wet tongue.

"I'll see how dinner's coming." Judith scurried from the room.

With Saber's enthusiastic kisses, the water glass nearly slipped from Chris's hand. She set the glass on the mahogany table and wrapped her arms around the dog's big furry neck. "I missed you too."

Geoff sat in the chair vacated by Judith. "Saber doesn't give a greeting like that to just anyone."

Chris hugged the dog, thankful for his distraction. "I'm honored to be held in such high regard," she said, giving Saber a scratch behind the ears.

"It may interest you to know that the last time I was in Boston, he wandered off. Judith said for the entire weekend. The neighbor's black Lab has puppies due in a couple of weeks. I guess our travels have something in common."

Chris couldn't help but laugh. She should have guessed that Geoff might resort to levity to ease the tension. "I've decided to keep the baby."

His forehead furrowed. "Is that wise?"

The question caught her off guard. "I'm not sure what you mean."

His calm gave way to annoyance. "Do I really have to spell it out? I think my mother had the seizures as well."

"Your mother?" she asked in confusion. "I thought she died in a car accident."

"She did, but I believe she may have had a seizure while driving. It explains why no one will say anything about what happened."

Their baby *could be* at risk. "Then I'll check the coroner's report."

Calm again, Geoff crossed his arms over his chest and leaned back in the chair. "Always the lawyer."

His hair was bleached by the sun and blonder than she remembered. A pink sunburn crossed the bridge of his nose to his cheeks. She could feel the sun on her face and wind in her hair just looking at him. He was doing what he loved best—working on the farm. "Would you expect me to behave any differently?"

"No."

Baffled by his lack of firm conviction, she asked, "Am I to understand that you'd prefer I have an abortion?"

"I didn't say 'prefer.' I merely want you to be aware of the possible consequences."

She waved at him to continue. "Geoff, stop beating around the bush and tell me what *you* would like me to do. I may not agree, but I would like to hear your opinion."

He met her gaze. "I think you already know my opinion. It hasn't changed since I left Boston."

So he still wanted to marry her. "What about Beth?" Chris responded without thinking and instantly regretting it.

His eyes narrowed in anger. "I see Judith has filled you with the latest gossip."

Chris glanced to the floor. "I'm sorry. I didn't mean to say that, but I can't stay here if I have no idea of where I stand."

"If it wasn't Beth, you'd find some other excuse." He stood. "I have some business to check on." His shoulders slouched as he left the room.

A minute later Chris heard her name, and she glanced up at Judith. "I saw Geoff leave. Are you all right?"

She clenched a hand. "Why does everything have to be so complicated? You know exactly what you want from life—a home, a family. I have a career, but I wonder where it gets me— more vacation time and more sick days that I never see."

"That bad?"

"Worse. I love him more than ever."

Unsurprised by the revelation, Judith remained sympathetic. "Then why don't you tell him?"

Laura stepped into the drawing room and announced dinner. Relieved for the diversion, Chris followed Judith to the dining room.

"I've had a feast prepared to welcome you back."

On an off-white linen tablecloth, a silver platter contained a scrumptious-looking herb roast beef. Fine china bowls were heaped with gravy, carrots, and au gratin potatoes. Woozy again, Chris clutched her stomach. "It looks wonderful, Judith."

A servant pulled out a chair. "Thank..." She met blue eyes—
Geoff, not a servant. "Thank you."

Without acknowledging her, he seated himself on the opposite side. The elder Cameron entered the room and greeted
her with a warm welcome. Geoff passed a china bowl. Chris
thanked him and dabbed some potatoes on her plate. The way
Geoff stabbed at the food on his plate, she could tell that he
was still angry. She glanced down. Thick cheese sauce made
her stomach constrict. *Where was the nearest bathroom?* As she
recalled, the reception room had a partial. *Not too far for a mad
dash.* The nausea faded, and she forced a smile. "Judith, when is
David arriving?"

"Not until Friday. He had a business trip to California.
It's probably for the best. You know what it's like trying to
get things accomplished when there are too many men in the
house."

Winston Cameron added lightheartedly, "I'll remember that
the next time you ask for a loan."

Judith laughed, then turned to Chris with concern. "You're
not eating. Would you prefer something else?"

Since she'd had a chance to speak with Geoff, she would
have to find a way to tell Judith—in private. "No, everything
looks great. I'm just a little tired from the trip." She picked up
her fork. The scent of gravy and cheese sauce made her stomach queasy. She cut some meat and took a tiny bite. Covering
her mouth, Chris ran for the adjoining reception room. Barely
reaching the bathroom in time, she leaned over the toilet and
threw up.

Someone patted her on the back as she vomited again. Even
before she looked, she recognized Geoff's gentle touch. He
handed her a glass filled with water to rinse her mouth. After
swishing the water around her mouth, she spit into the sink.
With a worried frown, Judith stood behind Geoff. "I'm fine, Judith, but if you don't mind, I'd like to speak to Geoff right now."

"As long as you're all right."

Chris reassured her that she was fine. Judith hesitated but
left the room.

Geoff helped her to a leather settee and sat beside her. "It's obvious that you haven't told her. Even with her poor math skills, she'll be able to figure out that one and one equals three." She detected his sense of humor returning once more. "I've been a fool. I haven't canceled my application. I can still take the July exam."

His eyes sparkled. "Does this mean I can finally ask the question?"

She giggled. "No, I'm going to ask you, but first..." She grew serious again. "I do need to know how serious it is between you and Beth."

He exhaled slowly. "I don't love her—not anymore."

"You've said that before. I believe you, but I don't want to start a marriage by getting caught in the middle of something."

"A valid concern," he agreed. "Chris, I have to be honest, I've been miserable the past couple of months. When I thought you were gone..." He clenched his right hand, then released it. "I blamed myself for leaving, but I couldn't find the courage to return to Boston. I spent a lot of time in a daze, and I guess I thought I'd find answers through the past. I didn't. You still weren't here."

Her hand went over his. If only she had taken the time to meet him halfway and visit Virginia before now, he might not have sought refuge in Beth's arms. "I'm sorry for not being here when you needed me. We can change that now."

A smile spread across his face. "Is this a proposal?"

"What would you say if it is?"

His grin widened. "That you do everything ass backwards up there in Yankeeland. Are you going to get on bent knee too?"

Chris grabbed a cushion from the settee and whacked him on the side. "Then again, I can tell my pa about the young'un, so he'll fetch the shotgun."

With a laugh, Geoff raised his hands in surrender, then hugged her.

"Does this mean yes?" she asked.

"Yes."

His hand traced along her side, and Chris stood.

"Was it something I said?" Geoff asked in confusion. "I thought we would fool around a while before I whisked you off your feet and carried you to your room."

She pressed a hand to her abdomen. "I might get sick again if you whirl and twirl me around like that. Right now, I've got some packing to do."

He stared at her in stunned silence for a moment. "Packing?"

She thumped him with the cushion once more. "I'm not returning to Boston, you fool. There's no sense pretending anymore. I thought I'd move my things into your room."

His smile returned as he got to his feet. "Need a hand?"

"I'd like that." With an excited yip, Saber bounced on his feet. "Is he welcoming me to the family?"

"I think so. Are you going to keep your name?"

"My name? Yes." With a laugh, she continued, "But I'll add yours to it. If I didn't keep my name in there, I'd end up with too many Cs. Christine Catherine Cameron is a bit much."

He embraced her. A throat clearing forced Chris to step away from him. Judith stood in the doorway and spoke to Geoff, "Sorry to interrupt, but T.J. called about a mare down and ready to foal. He'd like a hand."

Geoff nodded, but glanced to Chris first. "I'll be all right," she reassured him. "You've been patient with my work. It's time that I reciprocate." He gave her a kiss on the cheek before leaving the room with Saber on his heels.

Judith held a curious expression. "Well?"

"We're getting married."

Squealing with delight, Judith dashed over and hugged her. "We'll be sisters too!"

"There's more."

"More?" Her friend studied her as if expecting what was coming.

"You're going to be an aunt. And before you say anything, that's not why we decided to get married. Geoff wanted to some time ago. It just took me a while to come around to his way of thinking."

A broad smile came to Judith's face. "Chris, you don't need to explain your reasoning to me. When you first arrived, you looked miserable, but now . . . I guess I'll resort to a cliché, but you have a glow about you."

Chris took a deep breath. "You don't know how relieved I am to hear you say that. I thought you might be angry with everything that's happened."

"Angry? The only way I'll be angry is if you don't give me a chance to spoil the baby." Judith hugged her once more. "I hope it's a girl. I've already got a nephew, and girls are more fun to spoil."

"Just as long as you don't expect her to wear pink." For some reason, Chris had always felt uncomfortable with Judith's friendly touches, but now, she returned her hugs freely. Such a loyal friend only came along once in a lifetime. It finally dawned on her what Judith had said. Soon, they would also be sisters.

"Do you take this man?"

Beside the gently flowing fountain, Chris silently practiced reciting the words and glanced over her shoulder at the guests. The ever stoic patriarch Winston Cameron had a pride-filled smile. Even T.J. was in attendance. The crusty old stable hand had a neatly trimmed beard and wore a suit that formed a tight band, stressing the buttons at his waist. It was probably the only suit to his name. She scanned past him until locating Geoff. His gaze met hers, and she mouthed Judith's "I do." Happiness, more than she ever could have imagined, filled her. She quickly returned her concentration to the ceremony.

Instead of yards and yards of lace stretching down the brick aisle, Judith's gown transformed to a dirt path surrounded by dying weeds. Along the path came shuffling footsteps. Chris's breath quickened, and her knuckles turned white gripping the bouquet.

"I now pronounce you . . ."

She gazed into familiar blue eyes. His face was heavily bearded, and he wore a threadbare gray jacket and tattered trousers. Without shoes, he had wrapped rags around his feet. *George?* Chris blinked, but the double image refused to vanish as she watched David kiss Judith. Honeysuckle surrounded her, and a tired smile spread across George's face. Judith put her arm through David's, and the newly married couple waved. *Tears of joy filled his eyes as George took her into his arms. Instead of being elated, Margaret broke down sobbing.*

"Geoff!" Blackness engulfed her.

Saber charged ahead of Geoff. Thankfully, David had caught Chris before she hit the ground and, with Judith's aid, helped her to a wood bench. When Geoff reached her side, she clutched the sleeve of his suit jacket. Her other hand went to her head. "I feel dizzy."

Geoff held her to help steady her. "Just take your time to get your bearings." He glanced over at Judith. "Go ahead and see to your guests. I'll take her upstairs when she's feeling better."

Judith's expression remained one of concern.

"I said, 'Go.' She'll breathe easier if everyone isn't hovering around her."

"All right," Judith finally agreed, "but let me know if she needs anything."

"I will."

Judith's bridal gown swished against the path as she intertwined her arm with David's and returned to her guests. Most of the crowd that had gathered around dispersed, but a few onlookers remained behind. Used to being the center of such attention, Geoff resisted the urge to tell them to "get the hell away." "Are you feeling better now?" he asked Chris.

"I'm feeling like a fool."

"Don't worry about it. If you can walk now, I'll help you to the house."

"But I've never been the fainting sort."

"You've never been pregnant before."

A buxom woman with silver hair turned up her nose. Her name escaped him, but she was a friend of Greta's, one who was quite aware that he wasn't married. Let the rumors fly. He didn't care. They'd be married soon enough anyway.

"I think I'll be all right now," Chris said.

With a firm grip on her hand, Geoff helped her to her feet. She wobbled, and he put an arm around her waist. Although she remained unsteady, they made it through the garden. Near the steps to the house, Ken was hitching a matched team of horses to a carriage for the bridal party. Geoff guided Chris to the west wing and the door to the library.

Once inside, he led her to the stairs to their room. He assisted her with her gown and shoes, then helped her to bed. He plumped a pillow and placed it behind her back.

"All of this fussing really isn't necessary," Chris protested.

He sat on the edge of the bed and felt her forehead. At least she had no fever. "You're still looking a little pale. It might be best if I call the doctor."

She grasped his forearm. "It works two ways. You've objected when I've mentioned a doctor. I'm fine, and you'll have to trust my judgment on that."

Perhaps he had begun to overreact, but Chris could be too stubborn for her own good. "Then I'll let you rest."

Before he could get to his feet, her grip tightened on his arm. "Geoff, I saw him—George."

He should have guessed the visions would return. "In the garden?"

She nodded. "When he returned from the war. Anytime I envision some crucial turning point, I think that must be the reason why Margaret is letting me see so much from her life. First the scout, then the baby. I honestly thought that's what she wanted me to know, but now that I've seen George . . . There's more that she wants me to uncover."

Why did that thought suddenly make him uncomfortable? "I don't think this is a good idea."

"Do we have a choice? I can't control the visions. Doesn't it make sense to find out what she wants? The sooner we discover what it is, the sooner we'll be rid of her."

Everything seemed so simple and logical when she stated

it that way. Unconvinced, he shuddered. Maybe his uneasiness extended from seeing the photograph of George and knowing how he had died. But Chris was right. They needed to discover what Margaret was seeking.

Tessa poured the last kettle of hot water into the wood tub. After the servant scurried from the kitchen, Margaret helped George remove his clothing. The threadbare tatters nearly disintegrated in her hands. She would have Tessa burn the lice-infested rags.

Once he was naked, she realized how thin he had become. His ribs protruded, and his skin had taken on a sickly pallor. He must have used every ounce of energy to keep his promise of returning to her. George eased into the tub and set about to scrubbing with the lye soap, while she spread liniment to rid his body of lice. She had already helped him shave and sheared his matted hair close to the scalp, then she ran a nit comb through what was left.

As he bathed, he kept smiling at her. He was alive and finally home. Why couldn't she feel? "George, I . . ." Suddenly afraid, she couldn't bring herself to tell him about the Yankee scout. She loved him and would find some way to carry on as if none of it had ever happened.

When Chris woke, Geoff was leaning on the bed beside her, watching her. Fully recovered from her fainting spell, she sat up and clasped his hand. "I don't think she ever told him about what happened."

"You've had another vision," he stated matter-of-factly.

"A dream—she loved George so much that she wanted to spare him from the pain of finding out about the scout and baby."

Disengaging from her grasp, he stretched as if he had been in one position too long while she had slept. "Surely he must have sensed something was wrong."

"I don't know yet," she replied with a shrug. "It probably depended on his mental state. He looked like he'd been through hell after returning from the war."

Geoff's forehead wrinkled. "That's what worries me. He died by his own hand."

And Geoff looked so much like his ancestor. Chris wrapped her hand around his arm. "You're not like him."

His eyes narrowed as if in pain. "How do we know? I've thought about using a gun on myself."

A Civil War pistol. Her breath quickened. The gun must have belonged to George or the Union scout. "Geoff, what did you do with the gun?"

"Beth has it. She wanted to keep it out of my hands."

The fact that Beth had possession of the gun likely ruled out any possibility that she would be able to inspect it. Chris only hoped that it remained in a safe place.

Chapter Eleven

A WEEK LATER, GEOFF STOOD on the marble steps outside Poplar Ridge. "We've got to do this the right way." When he picked Chris up, her light-brown hair swirled in the summer breeze, and she wrapped her arms around his neck with a laugh. He carried her across the wood-floor threshold as Saber barked excitedly and nipped at her heels. He put her down in the hall and kissed her.

"Nancy told me I wouldn't be returning to Boston," she said. "I didn't believe her, but now it seems so right."

"I'm glad." He kissed her again.

She fiddled with his gold wedding band. "I still can't believe it's true, but we should tell your father. Judith said that she had warned him, but I doubt that he expected us to just run off and get married. He may not be pleased."

"I wouldn't worry about what he thinks."

"I know the two of you don't always get along, but he is your father."

He drew in a breath. "Now that you live here, I think you'll get a fair idea as to why we 'don't always get along.' " He grasped her hand and muttered, "We might as well get this over with." They traveled the halls until finding his father in the library, which tended to be a rare sight since his retirement.

Wearing his reading glasses, the old man sat behind the desk. Too old-fashioned to use the computer, he had papers scattered.

"Geoff," he said without looking up, "T.J. says that he needs feed delivered, but I can't find . . ."

"I'll take care of it. Business can wait, Dad." His father glanced up, and his unyielding jaw relaxed upon seeing Chris. At least that much was in his favor; the old man liked Chris. "I'd like to present my wife."

A broad grin appeared on the old man's face. "Chris." He got to his feet and came around the desk to give her a peck on the cheek. "I thought that I might get an invitation to the wedding, but welcome to the family. This calls for a toast."

Chris pressed a hand to her abdomen. "Water for me, please."

Uncertain how much Judith had repeated to the old man, Geoff watched him as he made his way over to the liquor cabinet. "You're going to be a grandfather again."

Without missing a beat, his father prepared the drinks. He handed a glass of water to Chris. "I see."

Judith hadn't informed him. "And that's all you have to say?" Geoff asked.

The old man gave him a Scotch and raised his own glass. "I presume the two of you have discussed the ramifications."

Geoff set his glass on the desk. "Ramifications?"

Chris sent him a look to be civil. "Geoff, we can talk about this later."

He glanced from Chris to his father. "I'd rather hear what ramifications we should be aware of. I've asked the question before but have never received a straight answer. Did my mother have epilepsy?"

"Now is a poor time to be asking. If you don't wish to drink a toast with me . . ."

"If you recall, I asked the same question when Beth was pregnant, but I never received an answer. If you won't tell me, then tell Chris. She has the right to know."

Gray eyes met his, then the old man snapped his shut. A reaction—Geoff had never known him to react before. He reopened his eyes and said, "If I knew of anyone else in the family with your affliction, I would tell you."

"Affliction?" With a cynical laugh, Geoff shook his head. "Do you see what I mean, Chris? He can't even say the word—*epilepsy*. How can I believe him if he can't even say the goddamned word?"

"Geoff..." Chris grasped his arm. "He did answer you—in his own way. We'll talk about it later, but right now, I'd like to drink that toast." She raised her glass. "To our baby's health." When their glasses clinked, the old man's eyes grew moist. All this time—his silence hadn't been from embarrassment. But what could it mean? Was he being totally honest in Chris's presence, or had his father been trying to shield them from the truth?

During the day when Geoff was generally working outside, Chris made a practice of retreating to the library to study for the upcoming bar. With the exam less than a month away, she worried that she had slacked off after Geoff had left Boston and wouldn't be prepared in time. Her eyelids grew heavy, and she closed her book on property law.

She needed a cup of coffee to get the circulation flowing or risk falling asleep. She hadn't realized that pregnancy sapped a woman's strength in the first trimester. She only hoped that she wouldn't doze off during the exam. Stretching her arms, she got to her feet and ambled into the hall. With Judith gone, the house seemed more like a catacomb. Occasionally, she'd run into Winston or Laura, but the rooms were deathly still until Geoff returned in the evening.

City girl—she feared that she might not make the transition to rural life. When she arrived in the drawing room, her stomach rumbled. No one had warned her how ravenous pregnancy made a woman either, and it was only half of another football field away to the kitchen. She reached the main entry hall. Instead of heading down the east wing to the kitchen, she placed her hand on the walnut banister and clambered up the stairs.

Upon reaching the second floor, she halted before the first door to her left. It was the same room that she had been drawn to on her first visit, as well as the one that Geoff had shared with Beth.

Would she be invading his privacy if she looked inside? Something compelled her to explore further. The room was stuffy from having been closed off from the rest of the house, and she had difficulty breathing. She opened the drapes to let some sunlight in.

Unlike the furniture in the room she shared with Geoff, the walnut-framed canopy bed with ornate leaves carved into the headboard hinted at a feminine touch. Had the room been decorated by Sarah or Beth? Chris ran a hand across the fine woodgrain of the dresser. While the surface wouldn't pass a white glove test, Laura definitely dusted it from time to time.

Near the fireplace, an aqua spoonback chair and matching ottoman brightened the room. A gold full-length mirror with rose and leaf carvings across the crest hung beside the bed. She moved toward it and suddenly felt as if she were prying. In the reflection, she saw Geoff. No, he was too thin for Geoff. He had to be George.

"Margaret..."

In the mirror's reflection, George slid the pins from her hair and it tumbled the length of her back. She trembled. When he grasped her arm, so that she faced him, she nearly screamed. More than a year had passed since she and Tessa had buried the scout. Why couldn't she rid her mind of his face?

"I thought of you each day. You are the reason I survived."

She took a deep breath and focused on George's blue eyes. He was here with her and very much alive. She should be thankful. A tear spilled down her cheek, and he gently brushed it away with his thumb. For his sake, she forced a smile as he made his way through the buttons of her dress. A lump formed in her throat, but he kept reassuring her that everything would be all right now.

Her dress tumbled to the floor, and he unhooked her corset. Why couldn't things be the way they had been before the war? So many carefree parties with fancy dresses. The last of his clothing fell away, and he led her to the bed.

Her heart thumped nervously as his hand traveled the length of her body, touching and fondling as he went. He kissed her again—this time more intimately. Absorbed in the sensations, she shoved her fear from her mind. Focus on his face. *If she did so, she wouldn't mistake him for the scout.*

He parted her legs and slid inside her. Breathe. *She panted for air. George, yes, he was George. Her life, her love. She clutched him so tightly that she bit her lip until it nearly bled.* George.

Then she heard him gasp. With a broad, satisfied smile, he kissed her. "Things will be different now, Margaret."

Tears streaked her cheeks. Could he ever forgive her?

Chris blinked back the reflection. George's image was still there, but scowling. *Geoff.* She buried her face in her hands. "Geoff, I'm sorry. I didn't mean to intrude, but this was *their* room."

His face softened. "Their room?"

"George and Margaret's."

He closed his eyes, obviously not realizing how much their lives ran in parallel. "What does she want?" he asked.

"Forgiveness," Chris whispered.

"For killing the baby?"

"No, she wants forgiveness from George."

His muscles tensed as if he were ready to take on the long-dead scout himself. "Why would George have blamed her for what happened? Did she ever tell him?"

She shook her head. "I suspect not. She was afraid. Even today, it's not uncommon for rape victims to refuse to admit that it happened. By doing so they empower the attacker, but until society stops blaming the victim, I don't see the denial changing anytime soon."

He placed his arms around her. "A good lawyer can help change things."

Chris pushed away from him, blinking in disbelief. "You're not suggesting that I switch to criminal law?"

"Why not?" he said with a shrug. "I seem to remember you complaining about the hours. If you're going to put in long hours, shouldn't it be for something you believe in?"

For so long, the corporate world had been her sole focus. One trip to Virginia had changed her life in ways beyond which she could have ever imagined. "I'll give it some serious thought. After I take the bar," she added with a laugh. "If I don't pass, it's a moot point."

"You'll pass," he reassured her, then shivered. "Now if you don't mind, I still feel uncomfortable in this room."

As Geoff turned, she caught his arm. "Have you told her—about us?"

"Not yet. Neal's been at summer camp, so there's been no reason to talk to her. He'll be home in a couple of days. I'll tell her then."

The fact that he wasn't going out of his way to speak with Beth was a good sign, yet his procrastination concerned her. *Stop looking for trouble where it doesn't exist.* But Chris had the distinct impression that the news wouldn't set well with Beth.

With Saber trotting beside him, Geoff strode up the walkway to the gabled Victorian. He raised an arm to knock and hesitated. He took a deep breath and rapped on the door. With a smile, Beth answered. "Neal is over at the neighbor's. I'll give him a call to let him know that you're here." She quickly dialed the phone and announced his arrival. As she hung up the receiver, she said, "He'll be home in a few minutes. Can I get you something while you're waiting?" She led the way from the foyer to the living room.

"No, thank you."

As she seated herself on the sofa, an uncomfortable silence descended between them. She motioned for him to have a seat. "Geoff," she said weakly, "you haven't called me in over a month."

He sank into a leather chair near the fireplace. "There's no way of saying this except straight out." Geoff cleared his throat. "I've married Chris."

"You what?" Her eyelashes fluttered, and she stared at him in stunned silence. Another flicker. "What about..." Her voice cracked.

"Us? There has been no us—not since you served the divorce papers."

Tears trickled down her cheeks. "I thought you had forgiven me."

First Margaret wanting forgiveness for something that wasn't her fault, and now Beth. "This has nothing to do with forgiveness. I don't blame you for what happened, but it doesn't change the way things turned out. I love Chris, and I think you sensed it when you first met her."

"I did," she admitted, brushing away her tears. "Neal thinks... well, you can guess what he thinks."

"Yes," he said with regret. Strife between parents was always hardest on the children.

Beth laughed, but sadness lingered in her voice. "I should have heeded your warning that anything new between us would be a mistake. But I wanted to prove to her that she was wrong."

"Her?"

She sent him a scorching look. "A friend. I do have a life outside these walls."

"I meant nothing by it. It might be better if I wait outside for Neal."

"I agree."

Geoff gave a light tug on Saber's leash for the dog to come along. At least they hadn't resorted to petty jabs again. In fact, the exchange had gone much smoother than he had anticipated. He hoped it was a sign that things might be calming down.

With the grueling, two-day bar exam finally behind her, Chris could relax—almost too much. Used to working for a living, she had too much free time on her hands. In an attempt to keep busy, she assisted Laura around the house. After she used regular dishwashing liquid for the dishwasher and duct tape for repairing a tablecloth, the maid banned her from helping. If she weren't pregnant, she would learn more about horse care, but the present didn't seem like the best time to start lugging hay around. And she had at least a couple of long and boring months before she learned the results of the exam.

Restless and unfocused, Chris padded down the hall of the west wing to the library. At least she'd be able to find a book to read. The mail had been placed on the desk, ready for Geoff to look over in the evening. She began leafing through the stack—mostly bills. Perhaps she could attend to some of the book-work. An official-looking envelope from the county government caught her eye.

She tore open the envelope and unfolded the reports on Sarah Cameron's death. The coroner's record stated that her death had been caused by internal injuries suffered in an automobile accident. She died two days later in the hospital. No evidence of alcohol or drugs was found in her bloodstream at the time of the accident. If she had been taking anticonvulsants, the pathology report would have certainly said as much. The police report wasn't much more helpful. Although conscious, Sarah had been too weak to give a full account. The investigating officer surmised the car skidded out of control and hit the tree.

"Chris," came Geoff's voice from the hall.

"In here."

Saber loped into the study and sat at her feet, staring up at her with his dark-brown eyes. Chris opened a desk drawer for a biscuit. Saber nearly chomped her fingers, snatching the treat from her hand.

"Where are your manners?"

Covered in grime as if he had been mucking stalls, Geoff entered the study. "You spoil him. He should have to work for treats."

She scratched behind the dog's ears. "Life shouldn't always be work."

He spotted the report on the desk. "What did you learn?"

"That your mother had no drugs in her bloodstream."

"None?" Geoff seized the report from the desk. "I thought . . ." He read through the papers.

He *had* been afraid to discover the truth. "That she was on anticonvulsants? There certainly was no evidence at the time of the accident. Geoff, I'm sorry. I didn't mean to dredge up old wounds."

"I've told you that I don't remember her." He glanced up from the report, and his eyes glimmered in a peculiar way—not the familiar absent look before a seizure.

Suddenly cold, she hugged herself. "What is it?"

"Loud voices—in here. My parents used to argue. The Colt .44 was in my mother's hand."

"You would have only been five. It's no wonder that you've forgotten."

He rubbed his temple, and the odd flicker returned to his eyes.

"Geoff?"

"Squealing tires. Blood everywhere."

Oh, God—*he did remember.* A child witnessing his mother's death. Chris gripped his hand. "I don't think this is a good idea."

With a blink, he shook his head. "It's all right. I don't remember anything else."

Ill to her stomach, Chris rubbed her abdomen until the feeling passed. She thought she spotted stains in the wood of the floorboards. She'd have to tell Laura about them. "Would you take me to your mother's grave?"

"Now?"

"If you don't mind."

"Let me take a quick shower first."

"You needn't worry on my account. I'm used to the smell of horse . . ." Chris wrinkled her nose. "On second thought, it's probably best if you take that shower—especially if you have any intention of kissing me later."

"I'll remember that the next time we take horses to the cottage," he replied with a laugh.

As Geoff and Saber left the library, Chris returned to studying the documents surrounding Sarah's death. Disappointed, she had hoped to gain more information. At least they could put to rest Geoff's fear that Sarah might have suffered from epilepsy. Winston had told them the truth, and the baby would be at no more risk than anyone else.

Feeling kinship to a woman that she'd never meet, Chris clutched her crystal necklace.

"Chris..."

She glanced up at Winston standing on the other side of the desk.

"I thought Geoff might be here."

"He'll be back in a few minutes. Winston, do you have any pictures of Sarah?"

"Sarah?" His mouth twitched slightly, and she hoped that she hadn't hit on a nerve. Finally, he smiled. "Unless Geoff has moved it, there should be a photo in the second drawer on your right."

Chris opened the drawer to writable CDs and various computer hardware. She rummaged through the cables and equipment until finding a folding picture frame. A woman with hair the color of sand held a baby in her arms. She had the same heart-shaped face and dimpled smile as Judith. Beside her stood a five-year-old, tow-headed boy.

"It was taken about a month before the accident."

Although Winston attempted to keep an even expression, Chris detected grief. His eyes watered. Even after more than a quarter of a century, Sarah's tragic death weighed heavily on him.

Granite spires and headstones covered the neatly mowed grass of the family cemetery. Purple-flowered wisteria climbed along the iron gate to the older section. As Chris knelt by his mother's grave, Geoff tried recalling what she had looked like. Nothing. The flashes of memory in the library had caught him off guard. Years before, the doctors had warned him the memories had quite likely survived intact and could resurface. *But after more than twenty-five years?* He stared at the headstone.

Sarah Cameron

October 15, 1954–May 3, 1979

Why couldn't he form an image of her in his mind? Loud voices in the library. She held the Civil War pistol, but why couldn't he see her face?

"I wish I had known her," Chris said.

Geoff blinked as Chris stood. "Me too."

"That was insensitive of me."

He took her into his arms. "I'm not taking it personally."

She glanced around the cemetery. "Where is Margaret buried?"

Afraid that would be her next stop, he gestured to the four-foot brick wall with the iron gate. "She's likely in the older section."

"Likely? You mean that you've never seen her grave?"

"No," he replied with a shudder.

A smile teased across her mouth. "All this time you've been hiding *your* fear of ghosts."

"Not ghosts," Geoff corrected. "Never mind, it's not important." Determined not to surrender to his foreboding, he grasped her hand and led the way to the older portion of the cemetery, shaded by mature oak. With sunset a couple of hours away yet, cicadas echoed a chorus. As they reached the gate, he broke out in a cold sweat.

A mockingbird mimicked the melodious trill of a robin, then switched to the imitation of a raspy wren. Geoff placed his hand on the gate latch but hesitated.

"If you prefer, I'll go alone," Chris offered.

"I can do it. It's totally irrational, but I've always had a strange feeling about this place." The iron groaned on its hinges as he opened the gate. On such a hot August day, he suddenly felt cold. They went through the gate, and his chill intensified. The names on the tombstones leaped out at him—Joseph Cameron and Susan Alden Cameron. *George's parents.* Thomas Cameron. *George's brother.* Mary Cameron Whitman. *George's sister.* The closer they got to George and Margaret, the more paralyzing iciness came over him.

"Here she is." On a small grassy patch beside the grave, Chris bent down for a closer look. "Geoff, are you certain you're all right? You look pale."

"You're standing on the spot where she was buried."

"She?" Chris looked around for a hidden marker.

"Georgianna."

Shirtless in the summer heat, George pounded a wood headboard into the ground, marking her final resting place. Georgianna Cameron. *Finished with the task, he grasped a cloth and wiped the sweat from his face and chest. "Margaret, I wish you had told me about the baby."*

Nothing could hide her shame. Pretending that Georgianna had been a Cameron failed to make it fact. And the blood of the baby and her father rested squarely on her hands. "I thought you were dead," Margaret said weakly. "She was sickly from the beginning." Lies— all lies—to hide her shame, but he must never know the truth.

George pressed a hand to her abdomen with a smile. "This baby will thrive."

A baby would be her salvation. He would rightfully possess the Cameron name. Tears streaked her cheeks as she collapsed to the ground.

Covering her mouth, Chris stared at the empty space between the graves and backed away. "George made a headboard and placed it here."

"I saw it."

"You..." Stunned by his admission, she glanced over her shoulder at Geoff, when Saber gave a warning bark. He *did* have visions before a seizure. "Geoff..."

As if trying to shut out the sound, he closed his eyes. "I heard."

"Do we have time to make it back to the house?"

His gaze smoldered. "How in the hell would I know?"

Saber yapped another high-pitched alarm. "I'm only trying to help," Chris said, attempting to remain calm.

Geoff placed his hand to his head. "I know. I'm sorry." Saber latched onto his arm. "I think . . . that answers your question."

He was growing confused already. Chris gripped his arm to help him remain steady. "You had better lie down."

"Not here. Please—not here."

"All right." She guided him through the gate and located a spot beneath a spreading oak. At least it was cooler in the shade. She wished she had a blanket for the ground. "I'll stay with you."

Geoff stretched his long legs on the grass and gripped her hand.

Only a few months earlier, he would have protested her presence. "Lie back," she said. He obeyed by lying on his side, and Saber snuggled against his back. "Geoff, what did you see?"

"George. He thought . . . Georgianna was his." He shivered. His hands were like ice. *On such a hot day?* "Do you remember anything else?"

"Margaret . . ." He swallowed. "She was pregnant. He . . ." Geoff touched his hand to Chris's abdomen. "He hated . . . to see her cry."

Curious. His vision had been the same as hers, except from George's perspective. *How much longer before the seizure?*

He tightened his grip on her hand. "Chris . . ."

"I'm here."

"She told him about the scout. But not . . . what he had done."

"Margaret told George?" she asked. He nodded. Geoff must be seeing George's life the same way she had been viewing Margaret's. But in Geoff's case, the seizures were triggering the visions—or burying them.

"Chriiis . . ." A blank stare crossed Geoff's face.

Chris held him and whispered words of comfort as spasms wracked his body. She checked her watch and counted minutes. One. Time seemed to stop—two. Three minutes. Three and a half. His shaking finally stopped, and she let out a relieved breath. What if someday the convulsions didn't stop? Saber got up from his resting spot and licked Geoff's face.

"Are you all right?" she asked, wiping tears from her cheeks.

Awareness slowly returned to his face. "Chris?" He groaned. "Has it happened?"

"Yes. It's over. Are you all right?" she repeated.

"I think so." Disoriented, he glanced around. "We made it out of the . . . cemetery in time . . . didn't we?"

"We did." As she helped him sit up, his eyes filled with pain—most likely a headache. He had been unnerved by their visit to the cemetery. Was it caused by learning the truth about the baby? Or had it been more directly related to George and Margaret?

His head was pounding. With each seizure, the headaches were growing worse. In the library, Geoff examined an old snapshot of Beth. Her hair was long and black like . . . After studying the photograph for a while, he took out the tintype Judith had found in the wardrobe on the third floor. He placed Beth's picture next to George. Had they been living parallel lives? Determined to learn the truth, he picked up the receiver and dialed.

"*Hello.*" Now that he had Neal on the line, he didn't know what to say. "*Hello?*" his son repeated.

"Neal, it's Dad."

"*Hi, Dad.*" Neal prattled on about swim class—an activity Geoff had never engaged in due to everyone's fear that he would seize and drown.

"I'm glad you're doing well. You'll stop by this weekend and go riding with the old man, won't you?" The invitation got an enthusiastic response. "Can you put your mom on now?"

"*Sure.*" The receiver thumped to a table at the other end.

"*Geoff.*" It was Beth. "*Why didn't you tell me that Chris is expecting?*"

"You didn't give me the chance."

"*I didn't mean to cut you off. The news that you had remarried took me by surprise, even though it shouldn't have. I thought . . . well, you can guess, that we might get back together.*"

Blinded by pain and bitterness for so long, he realized he hadn't given her the one thing that she sought. "Under different circumstances, it might have worked. Beth, I think I finally understand what you went through. I'm sorry for not listening to you sooner. But if I had forgiven after you had left, it wouldn't have changed how things turned out."

"*Then you forgive me for leaving?*"

"Yes, I forgive you," he responded, truly meaning the words. "*Geoff . . .*" Her voice choked. "*Thank you.*"

With love safely in the past where it belonged, *they* could proceed forward. Odd, but he had called to question her about what else she might know about Margaret. He'd no longer involve her. She had already suffered enough.

Chapter Twelve

IN THE SPOT WHERE MARGARET HAD KILLED the one-eyed ghost, Chris stared at the lapping waves of the James. Had the burial of the skeleton truly settled his restless spirit, and if so, how could she find peace for Margaret? Gazing across the river, which stretched nearly a mile across, she continued on the path along the bank. After walking more than a mile, she reached the off-white Gothic-style, two-story house. She went up the steps to the covered porch and knocked on the door.

Greta answered with a welcoming smile. The bony, silver-haired woman waved the way inside. "Chris, come in. Sit down, and I'll make some tea."

"The bother isn't really necessary."

"It's no bother." Greta motioned once again for her to sit and vanished from the room.

Chris made herself comfortable in a plush, velvet chair.

When Greta returned, she carried a silver platter with a black ceramic teapot painted with yellow and pink flowers. "I don't get many family visitors—not since Judith has left."

"I would have stopped by earlier," Chris explained, "but I was studying for the bar exam."

Greta poured the tea into cups matching the teapot. "Winston said that you had to drive to Roanoke for the exam."

Chris nodded with a laugh. "That was an adventure in itself. On the way to Roanoke, I got lost around Petersburg, and on the trip back home, I ended up on a country road that led to

who knows where. Thank God for cell phones. Geoff figured
out where I was and got me back on track."

The old woman smiled, making the deeply etched wrinkles
on her face stand out more prominently. She handed Chris a
cup, then seated her thin frame in the rocking chair. "As long as
you made the trip safely."

The days were much too warm yet for tea, but Chris relished
Greta's hospitality. Everyone in the area was kind and caring,
something that she had found lacking in the city. Still, if anyone had suggested to her a year ago that she would be making
her home permanently in Virginia, she would have dismissed
them as crazy. She sipped the hot tea, before setting the cup on
a coaster with a landscape of a forest along the James.

"Now that you've taken the exam, will you be heading back
to work?"

"I won't get the results until October." Chris rubbed her
thickening waistline. "With the baby due in January, I'll wait
until after the birth before I return."

"Good." Greta smiled broadly. "That'll give us some time to
get to know each other better. As I said, I get few visitors. Not
many have time for an old woman."

Chris detected loneliness in Greta's voice. "I will from now
on," she promised. "And next time, I'll bring Geoff."

"That would be nice. He hasn't called in years, but fine-
looking young men usually have their minds on pretty girls and
fast cars. When he was a boy, things were different." Crossing
her arms over her chest, Greta chuckled. "He'd ride over on a
spotted pony and help himself to my sweet potato pies. Now
that he's settled down, maybe he'll find time again." Greta's
gaze came to rest on Chris's throat. "That's an interesting necklace. May I see it?"

"Geoff gave it to me." Chris unclasped the necklace and
passed it to Greta. The old woman held it to the light filter-
ing through the window. Sunbeams captured the crystal and
reflected a prism. "Do you recognize it?" Chris asked.

"Of course. My grandmother gave it to me."

Chris swallowed hard. "Then it belonged to Margaret?"

The elderly woman nodded. "It was a present from my grandfather. As a girl, I had always admired it, and my grandmother passed it onto me before she died. I gave it to Sarah when she became part of the family."

Maybe Greta would be less afraid to speak about Sarah than Winston, so Chris could finally uncover how her tragic death related to Margaret's life. "What was Sarah like?"

Greta smiled in fond remembrance. "Soft spoken. She loved children and horses."

Sarah sounded a lot like Judith. "Do you know what happened on the day she died?"

"No. Winston would never tell me. He was too shaken when it happened, and after that, he clammed up. Initially, he spent every waking moment at the hospital. Then when Sarah died, he seemed to give up all hope for Geoff. To make matters worse, I think T.J. blamed Winston. There was friction between them before Sarah's death, but afterward, well, I'm not certain they've even spoken to one another since then, except what's necessary for the farm."

T.J.? Chris let out her breath slow and easy. Why hadn't she thought of asking him about Sarah? He might be as equally stubborn as Winston, but it was certainly worth a try. Unable to hold back, she felt comfortable in the old woman's company— to the point of sisterhood, and Greta had known both Sarah and Margaret personally. She began relaying her visions since her initial arrival at Poplar Ridge.

Peering over her glasses, Greta folded her hands across her lap and remained silent after Chris had finished. The old woman would certainly think that she was crazy. "Chris," Greta replied evenly, "from everything you say, my grandmother's not at rest. Maybe she feels cheated because of what happened with the scout or that my grandfather died so soon after the war. I always sensed there was much that she wanted to say, but even then, I think she was too afraid."

Chris swallowed hard—another ally. "She probably kept reliving the nightmare in her mind."

"Most likely. I'll check my bureau and see if there is anything else that I can find that may help. Since it's getting dark, it's time you should be going. We'll talk after I've had a chance to look through my things."

The old woman got up from the rocking chair. Gasping for breath, Greta brought Chris a flashlight. "This will help you see the path."

Damn, she had lost track of time. When she arrived, the sun had been shining. The river would seem imposing under darkness. Taking a deep breath, Chris exchanged a goodbye and shoved the door open to the warm evening. The flashlight guided the way as she located the twisting path along the river. The wind picked up and waves crashed against the bank. Poplar Ridge was over two miles away. Perhaps walking hadn't been such a good idea. Sometimes she was too independent for her own good. If she called from her cell phone, Geoff would send someone to pick her up, but that would mean retracing her steps to the road.

Chris continued along the path. After a mile, she breathed easier and waved the flashlight. Beams came to rest on the spot where she'd had the vision of Margaret killing the scout. The area was more overgrown with dense foliage than she remembered. She started forward, concentrating on keeping her feet moving. Get past the spot as quickly as possible. She increased speed. An overhanging branch caught her sleeve and tore the fabric in her shirt.

Awkwardly stepping over a fallen tree, she caught her breath. She was too pregnant for gymnastics. As she faced the bank, a scream caught in her throat. Several yards ahead stood a lone male figure. Unable to make out his identity, she held her breath. "Geoff?" No answer. If it was Geoff, Saber would be with him. Who else? "T.J.?" Silence.

Margaret glanced over her shoulder. It was too far to make a run for Poplar Ridge. She could hide in the swamp. Could a woman with child outrun a man? Escape was her only chance. She doused the lantern and bolted. She stumbled on a twisted root and slammed to the ground. Her belly ached. She clutched her abdomen. The scout with a hole where his eye should have been loomed over her. Abandoning the lantern, she was up and running again. Thorns cut into her hands. Ignoring the pain, she stumbled through the brambles.

Panting for air, she collapsed to the ground and huddled in the brambles. She curled to a ball and waited. Footsteps crunched against the drying summer grasses, and a man came to a halt almost next to her. She held her breath. He took a step away, and she breathed. A hand seized her forearm. She screamed. Lashing out, she kicked her assailant. The hand let go, and she ran blindly.

"Margaret!"

She fell to the ground, sobbing. "George?"

George limped over, gingerly rubbing a knee. He helped her to her feet, and she cried on his shoulder. "Margaret, why are you so afraid of me?"

She choked back the tears. "When you were gone . . ." She gulped to catch her breath. "I killed a Yankee . . . with his own gun. By the river. He wanted to . . . violate my person."

Mingling his tears with hers, he tightened his embrace. "That goddamned war. I should have been here for you. He gave you no choice."

She continued crying, and he hushed her with words of comfort. The scout was dead, she repeated silently to herself. But now she realized that his haunting image would be burned in her mind forever.

"Chris . . ."

The wind had calmed and the waves of the river lapped against the bank. Chris blinked. The solitary figure *had* been Geoff, not a ghost. "Margaret," she said, "told George about killing the scout, but not what he had done." If Geoff was having similar visions to hers, it would easily explain how he had known the scout had been entombed in the cellar. "I don't know whether the ghost haunted her, or if she was reliving the memory."

He grasped her hand and started back along the path to Poplar Ridge. "I doubt we'll uncover the answer tonight. Let's get back to the house."

"What were you doing here?" she asked curiously.

Saber sniffed the nearest tree before marking it. "Looking for you," Geoff replied. "Laura told me you had gone to Greta's on foot."

"I discovered some interesting things at Greta's." She had expected him to ask questions or display enthusiasm. When she got neither, Chris continued, "She told me about your mother."

His grip tightened on her hand.

"Geoff, are you afraid?"

He halted and faced her. "Yes. I now know the memories of what happened are there—buried deep, obviously—but they are there, nonetheless. I'm not certain any good will come from digging them up." He pressed his fingertips to his temple and rubbed it.

"The headaches are becoming more frequent, aren't they?" No response. "They must be caused by more than the medication. I wish you would see a doctor."

"They can't find anything wrong."

His news caught her off guard. Why hadn't he told her that he had been to a doctor? "When...?"

"When you were in Roanoke taking the bar." He laughed slightly. "They recommended a shrink." She opened her mouth to respond, but he held up a hand. "You were already stressed out enough with the exam. I didn't want to cause extra worry."

"Why didn't you tell me when I got back?"

He shrugged. "There was nothing to tell."

"All of these strange happenings have to be related. You have visions like I do, except the seizures make it difficult for you to recall them. You also don't remember an important portion of your life. Those buried memories are the key to uncovering the truth. In fact, I think it would be a good idea if you come with me to visit Greta the next time."

"I'll come, but, Chris—where is this going to lead? We already know how George died."

So, he was worried about the parallel lives they seemed to be leading. "But we don't know why. He might have suffered from posttraumatic stress. Margaret certainly did. The combination may have been too much for him. Even though they have been sharing visions of their lives with us, we haven't experienced the actual events. It makes us capable of dealing with it."

Geoff looked out across the waves. "Beth couldn't deal with it."

She should have realized that his fear went deeper than how George had died. "I don't pretend to know Beth's mind, but I believe I'm stronger willed than she is. I also think you and I are even stronger—together."

He gripped her hand. The moon cast shrouded light off the water, reflecting a shadow over his features. Chris felt a fluttering sensation in her abdomen—the baby. She pressed Geoff's hand to her belly. "Can you feel it?"

"I think so." He touched a little more firmly and smiled.

"It's going to be a boy."

"How can you be sure?"

"I just am." For a long while, they held each other, unmoving, and slowly, she felt his tense muscles relax.

By late October, Chris had received her bar results. She had passed and looked forward to working as an attorney again soon after the baby's arrival. In the meantime, she had completely taken charge of Geoff's bookwork, which alloted them more time together in the evenings. After a quick cup of coffee in the morning, she retreated to the library. While Geoff had been fairly organized with the various accounts, she streamlined unnecessary redundancies to make the entries more efficient. And she thought she had abandoned the corporate world. Behind the scenes, a working plantation was very similar.

By mid-afternoon she finished her work for the day and, from the desk, withdrew George's letters that Judith had discovered on the third floor. As she reread them, tears filled her eyes. Pregnancy was turning her into a blubbering idiot. Wiping her eyes and nose with a tissue, she returned the yellowed pages to the desktop. In each one, George poured out his love to

Margaret. Even with the great expanse of time separating them, she felt it. But what piece of the puzzle was still missing? She stared at the top letter, then blinked. Even though George's capital letters were ornate and looping, his handwriting looked vaguely familiar. The spacing and height of the lower case letters were similar to Geoff's. She shook her head. Just because they shared a common ancestry and similar appearances didn't mean that everything about them would be identical. Besides, the slope of George's angled to the left.

"Chris."

"Judith?" Jumping to her feet, Chris greeted her friend with open arms as she entered the library. "When did you get here? No one told me that you were coming."

They hugged. "I just got here," Judith replied. "I was hoping that I might surprise you." She took a step back and gave her a critical look. "I think you've put on a little weight since the last time I saw you."

Chris stretched her shirt across her expanding belly. "Four months to go yet, and I'm ready to get this acrobat kid out of me now." Judith laughed, and Chris continued, "Let's go into the other room where it's more comfortable."

Throughout the rest of the afternoon, Judith and Chris brought each other up to date. Over three months had passed since Judith had left Poplar Ridge. After spending a couple of months honeymooning in Europe, she and David had returned to his horse farm in Leesburg. The rest of the family joined them for dinner. Afterward they retired to the drawing room with the two women dominating the conversation.

After an hour of being lost among the endless chatter, Winston and David excused themselves. Around eleven, Geoff kissed Chris goodnight and retired for the evening. When he left the room, Judith gestured after him. "What a difference a year makes. You couldn't wait to get me out of the room so you could be alone with him."

"I guess we're an old married couple now. Besides . . ." Chris said with a laugh, rubbing her rounding belly. "I'm feeling anything but sexy these days." She covered her mouth and stifled a yawn. "I think it's time for me to get to bed too. I wish we could go riding in the morning, but I think it'll be a few months before I'm on the back of a horse again."

"Do you mean to tell me that Geoff hasn't taught you to drive?" Judith asked in surprise. "We'll hitch up the buggy, and I'll show you."

After an enthusiastic thank you, Chris exchanged a good-night. One more hug, and she trudged along the hall in the west wing to the stairs and up to the room she shared with Geoff. Thankfully, he had left the night-light on near the bed. She quickly changed into a nightgown. Still unused to a dog in the house, she nearly tripped over Saber lying on the rug beside the bed. The dog failed to budge. Switching out the light, she climbed over him and between the sheets.

As she cuddled next to Geoff, he placed an arm around her and mumbled goodnight. She closed her eyes and drifted. When she woke, the clock read 3:10. Nightly wakings due to a full bladder were becoming an irritating nuisance. With a groan, she made a quick trip to the bathroom. On her return to bed, she thought she heard a soft tinkling sound.

Curious, Chris grabbed a robe and stepped into the hall, following the sound downstairs. It wasn't tinkling, but notes from the piano. Judith must have been unable to sleep. Light touches on the keyboard from the player and the melody trembled a lament. Louder, like a beating heart, the vibration filled the main entry hall as the chords resonated the player's pain.

Outside the parlor, Chris waited by the door as the music wound down. She went inside. No one sat at the piano, and the keyboard remained covered.

After breakfast the next morning, Chris wandered ahead of Judith to the stable. T.J. led two horses to the outside yard to graze. "If ye're lookin' fer the lad, he's up ta the stallion barn. He'll be back shortly."

"Actually, I was looking for you, T.J. Judith is going to teach me to drive, so we'll need the use of one of the horses."

"I'll get ye Ebony." T.J. went to a box stall and pulled the dark bay gelding from it. He snapped the horse into a crosstie in the aisle.

"There was one other thing that I've been meaning to ask you." T.J. eyed her curiously, and she continued, "Sarah—what was she like?"

The grizzled old man smiled a broad grin. "Ye couldna' find a finer woman."

"What happened?"

Blowing out a breath, T.J. picked up a brush from the tack room and started grooming Ebony. "I don't right know, lass. When Sarah first began ta see Win, as he was called in those days, I saw red. I was certain he was tryin' ta take advantage o' her. Ye know—bein' a housemaid an' only eighteen."

Chris nodded that she understood his brotherly concern.

He finished brushing the gelding and grabbed a hoof pick. "When she told me that she was pregnant..."

"With Geoff?"

"Aye. I marched right up ta the big house, an' beat the shi— uh, crap—out o' ole Win. Nearly lost my job, I did. If it hadna' been fer Sarah, I would've. He must've felt somethin' fer her. A man o' his standin' doesna' marry a poor girl because he feels sorry fer her." Finished cleaning a hoof, T.J. moved onto the next one. "After they were married, Sarah grew poorly. She didna' speak aboot her health ta me. Kept sayin' she was fine, but before she died, she wasna' well at all."

"That must be why Geoff thought she had the seizures."

"I reckon so. All that doesna' matter now. The lad ne'er fergot his roots, an' there's a wee one on the way. Sarah would be proud."

Another dead end. "Thank you, T.J." Chris watched as T.J. finished picking the muck out of Ebony's hooves. When Saber dodged in next to her, wagging his tail, she knew Geoff couldn't be far behind. She turned, and his blue eyes sparkled as he approached her. Had it really been just over a year since they had first met on the road leading to Poplar Ridge? "I missed you at breakfast," she said.

He gave her an intimate good-morning kiss. "I needed to get an early start. Ken and I have fence mending to take care of. What are you and Judith up to today?"

"I'm teaching Chris to drive," Judith said, entering the stable. "Geoff, I can't believe you never showed her how."

He shrugged. "I haven't had much time. And if you'll excuse me, I must speak with T.J."

Chris caught his arm as he turned. "Did you hear the piano music in the middle of the night? By the time I got there, no one was playing."

Geoff exchanged a glance with Judith. "I didn't hear it."

"I did," Judith said, speaking up. "I'm surprised that you heard it all the way over in the west wing. Daddy never has."

At least Judith confirmed that she hadn't been dreaming. "Then you've heard it before?" Chris asked.

"Not since..." Judith cast a nervous gaze at Geoff.

They were keeping something from her. Chris tapped an impatient foot. "Well?"

"Not since Beth left," Geoff finished.

Judith drew Chris aside. "Let's have T.J. finish hitching Ebony while I show you something in the house." She then directed her question to Geoff, "Do you want to come with us?"

"I can't right now." He waved them on. "Go ahead without me."

As they retraced their steps to the house, Judith asked, "If I'm prying again, just tell me, but has Beth been any problem since I left?"

Uncertain what connection Beth might have with the piano music, Chris raised a brow. "Beth? She's dropped Neal off a few times, but otherwise, I haven't seen her. And if you're inferring that Geoff might have... He hasn't talked to her, except about Neal."

"It's not talking that I'm worried about," Judith muttered.

"No. I'm certain he hasn't been seeing Beth. Why?"

Judith breathed out in relief. "Because she used to play that terribly depressing music in the middle of the night. When I asked her about it, she always insisted that she couldn't play a piano."

They went up the steps of the columned portico. Chris shook her head. "I don't see how it could have been Beth. When I went into the parlor, no one was in the room."

"That's what I aim to show you."

As soon as they entered the main hall, Judith led the way to the parlor. The piano stood in the center of the room and the walnut-framed sofa rested along a side wall near the windows. At the far end of the room, Judith pushed aside a tea service cart. Behind it, she ran her hands along the wood panel until Chris heard a click, and the panel popped open. Inside, unpainted wood framed a doorway.

"There are a number of secret panels and passageways," Judith explained. "During Colonial times, my ancestors were paranoid of Indian and British attacks. There's one in every room in the main section of the house, plus under the stairwells. There may be others, but if so, they've likely been covered over and lost. Geoff used to love scaring my friends by sneaking up on us."

She easily imagined him playing such pranks with a boy's typically wicked sense of humor. "It sounds like something he would have done," Chris replied with a nervous laugh. She peered inside but was met with darkness. "Where does it lead?"

"It connects with other rooms. If necessary, a person can get to the cellar and tunnel."

And the river provided a means for escape by boat or a car for someone who was familiar with the grounds. "So, in this case, it wouldn't need to have been a ghost."

"Your ghost could be very much alive."

Puzzled, Chris frowned. "Would Beth be so jealous that she's suddenly resorting to trickery?"

"I don't know. I'm convinced that I never really knew her."

Ghost or human? In either case, Chris didn't like the implication, and she'd make certain that all of the doors and tunnels were sealed.

* * *

In mid-December, a dusting of snow had fallen during the night, giving Chris second thoughts about waddling across the path to Greta's in her advanced state of pregnancy. Bundling tight, she crossed the snowy lane to the stable. A sharp wind nearly blew her hat off, and she laughed aloud. At least the winters were less severe than those in Boston.

At the stable, T.J. greeted her. "Where ye be headin' on a mornin' like this?" He rubbed gloved hands together to keep warm.

"I'm going to visit Greta. She hasn't been feeling well. If you don't mind, I'd like Ebony hitched to the buggy."

"I don' mind, lass, but shouldn' ye be travelin' by a wee more modern mode these days?"

All of the men in the household had become protective of her of late. At times, she found the sentiment sweet, but then she'd grow annoyed. After all, she was pregnant, not sick, and had never felt better. "I like being outdoors. Besides, women used to travel by buggy all the time."

T.J. pulled Ebony from his stall. "Aye, because they had no choice." After harnessing and hitching the gelding to the buggy, he led the dark bay to the outside courtyard and helped her in the buggy. Bidding him goodbye, she covered her legs with a blanket. A light tap of the whip, and Ebony trotted forward. Wheels crunched through dried autumn leaves, making the first tracks through the snow-powdered forest floor.

Rhythmic thuds of Ebony's hooves and crackling leaves were the only sounds breaking the stillness. The sense of peace was something she had never experienced in Boston. As she neared Greta's house, several deer bounded from a clump of sycamore trees. Snorting, Ebony raised his head. A tap of the whip kept his mind on the path.

Near the house she heard a steady drumming like that of a horse and rider. She halted Ebony until the pair became visible through the leafless trees. Geoff cantered after her on the gray gelding with Saber next to them. "I thought you went into Richmond," she said as the pair pulled even.

"A change of plans. T.J. said you were on your way to see Greta. You know I don't like you going alone—not this close..."

"I'm not due for another month, but Greta will be pleased to see you."

He had walked straight into that trap and would finally fulfill his promise to visit Greta. With a triumphant grin, she tapped Ebony with the whip. The gray gelding trotted easily beside them, and she brought the buggy to a halt outside Greta's house. Geoff dismounted, then helped her down. Positive the hitching post had been used countless times throughout the years, she let Geoff tie the horses before he lent a hand up the snow-covered steps.

"I'll clear the steps for her."

Before Geoff could vanish to get a snow shovel, Chris caught the sleeve of his jacket. "After you spend some time with Greta. You've promised to visit for months."

He nodded, and a long while passed before Greta answered. More out of breath than usual, she gave their presence a broad, welcoming smile.

After exchanging greetings, Greta ushered them in. They hung their coats on a coatrack beside the door, and Greta gestured for them to be seated. "Chris, last night," she said, taking rapid, shallow breaths, "I found something jammed in a back drawer of the bureau that I thought you might find interesting."

Her recent visits had failed to bring new information, so with nervous anticipation Chris made herself at home in front of the fire. On a cold day, the warmth was especially welcome. Geoff joined her on the sofa, while Greta retrieved a tattered black book from the bureau. He stood when Greta returned, and Chris laughed silently at his quaint Southern manners. The old woman handed the book to Chris before plopping into the rocking chair. Only then did Geoff reseat himself.

Chris opened the book—not a book, but a picture with several smaller ones tucked inside. In the largest photograph, three small children were lined in a row with an older woman standing behind them. "I'm the only girl," Greta said, covering her mouth from a hacking cough.

"That cough sounds like it might be getting worse," Chris said. "I wish you would see the doctor."

"Nonsense." With a wave that she was fine, Greta pointed to the picture. "That's my grandmother."

Margaret. Chris held up the picture for Geoff to see. He stared at it curiously. "How old was she?"

"Let me see . . ." The old woman tapped a finger on her armchair. "I think she was in her eighties."

Eighties? That would have made the photograph from the early-twentieth century. Margaret's hair had gone completely white, and her eyes were etched in sorrow. She wore the crystal necklace. Chris touched the necklace about her throat.

"It was taken not too long before she died." Greta sifted through the remaining pictures before pulling one out. "Here's one of my grandfather."

Geoff's brow furrowed, and he rubbed his temple as if he had another headache. When Chris grasped his arm, he nodded that he was fine. She returned her attention to the picture.

The photo was older than the tintype. Attired in a Confederate uniform with a sash, a man had a saber strapped to his side. *George*—or a younger Geoff. On the back was ornate, feminine handwriting. During the intervening years the ink had faded, but the writing remained legible—*1861*, along with George's name. *Margaret.* Chris could almost smell the soft scent of honeysuckle. "Was this taken before they were married?"

"No. Because of the war, they married early. She was seventeen, and he was twenty-five."

Chris easily imagined a young couple in love, eager to get married, but the war had intervened, dashing their plans. "I still find it difficult to believe what they had to live through."

Greta frowned, imprinting the wrinkles deep in her face. "Chris, until you told me, I had no idea why she never spoke of that time. Do you think she ever revealed the truth to my grandfather?"

"She never told him."

Both Greta and Chris glanced in Geoff's direction. "What made you say that?" Chris asked. He shook his head, but his eyes were unable to hide the fact that he was in pain. Greta continued staring.

He stood. "I have to leave."

"Geoff?" Chris watched as he grabbed his jacket and disappeared through the front door. "I don't know what gets into him sometimes. It's especially bad before a seizure. Dammit, you don't think..."

"Chris, stop worrying. He just stepped outside for a breath of fresh air. See..." Her thin arm gestured to the window. "He's clearing the snow from the steps, and I don't hear Saber barking." Greta patted her hand, and got up to make tea, telling her once more to relax.

Chris sat back and studied the pictures.

With Tessa aiding her, Margaret traveled the weed-filled path behind George's brother's house to a tumbledown shack. A ragged rug hung in place of a door. When her servant called out, an elderly Negro woman lifted the rug. Her smile revealed missing front teeth. She waved them inside of the dirt-floor cabin. "What can I do for you, Miss Margaret?"

Margaret wrung her hands. "I can't have this baby."

"I keep tellin' her dat it ain't like afore," Tessa said.

The old woman pressed a withered hand to Margaret's abdomen. "Da baby quickens. It be too late to do what you askin'."

"Please, I can't go through it again." Margaret clasped her hands together, begging.

The old woman pointed a bony finger in the direction of the blanket. "An' if Mr. George fin' out? Da war be over, but white folks still hangs niggers. You be too far along. Now git."

Tessa tugged on Margaret's arm, but she resisted. "No, please, you don't understand. The baby will die, and then she'll lie in an unmarked grave."

"Mr. George make a fine, Christian marker for Georgianna," Tessa reminded her.

But Georgianna had red hair. How could the marker be Christian when she had been born from the devil's seed? Tessa tugged on her arm once more. Relenting, Margaret stepped outside and nearly ran into George.

Chris blinked back the vision, but blue eyes remained focused on her. Greta was busy making tea, and she reached out. "Geoff." She hadn't heard him return to the house. "Around back, there was a slave shack. Margaret tried to get an abortion, but the old woman refused to perform one. As she was leaving, she ran into George."

"Chris..." He kept his voice low so Greta wouldn't over-hear. "The answers you seek will bring grief. Let it drop before it's too late."

"I can't. You know that."

"Fine." Geoff stormed from the room, slamming the door on his way out. When Chris heard a horse gallop off, she cursed under her breath.

"Chris." Out of breath, Greta placed a silver tray with a teapot on the coffee table.

"I should have been helping you," Chris said. Rising quickly, she gasped and placed a hand to her chest.

"You stay put," Greta demanded. "You have someone else to look after, and a husband to care for."

"I don't think he'd call it caring. He just left in a huff."

"I couldn't help but notice. He's always been temperamen-tal. In that respect he's a lot like Winston—a Cameron trait. According to my grandmother, my grandfather was the same way."

Curious, Chris looked over at Greta as she poured tea. "George was similar?"

Greta nodded and handed her a teacup. "I think that's why my grandmother feels she's found him again."

Now there was something that Chris hadn't considered before—Margaret thinking that she had found George again, through Geoff. "Then I guess we'll have to prove to her that he's not George."

"That may be difficult, when she never gave him up in life. The baby will be here soon, and Geoff loves you. Why are you worrying about events that happened over a century ago?" The old woman's eyes glowed and her voice grew distant, yet unafraid. "I'm ninety-eight, and I've led a full life. Yours has barely begun. Once the baby arrives, you'll see something wondrous in yourself that you never dreamed possible. Just be sure to tell the baby about me."

With harsh realization, Chris swallowed hard. "You're saying goodbye..."

"I'm not. I won't live to see another spring, but I like to think of death as a new birth. We all have our beliefs whatever they may be, but it boils down to the fact that death isn't the end. I know it's not. Your experiences should prove that as well. Hopefully you can take comfort with that thought."

Positive she had missed some hidden meaning, she watched the wrinkles around Greta's eyes crinkle. At peace and accepting her fate, the elderly woman *was* saying goodbye. She had been so wrapped up in Margaret's life that she had never bothered asking Greta about her childhood. Remedying the oversight in the ensuing hours, Chris grew to know her in a way she never thought possible.

Chapter Thirteen

STILL REFUSING TO SEE A DOCTOR, Greta remained sick off and on throughout the following week. Chris visited the old woman daily to cheer her spirits. Christmas loomed, dampening her own mood. Judith was spending the holidays with David's parents, and her parents had held off visiting until after the baby was born. Away from home for the first time during the holiday season, she reasoned that her growing bulk added to her melancholy state. "Last year we were in Boston," she said, hooking a crystal star to the ten-foot fir tree in the drawing room.

"As I recall," Geoff said, replacing a burned-out tree light, "we had Christmas dinner in your apartment."

"It wasn't so bad," she said with a shrug, "a bottle of wine..."

"Half-raw turkey with the giblet package cooked inside."

Her hands went to her hips. "I don't see you cooking."

He raised a hand. "Chris, I was joking."

Aware that he was, she wondered why she had resorted to snapping.

"You miss your family. Why don't you call them?"

Her anger melted, and she planted a kiss on his cheek. "I will. Thanks for understanding when my moods go a little haywire."

With an affectionate smile, he patted her abdomen. "What's there to understand? You've put up with my moods."

For the first time that day she looked at him—really looked at him. His eyes flickered, reminding her of the face in the mirror on her initial visit. It was no longer a haunting image, and his deep laugh reassured her that all was well. A smile crossed her lips. "I'll go call my parents now."

In the hall, Winston Cameron carried something brown and fuzzy under his arm. She did a double take—a teddy bear. Heavily worn, the bear had bald spots near its head.

"It was Geoff's," he explained, somewhat brusquely. "I thought you might like it for the baby."

Never imagining him as the sentimental sort, she grinned in appreciation. "Thank you, Winston."

A smile of approval appeared on his face. "The sound of children is just what this old house needs."

Apparently the holiday mood had infected the ever-proper patriarch, which in turn lifted her own spirit. "I never thanked you for showing me the photo of Sarah."

As Winston stiffened to a proper stance, Chris worried she had hit his sensitive nerve again. "It was my pleasure," he responded with a waver.

She detected the grief that he must still carry inside and placed a comforting hand on his arm. "I can't say that I know how you feel. I've never lost anyone close, but from what little others have told me, Sarah was a generous woman. She'd want you to look back on her life with a smile, not sadness. She'd be proud of your children and grandchildren." Pain appeared in his gray eyes. "I'm sorry," she quickly apologized, lowering her arm, "I shouldn't have gone on like that."

"No, Chris, you're right."

"Right?"

Winston cleared his throat. "I have lived with the consequences for over twenty-five years. Sarah would have wanted me to repair the rift with Geoff long ago. Each seizure tears me apart. I'd give anything to trade places with him if I could, but knowing that I was the cause . . ."

Chris blinked in disbelief. "You? The cause?"

Geoff joined them in the hall. Winston clenched a hand and

spoke to Geoff directly. "Your mother and I used to argue about the fact that I had a gun in the house. It was an antique pistol that I kept in the desk. You were only five. I didn't think you could jimmy the lock. The gun misfired, and your mother found you. The wound was superficial." Winston's eyes misted and his hands trembled. "She died trying to get you to the hospital. When you were left in a coma, I thought I was going to lose you too."

With the confession, Geoff went pale.

"It was an accident," Chris replied. "Sarah would want you to forgive yourself."

Still speaking to Geoff, Winston added, "I never lied to you. Your mother never had any seizures. The doctors confirmed the accident caused them, but I never had the guts to tell you the circumstances behind it."

She gave Winston's hand a sympathetic squeeze. "Thank you for telling us. I can only guess how difficult it must have been."

Tears filled his eyes. "I meant to say something before now."

Without uttering a word, Geoff returned to the drawing room. Chris squeezed Winston's hand once more. "Give him some time. He needs to sort through his thoughts."

Winston shook his head. "I don't expect him to forgive me, but Sarah never wanted him to blame himself. I kept a loaded gun in the house. It's clearly my fault. The antique weapons, if they're not loaded properly, can misfire. Greta used to chastise me..."

"Greta?" Chris raised her head. The old woman needed her—now. "I must see Greta."

She scrambled as fast as her bulk allowed. In the drawing room, Geoff had poured a brandy. "Geoff, I need to see Greta. I know you need time to think about what's happened, but I need to see Greta. Now! Geoff, please..."

Dashing off, she grabbed her coat from a rack in the hall. The zipper no longer went around her large belly. Frustrated, she shoved her hat on her head and yanked mittens on her hands. By the time Geoff caught up, she was in the garage, opening the door to the Integra.

"I'll drive," he said, grasping her arm. He opened the back door for Saber, before climbing in behind the wheel. Relenting, Chris went around to the other side and got in. "Please hurry."

He backed the car into the drive, then sped the car down the lane.

"Faster," she insisted.

"It's not safe."

"I'm worried about Greta." She crossed her arms and sat back. Passing forest scenery was no longer a sight of solace. Greta needed her, and it was taking forever to get to her.

"Can't you go a little faster?"

"No."

His final word. Sycamore and poplar trees . . . A layer of dead fall leaves on the ground. Scenery that she normally loved, she could care less about now. Greta needed her. Nestled among the trees, the off-white house finally came into view. Geoff brought the Integra to a halt out front. Chris clambered from the car before Geoff could open the door for her. She knocked on Greta's door. No answer. She tried the knob. Locked. "We've got to get in. I'll try around back."

Geoff caught her hand. "I'll get you in. Stand back."

He clenched his right hand and poised it near the glass above the door.

"Geoff, you can't . . ."

"I said, 'Stand back.' " His gloved hand went through the pane.

Glass shattered, and Chris jumped. He reached through the broken pane and unlocked the door from the inside. He shook his hand.

"How is it?" she asked.

"Nothing serious."

"Good." Once inside, Chris searched the rooms until she found Greta in her bedroom, sprawled on the floor beside the bed. Chris rushed over to help. Shoving her hands under Greta's arms, she heaved. The old woman failed to budge. Geoff was by her side. He groaned from lifting Greta's prone form but managed to get her to the bed. Chris straightened the old woman's nightgown and propped a pillow behind her head.

A gnarled hand rested on Geoff's arm. Greta's glassy eyes stared, and a wrinkled smile appeared on her face. "Thank you," she whispered, "for everything." When Geoff nodded, she patted his hand one more time. "I must speak with Chris."

"I'll call for help." Taking out his cell phone, he left the room.

Chris sat on the edge of the bed. "He's gone, Greta. What is it you want to tell me?"

Weakly raising her head, Greta said, "I knew you would come."

Greta's voice was barely above a whisper, and Chris tilted her head to hear better. She clenched the old woman's hand. "I'll stay for as long as you need me," Chris promised.

The old woman's withered smile returned. "There's something . . . I must tell you." A hacking cough racked through her lungs. "I felt it . . . when he was here. He knew for a reason."

"Geoff? He knew what?"

Greta took another deep, gasping breath, but her smile reappeared. "My grandfather. I've finally met him. He's returned to reclaim what was taken away from him at much too young of an age before."

Her grip tightened on Greta's hand. "Greta, what are you saying?"

"The similarities . . . are more than coincidence."

Uncertain what message Greta was attempting to convey, Chris swallowed hard.

"In another reality—another lifetime if you will—he loved my grandmother. Think about the similarities. If you love him, you must fight for him."

Reincarnation? "That's not possible. Geoff isn't George."

Greta's voice grew softer and her breathing more labored. "I didn't say . . . he is." She licked her cracked lips and closed her eyes. With a gasp, Greta reopened them. "In a different lifetime . . . he was my grandfather. You've witnessed it. The memories are there, buried deep. Be forewarned—if you release them, he may choose the past over the present."

Greta closed her eyes, gasped for another breath, then fell silent. Her eyelids flicked open in the empty stare of death. Chris loosened her grip on Greta's hand and bit her lip so

as not to cry. *Geoff couldn't be George.* Only their appearances
were alike—a family trait. *Think like an attorney.* The evidence
pointed to the truth—Beth's similar appearance to Margaret, the
fact that they had led parallel lives, and the similarity between
George's and Geoff's handwriting. Were Geoff's visions memories? And why was Margaret sharing so much of her life with
her?

Chris bent her head as tears streamed down her cheeks. Not
far behind came a throaty sob. Strong arms went around her,
and she continued crying on Geoff's shoulder. Choking back
the tears, she brushed them away. His blue eyes held sympathy.
"Geoff, please don't ever forget how much I love you."

"I won't," he promised.

The soft scent of honeysuckle surrounded them. Chris broke
the embrace and struck out a fist. "Go away and leave us alone!"
Geoff drew her into the safety of his arms, holding her tight as
sobs of grief returned.

The funeral was the day after Christmas. Besides the family,
only a few of Greta's acquaintances bothered to attend the service, and being elderly themselves, they dispersed soon afterward. Seasons had changed since Chris had last visited the
cemetery with Geoff. The trees that had provided shade were
now leafless. Gray clouds hinting at possible snow made the
day seem ominous. She stared at the open hole of the freshly
dug grave. On the polished granite stones, Cameron names surrounded Greta.

With a dull ache, she spotted Winston paying his respects
to Sarah, then she turned to Judith and David. "I'm glad you
changed your holiday plans and came."

Judith dabbed a tissue to puffy eyes. "Geoff said you had
gotten close to Greta. Daddy had difficulty finding babysitters
when we were growing up because of a certain devilish brother,
but Greta was always there. Wild as Geoff was, I always suspected him to be a bit of a favorite."

Geoff left Chris's side without comment.

"I didn't expect him to take me seriously."

"This week's been rough, plus I think he's nervous." As Chris rubbed her full abdomen, she felt a kick. A tiny foot landed beneath her ribs, and she gritted her teeth.

"Three weeks to go? I'm sure this hasn't helped your nerves."

"I'll be fine, but I need to talk—obviously not here. Do you mind if I help you sort through Greta's things?"

Judith gave her a hug. "I'd be delighted to have your help."

"Thanks, Judith." Chris turned in the direction that Geoff had taken. A red-brick wall sectioned off the older portion of the cemetery. Dead leaves partially covered the headstones. Geoff had admitted to being apprehensive about passing through the gate, and the closer he had gotten to George's grave, the more nervous he had become. *But was all of the circumstantial evidence proof that he had been George?*

Arms went around her waist. Startled, she jumped.

"Chris, are you all right?"

Calming slightly, she faced Geoff. His eyes flickered in the tenderness she had recognized in the tintype—for Margaret. "Have you ever wondered why the older section makes you nervous?"

"A lot of people are uneasy about cemeteries."

"You're only apprehensive about that one. Why?" She gestured to the gravestones. "From the beginning, you've been afraid of the truth, but many of the answers are right through that gate."

With a frown, he dropped his arms to his side. "How can a few old stones reveal any answers?"

Chris negotiated the path over to the old section. Hesitating, Geoff held back. Her hand rested on the iron gate, and as if to prove that he was unafraid, Geoff followed her. "What were you feeling when we visited the time before?" she asked.

He swallowed noticeably. "When I saw the names on the stones, I thought of the people. It was almost as if I had known them."

"And the vision? You saw the same one I had, but from George's perspective."

He licked his lips. "I don't remember."

If only the seizures didn't bury his visions, the answers would likely be revealed. "You got very nervous when we approached George's grave."

Geoff closed his eyes momentarily. "What's this all about?"

"If you're up to it, let's try again, but tell me what you're feeling as we walk through." She held out her hand.

With a nod, he gripped her hand. After opening the iron gate, they stepped inside. "Joseph and Susan—they were George's parents. He had salt-and-pepper hair and was a strict disciplinarian. She always had a friendly smile and a melodic voice when she sang." His gaze darted from the headstones to Chris. "How can I know these things?"

Remain calm. Chris took a deep breath. "Continue on, Geo... Geoff."

He squinted his eyes in pain. "Thomas was George's brother. He lost an arm near the end of the war. Mary—she was George's sister. She wore her red hair in ringlets. When she was five, she nearly died from measles." As they got closer to George and Margaret's graves, his grip on her hand grew vise-like. Once they were within six feet, his hand flew to his head. "I can't. I'm sorry. I can't go any further."

"That's all right," she replied, struggling to sound reassuring. She had her answer. He *was* George.

When Chris entered the library, Saber raised his head and wagged his tail. Behind the massive desk, Geoff flipped the pages of a ledger. He acknowledged her with a wave, but continued leafing through the tattered pages. The heavy leather-bound volume was the same one from the mid-nineteenth century that she had searched through more than a year before when she had been seeking answers. "Dammit," he said, shoving the ledger across the desk. "Most of the records before the war are gone. I can't verify anything."

She sat in the chair across from him. *George.* Each time she looked into his eyes, she wanted to tell him, but Greta's warning held her back. "What are you searching for?" she asked, aware that her voice wavered.

"Whether what I said in the graveyard is the truth. Never mind." He forced a smile. "I thought you were supposed to be resting."

"I couldn't." *Tell him the truth!* "Geoff, Greta told me something that I thought you should..." The phone rang. Chris reached for it. "I'll tell them to call back." She switched on the receiver. "Mr. Cameron is busy right now. May I take a message?"

"Chris?"

Beth. Chris admitted only to herself that she got very uneasy anytime the woman contacted Geoff.

"Chris, please, is Geoff there? I must talk to him!"

Chris hit the mute button. "It's Beth. She sounds agitated. Neal probably has a hangnail."

He reached across the desk and lightly caressed her cheek, then took the receiver. "Jealousy doesn't become you, my dear. Besides, you're as sexy as when we first met."

"Right," she muttered to herself. Far from sexy, she felt unattractive, fat, and *insecure.* Pressing a hand to her abdomen, she focused on the dark stain on the floor boards. She had forgotten to tell Laura about it.

Geoff's voice grew louder and anxious.

Chris detected that something really might have happened to Neal. "Geoff..."

He waved at her to keep silent. "I'll be right there."

"What's wrong?"

A look of despair crossed his face as he hung up the phone. "Neal fell down a flight of stairs and was taken to the hospital."

"Oh, no!" Her hand went to her mouth. "Is he all right?"

"I don't know." He frantically searched through the desk drawer. "Where did I put the goddamned car keys?"

"Geoff..." Chris reached across and placed a hand on his arm. "I'll drive you. You were there for me when it was Greta. Where did they take him?"

"Richmond Medical."

Still relatively new to the area, she hoped he was calm enough to give directions.

Forty-five minutes later, Chris dropped Geoff off at the emergency room door, while she parked the car. She went inside to the sound of buzzing intercoms. No sign of Geoff. She inquired at the desk as to where Neal had been taken. Locating the waiting room, she paced.

After nearly an hour, Beth greeted her. Her black hair was in disarray and her eyes puffy and red like she had been crying. "Geoff's in with Neal."

"How is he?"

Beth placed a tissue to her face. Her sides heaved, but no tears appeared. "They want to keep him overnight for observation to rule out the possibility of any internal injuries, and his right leg is broken. It could have been much worse."

"Then he'll be all right?"

"The doctors think so. Chris, thank you for bringing Geoff."

"It's the least I could do," Chris said, swallowing nervously.

No longer shaken, Beth stared at her a moment—those violet eyes still made Chris shiver—then she glanced at Chris's thickened waistline. Beth's eyes glazed, and Chris smelled perfume—honeysuckle—emanating from Beth. *Had she been the one playing the piano?*

Beth blinked, then sent her a tired smile. "When did you say the baby was due?"

Chris's blood chilled. "Another three weeks." She barely managed to keep her voice even.

"Neal is thrilled about having a brother or sister. He's already talking about reading to the baby and playing with it."

"That's wonderful," Chris said weakly and wondered exactly what connection Beth had to Margaret.

With Beth's help, Geoff had moved their son to the spare room downstairs, so Neal wouldn't have to negotiate the stairs to his bedroom on the second floor. Geoff waited by Neal's bedside.

His son's right leg remained in a cast. The boy's eyelids flickered open and a smile crossed his lips. "Dad, you're here."

Geoff forced a smile. "Where else did you think I'd be? You had us mighty worried the last few days, but the doctor says you're going to be fine. By the look of things, it'll be a while before we'll be able to go riding again."

"Can I still play with Saber?"

"Of course."

The black sheepdog placed his front paws on the edge of the bed, and Neal giggled. "Did you see my cool cast?"

Kids—they had such resilience. "That's a dandy. Neal, you were a bit groggy in the hospital. What happened?"

A sudden look of sheer terror crossed the boy's features. "Nothin'."

"Neal..."

"Nothin'," Neal insisted.

"He was running in the house."

At the sound of Beth's voice, Geoff straightened.

"I don't know how many times I've told him not to run in the house. But he ignored my warning, then tripped and fell down the stairs."

Geoff stood. "I need to be getting home. I'll stop by to see you tomorrow, Neal."

Neal tugged on his arm. "Dad, could you read me a story before you leave?"

"Sure."

His son pointed to a bookshelf. "The one about King Arthur."

King Arthur again—knights and castles. At least Neal didn't seem to dwell on the Civil War era like he did. Locating the book, Geoff settled on the edge of Neal's bed and began to read.

Beth smiled. "I'll fix lunch."

Geoff nodded an acknowledgment but continued reading. Beth vanished from the room.

"Dad?"

He looked up from the pages.

Neal had a pensive look on his face. "Mom's been acting weird lately."

"Weird? In what way?"

"She goes to the attic and talks in a funny way."

"Does this have anything to do with why you fell?"

"No," Neal said abruptly, glancing to the door.

Beth stood in the frame. "I hope I'm not interrupting. Geoff, you're welcome to join us for lunch. I'll set an extra plate."

"I've already told you that I need to get back home." Annoyed, Geoff closed the book and softened his tone. "I'll see you later, Neal."

His son's tension melted, and he sent Geoff a round of goodbyes. Was there something peculiar going on? Now his imagination was getting the best of him. In spite of their problems, he had never known Beth to lie, and more importantly, she was a good mother. He stepped into the foyer with Saber at his side.

Beth met him and rubbed her arms. "I'm frightened."

"He'll be fine."

"The doctor said there's a possibility of infection."

"Do you want me to send someone to help you?"

She shook her head, but continued rubbing her arms. "We'll be fine."

"Just give me a call if you change your mind." She mumbled her thanks, and Geoff turned to leave but halted before he reached the door. "Neal says that you went up to the attic and talked in a funny way."

An embarrassed smile appeared on her face. "I've been moving the furniture and cleaning the place up. It was a filthy mess. I think I let a few words fly that I've scolded him for using in the past."

A logical explanation. As he said goodbye, he realized how the tension that formerly was commonplace between Beth and him had melted. Their relationship must have finally reached the plateau of acceptance of what had gone between them. He liked that. In the long run, it would certainly be better for Neal.

* * *

Two and half weeks after Greta's death, Chris finally found the enthusiasm to accompany Judith to sort through the old woman's belongings. Papers, letters, brightly colored glass knickknacks. She had never known anyone who collected so much junk. Chris immediately chastised herself for the thought. To Greta, the items had been treasured, and if she was honest with herself, she'd admit that she had difficulty hiding her disappointment at finding nothing on Greta's grandparents.

After breakfast the following day, Chris kissed Geoff goodbye, sending him with her best wishes for Neal, then grabbed a cup of coffee on her way to the library. Her stomach felt queasy, and she damned herself for being a glutton and taking that second helping of pancakes swimming in maple syrup. What had possessed her? Now, even the thought of the sticky, sweet goo made her want to vomit.

The muscles in her abdomen tightened slightly. A contraction? She resisted the temptation to call the midwife. If it had indeed been a contraction and not nausea, Ruth would prefer to receive her call when they became regular. Chris wandered into the library and switched on the computer, spending the next couple of hours paying the farm bills.

Ready for another cup of coffee, she returned to the kitchen, where Judith was helping Laura bake an apple pie. A mild contraction caught her off guard, and she placed a hand to her abdomen.

Alarmed, Judith stared at her in concern. "Chris?"

The spasm passed quickly. "I think the baby may be coming. I've been feeling unsettled all morning, but thought it was caused by the pancakes I had for breakfast."

"I'll call Ruth. You may want to get in touch with Geoff."

"The contraction was mild. Won't Ruth want them to be a little stronger and more regular before she comes?"

"That's what I aim to find out."

Chris took a deep breath. "I'll be in the library finishing my bookwork. I won't bother Geoff until you let me know what Ruth says." She padded in the direction of the west wing hall.

Before Chris reached the library, Judith caught up with her.

"Ruth's assistant says keep her apprised of the contractions. As long as they're short and mild, go about your normal business, but no more caffeine."

With nervous excitement, Chris laughed. "Normal business. How am I supposed to keep my mind on normal business, especially without caffeine?" She glanced out the window and pointed. "When did it start sleeting?"

"A few minutes ago, but don't worry, the roads are clear, and we're only supposed to get the fringes of the storm."

By late morning, her contractions grew more regular. Although they remained mild, their frequency made it more difficult to concentrate. Chris climbed the stairs to the bedroom and lifted the drape. The sleet hadn't eased, and she began to worry. The midwife was aware of the situation. If the weather made travel difficult, Ruth would arrive early, rather than leave her to fend for herself.

Deciding that she would feel more comfortable with Geoff's presence, Chris picked up the receiver and dialed his cell phone. The line had static when he answered. "I'm having frequent contractions," she said in a collected manner.

"*I thought these things always happen at night,*" he responded excitedly.

"Nights or winter storms." A sense of extreme isolation finally dawned on her. Unless the weather cleared, Ruth might not be able to make it in time. "Geoff, I'm not sure what to do. The midwife isn't here yet."

"*Chris, relax. Call an ambulance if necessary.*"

His strength was what she had needed. She calmed slightly.

"*I'll be there as soon as I can.*"

"Please hurry . . ."

"*I will.*"

The phone went dead, and Chris dialed the midwife's office and gave an update. The receptionist assured her that Ruth had already left. Despite all of the reassurances, her calm slowly gave way to panic. She dropped the phone and called for Judith. When she got no answer, she shouted again.

Out of breath, Judith rushed into the bedroom. "What is it?"

"Look at the conditions outside. The midwife is on her way, but what if she can't get through?"

Judith waved at her to relax. "You'll be fine. Women have given birth to babies for millions of years."

"That may be true, but my timing for becoming a country girl stinks. A crowded city hospital sounds very attractive right now."

"You'll do fine," Judith replied. "How far apart are the contractions?"

Relieved that Judith had stayed for the birth, she answered, "About ten minutes, but they've gone from mild to much stronger."

"It sounds like there's plenty of time for you to get comfortable. While I make up the bed, maybe you should take a shower and relax." Judith gave her hand a reassuring squeeze. Unconvinced, Chris nodded. "Just remember, a lot of Cameron women have given birth in this house."

Tradition—hadn't that been part of the reason why she had decided to have the baby at home? She would have her baby just as Margaret had. But Margaret had killed her baby. *Don't think about Margaret.* "I did get through to Geoff. You'll let me know when he arrives?"

"Of course."

Chris stepped into the bathroom and undressed. In front of the mirror, she rubbed her abdomen. She'd be holding the baby in her arms soon. A son . . . Would he have blue eyes and blond hair like Geoff? Be a towhead like Neal? But first, she needed to get past the birth.

"Are you all right?" Judith called from outside the bathroom door.

"I'm fine."

"The midwife just pulled into the drive."

Breathing out in relief, Chris turned on the faucet and stepped into the shower. As her abdomen tightened, she held her breath. The pain grew worse. Wrong reaction. *Breathe.* She let out her breath, and the contraction ended. Blood spotted the porcelain floor. "Judith!"

The bathroom door banged, and Judith opened the shower curtain.

"I'm bleeding!"

Judith smiled. "That's normal."

Crimson drops whirled like a rivulet down the drain. "Are you sure? You've never had a baby."

"I've helped deliver a number of foals. Most of us in the family have at one time or another."

"Am I supposed to be comforted by that fact? Maybe you should make me a bed of straw." Like a mother grasping a toddler's hand, Judith helped her from the shower. "Where's Geoff?"

"You said that he was on his way. He'll be here." With a towel in hand, Judith dried Chris's body in gentle, soothing strokes, then dressed her in a short cotton nightgown as if she were a small child.

Chris's contractions grew stronger and more frequent, and she returned to the bedroom as Laura showed Ruth in. Judith stayed by her side and coached her through the contraction while Ruth set her instruments, syringes, and gloves on a cookie sheet. Once Chris's contraction ended, Judith opened the drapes. The sleet was coming down heavier. "What were the roads like, Ruth?" Chris asked.

"Slick, but passable."

"When is Geoff going to get here?"

"Soon," Judith assured her.

Spasms raked her abdomen. Chris began to pace. That didn't help the pain, and she lay down. Ruth encouraged her to lie on her side and massaged her legs. The contractions felt worse, and she returned to her feet. Walking helped some of the discomfort. By the window, she looked for Geoff. The wind howled, and the sleet grew blinding. If Geoff was out there, he might be lost. No time to worry. Her muscles cramped, warning her of another contraction.

Gusts of blowing sleet became her focal point. Ruth was by her side, holding her hand. *Breathe—in, now out. Again.* The contraction ended, and she saw a shape in the swirling cloud. A man's profile, and he trudged to the house. *Geoff.* She pointed for Judith to look.

Judith craned her neck. "Sorry, I don't see anything."

"I thought I saw Geoff." Chris got up to check again, but a river of water gushed between her legs. "Dammit," she said in disgust, "I think my water broke. Judith, could you see if that was Geoff?"

"I will—later. You need me here."

"Ruth's here." Silence ensued. Then, three minutes after the last contraction, she felt another. The intensity was building, and Chris groaned. She lay on her side again, and her muscles finally relaxed. "I should have gone to the hospital."

Ruth reassured her that she was doing fine. The wind howled, and the lights flickered. Another flicker, and the lights blinked out. Ruth and Judith scrambled to light candles.

Already exhausted, Chris struggled to get comfortable. Her break was short. With each contraction coming closer together, the pain intensified, affording her little opportunity for rest. A knock at the door irritated her. Breaking her concentration, she let out a cry. "Who the hell is that?"

Laura tiptoed into the room, and Judith waited for the contraction's end before acknowledging her. She placed a cool cloth on Chris's forehead as Ruth checked her dilation progress. Chris mumbled incoherently.

"Mrs. Markey, you're needed downstairs," Laura said.

"Whatever it is, it can wait," Judith snapped.

Cupping a hand next to her mouth, Laura leaned over and whispered in her ear, "Your brother is downstairs. I can stay with Chris and Ruth."

"Thanks, Laura. Ruth, would you like me to have the generator started?"

"I have enough light for now, thank you."

Intent that her absence would be brief, Judith picked up a candle and rushed down the stairs and through the hall.

Beside the drawing room fire, Geoff sat in the wing chair with a blanket wrapped around him. His eyes were half closed, and he shivered. A soggy Saber lay curled on his dog bed, while Daddy paced the floor in a more time-honored tradition.

"Thank goodness, it really was you," Judith said to Geoff. "Chris saw you from the window. I was beginning to worry."

Geoff opened his eyes. "You and me both. Roads were iced over. I walked the last couple of miles, but Saber got us through."

"I know you probably need time to warm up, but babies don't follow time schedules. Ready or not, it's going to be here soon."

Drawing the blanket tighter, he stood. "I'm as ready as I'll ever be."

"This is Chris's first. She needs your support."

Her message was clear. He repressed a shiver and went upstairs to their room. His hand rested on the doorknob, and he hesitated. A baby could care less if he was cold, and Chris needed him. Breathing deeply, he went inside. Kneeling beside Chris, he grasped her hand. She failed to notice his icy fingers. "Chris, I'm here."

Grimacing, she took a relaxation breath as a contraction ended. "If you ever put me through this again, I'll kill you."

Delirious, he reminded himself. *It was her pain speaking.* He held her and stroked her hair. "You're doing great, Chris."

Ruth nodded that he was doing the correct thing, while checking the baby's heart rate. "Everything looks fine," she reassured.

Her fingernails dug into his hand, and Chris yelped at another contraction. Her grip loosened, and she wailed, "I think we should go to the hospital. I can't go through with this."

"Yes, you can."

"Easy for you to say," she snapped.

"Just tell yourself that our son is almost here."

"Our son . . ." A smile appeared on her face, but the next contraction caught her off guard. "Is it time to push?" she moaned.

"Whenever you feel the urge," Ruth responded, checking Chris. "You're fully dilated."

"I need to go to the bathroom." With Ruth's assurance that it was okay, Geoff helped Chris to her feet. She shook off his hand and shuffled to the bathroom. "Alone."

"She'll be fine," Ruth said with confidence.

Two minutes later, a call came from the bathroom. "Ruth!" Ruth requested that he should accompany her.

Chris leaned on the bathroom counter with her head down. "I have to push."

"Where do you want the baby to be born?" Ruth asked calmly.

"I'm comfortable right here, if that's all right."

Ruth placed a layer of absorbent pads on the floor and gestured to Geoff to remain at Chris's side. The midwife placed enough candles about the room to see by. Chris's face wrinkled, and she clenched Geoff's hand and gritted her teeth. Another groan, and blood ran down her legs, turning the white pads red. Even after witnessing Neal's birth and assisting with mares, he hadn't expected quite so much blood. Suddenly dizzy, he shook his head to clear it. She needed for him to be alert and thinking coherently.

Her eyes brimmed with tears, and Chris whimpered. "I can't go on."

"Yes, you can," he reassured her.

"Don't tell me what I can and can't . . ."

Ruth applied warm towels to Chris's genitalia and gently massaged the area.

Chris bit her lip to keep from crying out. Ruth motioned for him to be ready to catch the baby. The flickering from the candlelight and seeing Chris pant in the mirror made the whole scene seem surreal. The baby's head appeared between Chris's legs. Another push, and the baby's head was free. Geoff held it in his hands. Chris strained with another contraction, and a blood-covered form slid into his arms. A girl—but she wasn't breathing. Why wasn't she breathing? He exchanged a glance with Ruth. The midwife grasped the baby and cleared her nostrils and mouth with a bulb syringe, then rubbed the tiny body briskly.

"What's wrong?" Chris asked, straining to see the baby. A cry pealed through the room. "Let's get them to bed," Ruth said. "I'll take the baby, while you help Chris."

"It's a girl," he announced, taking Chris's arm and supporting her about the waist. "Are you sure?" she asked. As soon as Chris reached the bed, Ruth placed the baby on Chris's belly, and she checked the baby's genitals.

"I think I know the difference by now," Geoff said. "I hope you're not disappointed."

Satisfied he was telling the truth, she clutched the wriggling baby. "Of course not. I just thought for sure . . . Oh, God, Judith just better not get the idea that she's dressing her in pink."

The lights flickered back on, and Ruth blew out the candles. "That's a welcome relief. I was about to ask you to start the generator." She clamped off the umbilical cord and handed Geoff the scissors. He cut the cord. "Geoff," Ruth continued, "can you take the baby for a few minutes?"

"Of course." He gathered the baby in his arms. "Everything's all right, isn't it?"

"Chris has a minor tear that needs a couple of stitches."

Geoff paced the floor while the midwife tended to Chris. Finally, he was able to return the baby to Chris's waiting arms. Chris lowered her gown, and the baby sought her nipple and began to nurse. Her hair was reddish brown. "She has blue eyes," Chris said with pride.

"All babies have blue eyes."

"They're like yours. Trust me, I know."

"Like you knew she was a boy?"

Chris stroked the damp hair with a loving smile. "Sarah."

A lump rose in his throat, and he touched the baby's tiny hand while she suckled. "Sarah? You were so certain that she was a boy that we didn't take the time to agree on any girl's names."

Chris's eyes glowed. "Sarah Cameron—it's the way things were meant to be." She looked up at him. "Geoff?"

He swallowed. "I'm all right." Overcome with emotion, he placed his arms protectively around them.

Chapter Fourteen

TWO DAYS LATER, AN INFECTION HAD SETTLED in Chris's lungs. In conjunction with a fever, she had become too weak to nurse. Sarah required the rest of her attention. Thankfully, Geoff had helped with the baby's care. At dawn, Chris rose on an elbow. She watched Geoff's even breathing and smiled. Reaching out, she stroked a finger through his moustache. With a mumble, he turned to his side.

Stepping over Saber on the rug, she stretched and went over to the crib to check on Sarah. The baby's face puckered in a sucking motion. Chris covered the week-old infant with a blue rocking horse blanket. She had been so certain that Sarah would be a boy.

Without bothering to change from her nightgown, she stepped into the hall and wandered along until she arrived at the guest room that she had stayed in on her first visit. Opening the door, she blinked. The heavy-bodied mirror stood in the corner. With her balance slightly off, Chris trudged toward it. No heat. A chill pervaded the room. She caressed the wood-carved horse heads and smelled honeysuckle.

Margaret crossed the floorboards and placed the sleeping baby into his crib. Jason Cameron. For a brief second, she thought she saw red hair. She blinked back Georgianna's image. This baby's hair was blond like George's. He was a true Cameron.

A hand patted her on the posterior, and she jumped with her heart racing wildly.

"It's only me, Margaret." George kissed her on the mouth.

Over two years had passed since she and Tessa had buried the scout. Why couldn't she rid her mind of him? George was here now. His kisses and touches grew more intimate. She envisioned the scout probing her mouth with his tongue and shoved away from George's embrace.

His brow furrowed in confusion. "Jason is over two months old."

Throughout her pregnancy, she had made excuses to keep him distant. Now . . . "The doctor . . ." Her throat closed off, and she gulped for air. "He said that I can't have anymore children."

He studied her a moment, then narrowed his eyes. "Why didn't you tell me earlier?"

"I was afraid. Please don't hate me."

"I could never hate you."

He moved to take her in his arms, but she stepped back. "From now on, I shall make my room in here where I'll easily be able to care for Jason."

His patience faded, and she spotted anger in his eyes. With a curse, he stormed from the room. She cast a glance into the mirror. Frowns and tears—she had forgotten what it was like to smile. She placed her arms on the dresser and lowered her head into them. Lord forgive her, not only had she lied to cover her shame, but she had forsaken her husband.

"Chris."

At the sound of Geoff's voice, Chris blinked. She looked over at him, standing in the doorway. *Shouldn't he remember what had happened?* He was Geoff, not George, she reminded herself. "Margaret kept withdrawing from George, rather than telling him what had happened."

He pressed a hand to her forehead. "You're burning up. I'm getting you to the hospital."

"She moved out of their room, telling him that she couldn't have anymore babies."

He picked her up in his arms. "We'll worry about that when you're better."

Cold—her arms, legs, all of her. Chris placed her arms around his neck. "I smelled the honeysuckle."

"Right now," he said, carrying her down the stairs, "I'm more concerned about getting you medical attention."

When they reached the hall, Geoff put her down gently and threw a wool coat over her shoulders. He called for Laura to check on the baby. Winston joined them and supported her left arm, while Geoff remained on her right side.

On the outside steps, she said, "Geoff, I think she's trying to make amends to George. You look so much like him that you could be twins. Greta thought you *were* him in another lifetime."

The men exchanged glances as they helped her to the Mustang. While Geoff snapped on her seat belt, Saber jumped onto the back seat. "I'm not George." He closed the door behind her and slid in on the driver's side.

"What about the evidence to the contrary? You know details about George's life that could have only been possible if you had lived it. That's why you smell honeysuckle before a seizure. You're remembering *her*—Margaret."

After pulling the car out of the drive, Geoff gunned the engine down the lane. "You loved her in another lifetime."

"Chris, I have never lived a past life."

"Think about the evidence. You're terrified to go near George's grave."

She saw it—at the same moment Geoff braked. As the Mustang screeched to a halt, she screamed. Directly ahead, a black stallion with a woman riding sidesaddle jogged across the road.

Chris had been home from the hospital for several weeks. After her bout with pneumonia, she tired easily, but with each passing day, she was regaining her strength. Seated at the desk in the library, Geoff studied the letters written by George. The handwriting *was* similar. He laid the top letter flat on the desk, then picked it up again. Actually, George's handwriting was quite different with ornate loops in the capital letters.

Geoff turned his attention to the photos. The first picture was of a young man wearing a sash and sword, ready for war. The face staring back at him could be his. But it wasn't. He wore a pistol on his hip with the holster facing backward. The reverse holster wasn't simply due to the style of the time, but George had been left-handed. *How had he known?*

He returned to the correspondence. Except for the capital letters, stylistic differences were slight. The slant was the major variant from his own handwriting. He picked up a pen, forcing himself to use his left hand. Even though it felt awkward, he placed the pen to paper and began writing. At first, he produced scribbles, then the letters became easier and more fluid until it felt natural.

"Geoff?" Chris stood in the doorway with Sarah in her arms.

"I think you were right," he said.

"About what?"

"That I was George."

"I was feverish."

Closing his eyes, he lowered his face to his hands. "How do you explain that Greta felt it as well?"

"She was an old woman seeing what she wanted to before she died."

He slammed a fist to the desk. "But she never met me then." Stay calm—the evidence was circumstantial. A portrait of a distant ancestor and a fascination with a Civil War revolver failed to prove reincarnation. Calm again, he said, "You said it yourself, I'm terrified to visit George's grave."

"Geoff..."

"Never mind, I have chores to tend to." Geoff strode from the library. By the time he reached the barn, he found T.J. holding a compress to a chestnut mare's leg. "I was just aboot ta call ye. She was kicked by sassy Tiffany."

Geoff knelt to check the gash. It wasn't deep. A couple of stitches and she'd be as good as new. "Have you called the vet?"

"Aye."

Before Geoff could say anything further, his cell phone rang. "Hello."

"Geoff, where are you?" came Beth's furious voice.

"In the barn, checking an injured mare."

"You promised Neal that you'd stay with him while I went to the eye doctor."

He had been so wrapped up in proving that he wasn't George that he had forgotten Neal. Dividing his time between two families had become wearing. "Tell him that I'll be right there."

"I'll see ta the mare."

"Thanks, T.J." Geoff went to the garage and hopped into the Mustang, with Saber landing in the back seat. After a thirty-minute drive to the city, he pulled up to the yellow Victorian with the brick walk lined with daffodils. Ever since Neal had broken his leg, Beth had kept him informed, and his son had made no further complaints about her going up to the attic and acting "weird." He knocked on the door.

"It's about time you got here."

Geoff bowed. "Good day to you too, ma'am."

"Never mind your gentlemanly crap. Thanks to you, I'm late."

He straightened. "I'm sorry. I truly forgot."

Her expression softened slightly. "Neal's inside playing video games. I'm sure with Saber here, he'll prefer to play with the dog. If you need anything, just ask Neal where it is." She shouted over her shoulder, "Your dad's here. Bye, Neal."

Geoff heard his son respond with a "bye" from inside. He went into the foyer. Other times, he would have taken Neal to the park. While his son's leg was out of the cast, he walked with noticeable difficulty. Even then, Geoff had to break up a game between Neal and Saber that got a little too physical. By the time Beth returned, Geoff was making lunch—macaroni and cheese from a box.

"I see that you found something nutritious in the pantry," Beth said with a laugh.

At least her foul mood had faded. Geoff stirred the bright-yellow powder over the macaroni. "It was the best I could do. You know that I'm not a cook."

With a smile, Beth held up two cardboard containers. "And Chinese for the grownups."

"I really need to be getting home." He set the packet on the counter, and yellow powder puffed from the bag.

"Geoff, I'm sorry about earlier. I didn't mean to snap. I've been on edge since Neal's accident. Can you blame a mother for worrying?"

He shook his head and spooned the macaroni onto Neal's plate.

"Neal would like for you to stay. Certainly, you can spare a few extra minutes with your son."

"I'd spend more time with him if you'd allow him to visit me again."

"I will, when he's completely recovered from the broken leg. If I know Neal, he'll want to go horseback riding too soon. And you'd most likely let him."

He sensed an argument brewing. "Beth..."

"Next weekend," she promised.

He called Neal for lunch. "All right, I'll stay."

Saber charged into the kitchen, followed by Neal. His face lit up. "Oh, boy, mac and cheese."

Beth got two more plates from the cabinet. Throughout lunch, they talked to one another like old friends. Geoff liked the transition—no tension, no heated conversations. Beth even asked about Chris and Sarah. At one point, he caught Neal feeding Saber under the table with boyish giggles.

"Geoff," Beth finally said at the end of lunch, "I've got some furniture in the attic that I was wondering if you could help me move before you leave."

The attic? Even though Neal had made no further complaints, it would give him the opportunity to examine the room without arousing suspicion. He checked his watch. "Sure. Neal, why don't you join us?"

The boy furiously shook his head. "My leg hurts."

The boy's fear was evident. Geoff should have checked the attic sooner. "Lead the way," he said, motioning to Beth. To Neal, he continued, "I'll leave Saber here to watch over you." Beth showed him to the second floor. Behind a door, steep stairs went to the third floor. At the top, another door creaked on hinges. An old brass bed was in the center of the room. A dresser and an antique mirror stood off to the side. "What is it that you want moved?"

"We sneaked up here before we were married," Beth said with a flirting smile.

He shook his head. "You're mistaken. Beth . . ."

"No, George. You know who I am."

Not Beth. She was . . . Geoff snapped his eyes shut. "I'm not George."

"You know in your heart otherwise. After we consummated our love here, Papa said that we needed to advance the wedding date to before your leaving. He gave you a lecture that young couples in love often did foolish things before a war, but you needed to face the responsibility that went with our actions."

For some reason, the image of a man with a beard and a gray pin-striped suit popped into his head. "Beth . . ."

"George, look at me. I can prove to you what I'm saying."

He glanced in her direction. Over by the mirror, she twisted her black hair and pinned it into a knot at the back of her head. He still saw Beth. "Even if what you say is true, I don't remember any of it."

"You do," she insisted. "Even as a child, you recalled the truth, but your mind wasn't mature enough to accept it then. You blocked it out." She moved closer and stroked his cheek.

Her words made no sense. He drifted through hazy layers, not unlike before a seizure. He should have brought Saber along.

"Like today, it was spring. Virginia announced that she had seceded from the Union. You came to tell me that you had enlisted in the cavalry."

His hands went to his head. "Stop it!"

"George . . ."

"No!" The pressure in his head intensified, and he collapsed to the floor.

"George." She was beside him, helping him to his feet. "I've waited all of these years for this day. I wanted to make things up to you."

"But I'm not . . . Beth, I think I'm going to seize."

She led him over to the bed and helped him lay back, then massaged his temples. "There shan't be any fits today. It's the memories. Stop fighting them and let them through."

He groaned. "I can't. I'm not George."

She left his side and poured some water from a porcelain pitcher. A cool cloth went to his forehead. Spring—Geoff thought he heard the clip-clop of hooves on the street below. He had come to the house, dressed in his fine new uniform with a yellow sash to announce the news. He resisted. Beth had planted the thought into his head. But there was more. She had been alone that day, and they had climbed the stairs to this room.

"Margaret?"

"Yes, George. I'm here."

"We weren't going to be married until summer."

"That's right, but Papa caught us together."

He had loved her. The war was supposed to only last a month, and he agreed to marry her early, even though there had been the chance that he might never see her again. "I remember." He kissed her lightly on the lips. She returned the kiss and joined him on the bed.

Leave, now. He wasn't George! But he was. Finally acknowledging the truth, he slid the pins from her hair. Her hair tumbled the length of her back, and he envisioned a long dress. He helped her remove it, and she smiled shyly. His muscles tensed, but she reassured him that everything would be all right. When the last of their clothing fell to the floor, he whispered, "I love you, Margaret. The war can't last forever."

"Promise me . . ." She swallowed hard. " . . . that you'll come back alive."

He twisted her hair between his fingertips. "I promise."

They kissed and fondled. Soon, they were on the bed, tumbling in delight. Reaffirming there was life, her heart beat against his chest.

As he rose above her, her legs wound around him. Clinging, almost desperately, they united in rhythmic unison. He intertwined his fingers in hers, and she gripped him as if she would never let go. Honeysuckle engulfed them, and the warmth of tears streaked her cheeks in a shuddering response.

The memories remained murky, like recalling a dream. In the library, Geoff stared at the computer screen, but kept thinking of Margaret. He remembered courting her, and the intensity of their love and passion. Nothing could have separated them—if there hadn't been a war. *Were there more images from the past buried within the recesses of his mind?* She had assured him there were. Even though he was undeniably drawn to her, that fact frightened him. After the war broke out, their lives had been filled with turmoil. And George had died several years later.

"Geoff, I've put Sarah to bed." Chris entered the library, beaming. "I have some good news. Starting next week, I'll be working as an attorney at an all-female firm in Richmond. They have a convenient daycare for Sarah, so I can just take her with me. They said I can start off half-time until I've gotten my strength back from this nasty bug." When he gave no response, her smile faded. "I thought you'd be pleased."

"I am. I've just got other things on my mind right now." He glanced at the stain on the floor.

"I've noticed it too. I keep forgetting to tell Laura about it. What do you suppose it is?"

"Blood. George died there." *By his own hand.*

Chris trembled noticeably. "You're scaring me. How is Neal doing?" she asked, quickly changing the subject.

"Better." But he could think only of Margaret. Her scent—the honeysuckle. He no longer feared the smell. It was the scent of the woman he loved. He needed to clear his mind, but he was growing aroused.

"Is there something wrong?"

He blinked and briefly thought about telling Chris what had happened. She could help. *Stupid bastard—you don't tell your wife that you've been screwing another woman.*

"Geoff, have you had a seizure?"

"A seizure?" He shook his head. "No."

She glanced at Saber, resting on his back with his feet in the air on his dog bed. "I don't care whether he senses it or not. I think you may be about to have one."

"I'm fine—merely distracted."

"You're still thinking about what we talked about this morning, aren't you?" She edged her way to his side of the desk.

He needed to tell her, but he'd lose her. "I love you."

She wiggled onto his lap and kissed him on the mouth. "I love you too. Why don't we go upstairs? Unless you'd rather stay right here and reminisce." She caressed his groin.

"Not now."

She continued fondling. "I thought a little fun might help you relax."

"Chris . . ." He grasped her wrists. "I said, 'Not now.' "

"This whole George bit has you really upset." She stood and extended an arm. "Let's go over here and talk about it." He grasped her hand, and they went over to the sofa. "Now tell me what's bothering you," she said.

"Why did it take a fever for you to tell me what Greta suspected?"

Ashamed, she looked away. "Because I was afraid. Greta said if you remembered the truth that you might choose the past. I don't want you to die like he did."

She must be worried if she was making an open admission of being frightened. "I'm not sure what to do about it. Maybe you should lock me away in a padded cell somewhere."

"Geoff, no." She clutched both of his hands. "Even if you were George in the past, you're not him now."

But the memories—how could he be rid of them? He nearly laughed to himself. What if George had killed himself because he had been haunted by memories from a previous lifetime?

Not willing to give up yet, he had to find a way to avoid Beth. But how? She was susceptible to Margaret's control. The visions—Chris had said they were the key to providing answers. "I need your help."

"I'm here."

Stretching out on the sofa, he put his arms around her and let his head come to rest on her lap. After a long while his tense muscles finally relaxed. "Tell me about the visions—all of them."

"All of them?"

"I think only by knowing what happened will we be able to avoid the end result."

Chris swallowed and began recounting the visions, starting with her first visit to Poplar Ridge. Margaret was allowing Chris to see into her life, but she didn't seem to have the hold over her as she did Beth. And he was such an ass. She'd eventually figure out what had happened and confront him anyway.

As he sat up, he avoided her gaze. "I remember her."

"Margaret?"

There had been a waver in her voice, and he managed a weak nod. "George loved her."

"And now?"

He briefly glanced in her direction and saw tears filling her eyes. Unlike Margaret, Chris didn't normally ruffle easily. "I don't know. Before George married Margaret, she lived with her parents in the same house as Beth's. She has some kind of influence over Beth, and I suspect that's the reason she moved there after we split."

"What are you trying to say?"

He clasped his hands together and closed his eyes. "When I saw Neal today, I began to remember George's life. For a short time, the memories were as clear as if it were spring of 1861 again."

"That's when George and Margaret first became lovers," she easily concluded.

"They were engaged to be married, but the war . . . No one expected it to last four years."

"I understand that. Does this mean that you and Beth . . ."

Her voice faltered once more. He shook his head. "Not Beth, but Margaret."

"Dammit, Geoff!"

"I'm sorry," he whispered without looking at her. "If you decide to pack up and leave, I wouldn't blame you because I can't give you any promises that it won't happen again."

Beside him, he felt her weight leave the sofa. As Chris reached the door, Saber raced over and latched onto the edge of her skirt with his teeth. Shouting the dog's name with a curse, she wheeled around on him. His ears were alert, and he sat obediently at her feet, while she checked the skirt's hem. "You've ripped my skirt you pointy-eared devil." Chris glanced over at Geoff. Her gaze softened. "He may be the smartest one of all of us. I was ready to walk out, but Greta said that I would have to fight. You should know by now that I don't give up just because the going gets rough. I intend on taking her advice. We *can* fight this, but it's got to be the two of us—together."

All traces of wavering had faded from her voice; only firm conviction remained. "Chris . . ." His voice broke.

Forcing a smile, she returned to the sofa and gripped his hand. "Let's start by making a plan."

"How?"

"First," she responded, taking charge, "you mustn't see or talk to Beth—under any circumstances."

He fully expected that condition. "What about Neal?"

"We'll include the family on a need-to-know basis. With their cooperation, we'll make certain that he's all right. We can shuttle him back and forth, so he can spend time here, and you'll use one of us as a go-between for contacting Beth. If you think we need to get him out of there for his own protection, things might get a little sticky, but it's doable."

"He should be fine. He fell down the stairs because he was frightened by Margaret. I'm not even certain Beth is aware of what's happening."

Chris let out a breath. "I suppose the next question is—is Margaret capable of harming him?"

Margaret wasn't sane. She couldn't be. "Beth is stronger when it comes to Neal."

"Good. Then let's get some sleep. We need rest if we're going to meet this head on, and I think we can count on Sarah waking early."

He tightened the grip on her hand and followed her upstairs.

A high-pitched bark from Saber startled Chris from a deep sleep. She tugged on Geoff's elbow. "Are you all right?"

He groaned and clutched his head. "The voices . . . I can't get them out of my head."

After switching on a light, Chris sprinted to the bathroom for some Dilantin and a glass of water. "Here, take this," she said, returning to his side. She helped him drink to wash the pills down. "I think you should lie on your side."

He followed her suggestion, and Saber placed his head on the edge of the bed.

"Thanks, Saber. You've done your job." She scratched the dog under his chin. "Who are the voices?"

Geoff continued clutching his head. "Screams. Make them stop!"

Chris held him, reassuring him that everything would be all right, then she felt his muscles go rigid and the twitching. There was little she could do once the seizure began, except count the minutes until he came out of it. One minute, two. Her heart pounded. After several months without any seizures, they seemed to be returning with a vengeance. Three minutes. If he didn't come out of it soon, she'd have to call 911. *Keep calm.* She reached for the phone, and his thrashing stopped. She checked his pulse and breathing rate. Thank goodness, everything was returning to normal. Some blood trickled from his mouth. With a tissue she wiped it away.

"Goddamn."

"Geoff, are you all right?"

He stared at her as if not really seeing her, then blinked before grasping her hand. "I think . . ." He nodded.

More blood dribbled from his mouth. She dabbed at it. "It looks like you may have bitten your tongue." He closed his eyes, and she wrapped her arms around him. What was she to do? After his confession, her first impulse had been to return to Boston, but she loved him and would fight Margaret. She drifted, and when the light of dawn filtered through the window, she woke to the gaze of his blue eyes. "Feeling better?" she asked.

"A little."

At least he seemed coherent again. "Good. I need to feed Sarah."

"I'll be fine," he reassured her.

She got up.

"Thanks, Chris."

"Of course."

After Chris's illness, Winston had moved into the main section of the house, so Sarah could be in the room next to theirs in the west wing. She meandered into the hall. Sarah's bright-blue eyes stared up at the horse mobile hanging over her crib. Her legs kicked and she squealed in delight when the horses twirled above her. Chris quickly changed her daughter, then fed her a bottle. By the time she gathered up Sarah and made it down to the breakfast room, Winston sat alone at the table. He stood when she entered the room. "Geoff isn't here yet?" she asked.

"He's already come and gone," he answered, extending a forefinger to Sarah. The baby latched onto his finger with a gurgle. "He grabbed a quick bite and said he had chores to see to."

Suddenly suspicious, Chris asked, "Can you watch Sarah for me for a few minutes?"

He took the baby into his arms. "If something is wrong, I'd like to help."

Relaxing a little, Chris seated herself at the table and Winston sat beside her. Although Winston's confession at Christmas hadn't automatically mended the rift between him and Geoff, they occasionally conversed on topics besides the farm. She was convinced that time would narrow the gap. "Geoff had a seizure last night."

Winston winced.

"He's fine in that regard, but..." How much should she tell him? She absolutely needed his assistance and decided to tell him everything—from her first visit to Poplar Ridge to the relationship between Beth and Margaret.

When she finished, he returned Sarah to her arms, then strode over to the window and gazed out. He clasped his hands behind his back. His voice was barely above a whisper when he spoke. "One can't live in this house for any length of time without realizing that it's unsettled. I too have seen the one-eyed ghost," he admitted, facing her. "Sarah used to be terrified of him. She never mentioned any 'visions,' but she composed a piano piece entitled 'Margaret's Lament.' "

Chris's jaw dropped. "Sarah played the piano?"

"She was quite gifted."

"Have you heard her music since her death?"

The muscles around his mouth twitched, and his eyes grew incurably sad. "That's why I originally moved to the room in the west wing. Someone played the lament nightly. As far as I know, no one heard the music again until Judith was about sixteen. She complained about it for several years, then it stopped as suddenly as it had started."

Maybe Beth hadn't lied to Judith about her inability to play the piano. *Sarah must be trying to tell them something.* "Winston, I've heard it too." His eyes widened with the news, and Chris placed the baby in his arms once more. "If you don't mind, I'd like to see how Geoff is."

"Of course."

Chris hurried from the breakfast room. After cutting a path through the dining room and entry hall, she jogged outdoors to the barn. Out of breath by the time she arrived, she was relieved to find Geoff helping Ken unload hay from a wagon onto a conveyor belt to the loft. His shirtless form glistened in the morning heat. Wasn't the fact that he was unafraid of physical labor part of the reason she had fallen in love with him? He turned, and her heart pounded. He had shaved his goatee—only a moustache remained.

"Chris?" With a surprised smile, Geoff tossed another bale of hay to the conveyor belt, then came over to the fence to meet her.

"I just wanted to make certain that you're all right."

"I'm fine."

"Geoff, your face."

Confusion crossed his features.

"Why did you shave?"

He touched his smooth chin. "I don't remember doing it."

She held out a hand. "Give me your cell phone."

"My cell . . ." He withdrew his cell phone from his pocket and relinquished it to her. "If Beth calls, I want her to speak to me."

He lowered his head in shame.

"Have you already contacted her?" she asked, attempting not to sound accusing.

"No, but I wanted to."

At least he was being honest, and he finally met her gaze. Although he tried to keep his expression emotionless, she spotted confusion and defeat. "We *will* get through this."

"I need to get back to work."

She watched him as he returned to the wagon and lifted another bale of hay. Her heart ached. How long could he fight the memories? And she had yet to come up with any sort of real plan.

Chapter Fifteen

TWO WEEKS LATER, AS CHRIS PACED the length of the library, Judith seated herself in the wing chair near the fireplace. Something had definitely upset her friend. Upon Judith and David's arrival from Leesburg, Chris had been anxious to detach herself from David and Geoff to speak in private.

"Calm down, Chris, or you're going to carve a rut into the floorboards."

Chris halted and sat on the sofa, taking a deep breath.

"Now tell me what has you so worked up."

Chris placed a tissue to her eyes. "I can't let Geoff see me upset. He looks to me for strength, but I think I'm losing him."

Ordinarily, Chris wasn't the sort to come unglued. Confused, Judith asked, "Losing him?"

In control of her emotions again, Chris stood. "It's unfair of me to drag you into this mess when you only get a chance to visit us every couple of months."

Her friend's silence gave her a clue to the source of the problem. "Beth," she breathed out in disgust.

"Yes. I mean, no."

While she had accused her brother of many things over the years, she hadn't thought that he would carry on an affair, especially when he had seemed so in love with Chris. "It can't be both," Judith replied, keeping her voice calm.

"She's trouble, all right," Chris said with a cynical laugh, "but that's not what I meant."

"Then what?"

"No, Judith. I meant it when I said I won't involve you."

"You're my best friend. If Geoff is behaving like a jerk, then he should be treated accordingly." But her friend refused to elaborate further, and at supper, the family chatted, bringing everyone up to date since their last visit. During the meal, Judith observed Geoff closely. Although he appeared somewhat withdrawn, he took time to play with Sarah. After the meal, Chris carried the baby upstairs.

When Daddy and David excused themselves for brandies in the drawing room, Geoff retreated to the library. There was no time like the present. Judith tossed her napkin to the table and followed him. "Geoff?" She knocked on the library door and went inside. "Is everything all right?"

Seated behind the desk, he looked up at her. "Why do you ask?"

Should she come straight out and say what was on her mind? She imagined him in bed with Beth and her blood simmered. "Why is Chris suddenly making excuses for you?"

He stared at her a minute. "I don't know. What did she say?"

"I don't like being answered with a question." Judith pointed an index finger in his direction. "Beth. I know it's been an on-again, off-again thing between the two of you over the past year, but I honestly believed it would stop once you married Chris, especially after Sarah arrived." She continued jabbing her finger in his direction for emphasis. "Beth may be Neal's mother, but besides your son's well-being, anything else between you and her needs to stop. You have no right dragging Chris through the middle of your sordid affair."

"Judith, I'm not sleeping with Beth."

Surprised by his response, she lowered her arm. "Are you sure?" Even before she finished the question, she realized how stupid it had been.

He folded his arms over his chest. "I think I would remember."

Watching him closely, she tried to detect any sign of lying. She spotted none. "I'm glad to hear it. Then what's wrong?"

All pretense vanished, and Geoff clamped his eyes shut.
"Geoff..."
With his left hand, he grasped a pen from the desk, then raised his arm. "Meet George."
"George? You can't be serious." She expected one of his prankster grins to cross his face. When none did, she sank into the chair across from him. *Losing him.* That's what Chris had meant. "What makes you think you're George?"
He withdrew a blank piece of paper from the drawer and began writing. His strokes were fluid and without hesitation. After jotting down a few lines, he handed her the sheet along with a letter from George. "Compare them."
Judith breathed in sharply. His handwriting was identical to that on the yellowed paper dated 1861. "I'm no handwriting expert, but they do look alike," she agreed. "That doesn't prove you were George."
The pen quivered in his hand, and he gave a sarcastic laugh. "Ask Chris. Even she admits it. She's afraid to let me out of her sight because of what I might do. With each day, the memories become clearer. They're blending with my own." The pen fell to the desk with a click, and he lowered his face to his hands. "Sometimes—I don't know what century it is."
She placed a hand on his shoulder. "I'll talk to Chris, and if necessary, I'll stay longer than the weekend."
He exhaled slowly. "Thank you, but that won't be necessary."
"I'll decide what is and isn't necessary—*after* I talk to Chris." Thankful that he gave no further argument, she turned to leave. He had reclaimed the pen and was writing with his left hand. *George?* Eager to speak with Chris, she rushed from the library.

Two days later, Chris awoke to bright May sunshine streaming through the window. She stretched and glanced at the clock. *Nine o'clock!* How could that be? She hurriedly dressed. Sarah wasn't in her room. Geoff must have taken the baby downstairs to let her sleep. She found them in the drawing room with Judith. Sarah squealed when she entered the room. "I can't believe I slept this late," she said, taking Sarah into her arms and bouncing the baby on her hip. "She's been fed?"

"And changed," Geoff responded with a good-morning kiss. "Now, if you don't mind, I have some painting to do."

If she took the idyllic scene at face value, Chris could almost pretend that it was a normal day. After Geoff and Saber left the room, she sank to the sofa.

"Another bad night?" Judith asked.

Chris gave Sarah a yellow and green rattle in the shape of a lollipop. "He keeps waking to the voices, and the headaches are becoming more frequent."

Judith sat beside her and tickled Sarah, making the baby giggle. "At least you've been successful in keeping Beth away."

Her stomach knotted. "For how long? It's only a matter of time before Beth realizes that we're monitoring his calls, or that Geoff..." She swallowed hard. "...can't control George from seeing her."

Judith squeezed her hand. "We'll find a way to keep them apart."

"And I've got two weeks to find a solution. They're not going to hold my job indefinitely."

"Chris, relax. I stayed on to help." Judith gathered Sarah in her arms. "In fact, why don't you get some breakfast, then take a bubble bath, or anything else that will help calm your nerves? We've got a family network. T.J. will let us know if anything is amiss, and I'll watch Sarah the entire day if you like."

"Thank you, Judith." Chris gave her friend a hug. The show of affection that she used to find difficult came easily now. Deciding to skip breakfast, she ambled upstairs for a leisurely shower. After blow drying her hair, she went down to the kitchen and gathered the fixings for a picnic lunch. Bread, cheese, turkey, ham. What was she forgetting? A bottle of wine. She packed plates and napkins into the wicker basket, then headed outside.

As she approached the stable, she heard chattering from the

roof. Geoff and Ken, both shirtless, were painting the cupola. His tongue lolling from the warm day, Saber remained protected from the sun beneath the overhang. Chris only hoped the dog was close enough to warn Geoff, if necessary. *Never mind.* Geoff wouldn't approve of any interference. She raised the picnic basket for Geoff to see. He shaded his eyes, then descended the ladder.

He grasped a towel from the ladder and wiped the sweat from his face. "What's this?"

His finely muscled chest glistened. "Lunch," she responded. "Although if you partake in any of the wine, I suggest that you find a safer chore than spending your time on a barn roof this afternoon."

"Lunch. Wine." With a growing smile, he checked his watch. "What's the occasion?"

"Simply that we've had so little free time since Sarah has been born. I thought we could picnic in the meadow, then ride out to the cottage afterward."

Intrigued, he grinned. "Give me a few minutes to clean up."

"I'll have T.J. help me saddle a couple of horses." She proceeded to the stable. A loud curse guided her to T.J. in a stall beside a brown mare.

He raised his head. "I beg yer pardon, lass. I didna know ye were standin' there."

Dismissing his apology, Chris silently thanked Judith one more time for giving her a chance to unwind. "I think I've heard such words before—from trial lawyers, no less. What's wrong?"

"Nothin' I canna handle. What can I do fer ye?"

"Geoff and I are going for a ride. Could you saddle one of the horses for me?"

T.J. pointed to the mare. "Aye, but I'll warn ye. Tiffany is in heat an' in one o' her moods. She got me foot."

PMS—even horses suffered from it, and now she understood why T.J. had been swearing. "Then maybe I should ride Ebony."

"Only if ye want ta spend thirty minutes catchin' him. He's out in the field, lass."

She set the picnic basket on a bale of straw. "Then Tiffany it is." After brushing the mare, Chris saddled her, while T.J. readied the gray gelding for Geoff. As she tightened the girth, she realized she had twisted it. She heard her father's voice chastise her for the stupid mistake: "*Christine Catherine.*"

T.J. jerked his head around, staring in her direction. "What did ye say yer middle name is?"

Middle name? She hadn't realized that she had muttered out loud. "Catherine. You must have heard something about the family history."

"I ne'er shared Sarah's enthusiasm aboot the family history. We'll talk aboot it ano'er time."

Peculiar. Before she could inquire further, Geoff strode into the barn with Saber at his side. Chris strapped the picnic basket to the saddle, then handed him a helmet, while slipping her own on her head. "All saddled and ready to go."

He led the horses to the outside yard, then boosted her on Tiffany's back. "No racing."

A reminiscent smile suggested that he was thinking of the first time they had taken a ride to the cottage. "No racing," she promised. "I wouldn't want to break the wine bottle."

Hooves clattered against the stone courtyard as they headed in the direction of the grove of oak and sycamore trees. Geoff rode beside her as the path changed to dirt surrounded by knee-high grass. Seasons had changed, and no chicory or black-eyed Susans bloomed in the meadow. Spring grass waved gently in the breeze.

They halted beside a towering oak and spread a blanket beneath it. Geoff stretched out his long legs as Chris served the sandwiches and wine. His expression remained relaxed, and she cursed silently to herself for not thinking of a picnic sooner. As she ate, Saber plopped beside her and stared. She broke off a bit of cheese from her sandwich, and he snarfed it from her fingers. The dog continued to watch her.

"He won't stop begging if you keep feeding him," Geoff reminded her.

She threw her hands up in surrender. "Okay, I'm guilty, but you don't feed him enough."

Amusement crossed Geoff's face. "He's gained five pounds since you first arrived here. I can't find his ribs anymore."

With a dismissive laugh, Chris took a sip of wine. "Which proves he was too skinny."

A tiny white grub dropped to the blanket. Geoff's gaze fixated as it inched toward him. "The maggots got into the wounds—crawling over and eating rotting flesh."

"Geoff..." She shoved her sandwich back into the basket and brushed the grub from the blanket.

He blinked. "Each day, I recall more."

"The voices?" she asked.

"They're from the war. I don't know how to keep them from taking over."

The mood of the carefree picnic suddenly dissolved. She gripped his hand. "Continue telling me about the memories when you have them."

His forehead furrowed in pain. "We weren't supposed to remember."

She withdrew her hand. "We may need to change tactics. Trying to suppress the memories doesn't seem to work. Have you stopped to think that George might be trying to tell you something?"

The tension on his face relaxed slightly as if he were pondering her question. "Possibly," he agreed, "but what?"

Further suggestions on her part could be a risk. George might be the stronger entity. "A way to cope with whatever it was that he could not. If you recall what happened, then we can do something to prevent it."

"So you're saying I should open my mind to George?"

"Yes."

His gaze met hers. "Haven't I already given you enough heartache?"

"We'll never know what was truly ours until this is resolved."

"Truth?"

"Truth," she replied firmly.

He searched her face. "What if . . . Never mind. I asked you to face the truth, and you did—head on. It's only fair that I should do the same."

She gripped his hand once more. "It's not about what's fair, but what we must do. You can't go on the way you have been. Now, I believe we had a date."

"A date?"

Standing, she tugged on his hand. They hadn't made love since his confession. "At the cottage. Or have you forgotten?"

"Chris . . ." When he got to his feet, she thought he would reaffirm his love, but the words were best left unsaid until they knew exactly what they were up against. All this time, she had mistakenly thought the problem lay exclusively with Margaret, but George had a role that couldn't be ignored. And neither would rest until the past was resolved.

Wood creaked under her feet as Margaret went up the steps to the cottage. As she reached the door, her hand trembled. Go back. *If she did, she could pretend that her imagination had got the best of her. But Tessa was aware of what was going on, and she was being made to look like a hysterical fool. Determined to discover the truth, she cracked the door open. Clothes lay strewn about the floor. The shadows across the bed played tricks. A throaty moan, and a mass of arms and legs. She spotted a woman's slender, naked back. Light brown hair draped across a man's bare chest.*

She bolted down the steps.

Chris ducked to Geoff's chest as if she had seen someone standing in the door frame. Shaken, she moved to his side and covered herself with the sheet. "I saw her too," he admitted. In resignation, he got up and tugged on his jeans before slumping to the chair beside the bed. "I guess I'm not much different in either lifetime. Margaret had become distant. By the time I understood why, it was too late."

"Geoff . . ."

George. Even though she hadn't said the name, he heard it all the same.

"You're getting closer to uncovering what happened."

And if he was meant to die, so be it. At least he could make peace with whatever was raging inside him. "After Margaret moved out of our bed, I had an affair. I never meant for it to happen, anymore than..." Damn, he had made a mess of things in two lifetimes. "Although Margaret was distressed at discovering me with another woman, she was relieved. For reasons that are quite obvious now, she never cared for any physical contact after the war."

Chris sat up but kept the sheet wrapped about her body. "Was the other woman's name Catherine?"

Catherine. He repeated the name, trying to visualize her, but drew a blank.

Chris got up and pulled on her silken underwear. "You called me Catherine when we first met—before a seizure."

He now understood why Beth had accused him of cheating. "The seizures are more frequent when I remember the past."

"The stress from recalling a past life," she said, breathing out in realization. She hooked her bra and her breasts vanished from his view. "So, her name was Catherine."

"Yes, her name was Catherine." Why hadn't he seized now? He glanced at Saber calmly resting beside the bed. "Saber..." With alert ears, the dog raised his head, and Geoff gave a sarcastic laugh. "Where do you think he got his name? I remember the weight of the saber in my hands. I used it in battle..." He closed his eyes. "And cleanly removed a man's hand."

Finished dressing, Chris sat on the bed across from him. Saber nudged her with his long black nose, and she hugged him to her. "Have you realized that you've begun to speak of George in the first person?"

First person? Would he reach a point where he'd only answer to George? "Saber likes you. If anything should happen..."

"Don't say it." She patted the dog on the top of his head.

"Someone needs to look after him."

"You," she insisted, then she added with a nervous laugh,

"He only likes me because I give him treats when you're not looking—and sometimes when you are."

Not really seeing her, he stared at Chris a moment. "He'd become fat and lazy."

"You just winked out."

A seizure *was* near. How long? Hours? Minutes? No, he reassured himself that Saber would alert him when the time came.

"Can you tell me anything else about Catherine?"

Catherine. "Not yet, but the war . . ." Frantic shouts came from the depths of his mind. A cannon boomed. Blinking back the echo, Geoff broke out in a sweat. The acrid smoke was so thick from muskets firing at close range that his eyes burned. Barely able to see through the dense woods, bodies lay everywhere. Stumbling, he nearly tripped over one. Separated from his regiment, he pushed forward using his saber to cut through the dense undergrowth. A bloody hand reached out, and he bent down to help.

The uniform of the dying soldier belonged to a Union lieutenant—equal in rank to his own. They were in hell together, and he felt no animosity. He placed a canteen to the man's cracked lips and let him drink until his thirst was quenched. He helped him to his feet. Spotting a clearing in the smoke, he pulled the man's arm over his shoulder. As they neared it, he saw a line of blue coats. Before he could react, he felt a sharp sting in his head. He heard a dog bark, and another voice called him—again and again. He clamped his hands over his ears, trying to block out the sounds.

After the long day, Chris turned on the ivory handles of the claw-footed tub. Undressing in front of the mirror, she glanced at the image. The skin was taut around her eyes, and dark bags had formed. She removed the crystal necklace and placed it on the counter. Geoff's seizure at the cottage had lasted four minutes. While he slept, she had stayed with him into the late afternoon until he was capable of returning to the house. He then had climbed the stairs to their room and proceeded to fall into another deep sleep. Water dripped. The tub was overflowing, and she snapped the faucet off. Without bothering to mop the puddle, she stepped into the tub and leaned against cool porcelain.

Water trickled over her skin as she sponged her body. Each drop soothed her fatigued muscles. She stretched to reach the middle of her back, and the sponge disappeared from her hand. Gentle massages went between her shoulder blades. Geoff smiled.

Geoff? Yes Geoff, not George. "You've had me worried," she admitted.

He sponged her back, then leaned forward to kiss the nape of her neck. "You don't seem too worried now." His blue eyes watched her naked reflection.

"I have a good idea what you're thinking."

His grin turned sly. "I must be as transparent as the water you're sitting in." His grin vanished. "Chris—I remember more than you can imagine."

"Share with me. You promised," she reminded him.

"Maggots climbed the walls."

Fort Delaware—she closed her eyes to George's memory.

"I never got the stench out of my mind." Standing, he slammed a fist against the wall.

"Geoff..."

He looked in her direction. Relieved that he continued to respond to his name, she gulped back a breath.

"I'm sorry," he whispered.

"Don't be. You didn't ask for this."

He extended a hand and helped her from the tub.

Water trickled down her back and onto the floor. Chris giggled. "How come you didn't join me?"

His eyes grew fixed.

"Geoff—what do you see?"

"Mile after mile. I had no shoes, but the thought of Margaret waiting kept me going, only to find she had changed." His arms went around her, and he kissed her, almost desperately. Like twine, he held on, but he was slowly unraveling. She stroked

her fingers through his thick, blond hair, and he gradually relaxed. On the steamy mirror, letters formed. G followed by an E.
As the scent of honeysuckle filled the room, a scream caught in
her throat. O . . . R . . . G . . . Another letter formed—E. The word
was George.

More letters. F . . . O . . . R . . .

Geoff rushed over and wiped the letters from the mirror.

"It could have provided a clue as to what she wants." No
more letters formed. For? The beginning of a prepositional sentence? Or foretell? Foregone? *Forever.* No wonder Geoff hadn't
wanted her to see it. Margaret had committed to George forever.

The next day was a warm spring day, and Chris served lunch in
the gazebo. Shortly after the letters had appeared on the mirror,
Geoff had suffered another seizure. The doctor's response was
to increase the dosage of his medication, which left him in a
stupor. As she fed Sarah a bottle, T.J. joined her and Geoff. "T.J.,
what a pleasant surprise," she said, forcing a smile.

Geoff attempted to stand but swayed on his feet and reseated
himself.

T.J. removed his cap. "I heard the lad wasna feelin' well." A
broad grin crossed his face when he spotted Sarah.

Chris held up the baby. "Sarah, say 'Hi' to your great-uncle."

T.J.'s grin widened as he extended a finger for the baby. Sarah
latched on and gurgled. "An' a bonny lass she is."

"Please join us for lunch, T.J.," said Chris, relieved to see the
older man. He was just the recipe for Geoff that she had hoped
for.

He seated himself at the table. "Geoff, I wanted ta see if there
is anythin' I can do fer ye."

"I appreciate the offer, but I'm fine, although I don't think I'll
be climbing any ladders in the near future."

Sarah began to cry. "If you'll excuse me," Chris said, rising
from the wicker chair. "I think someone needs changed." As
she approached the house, T.J. followed her and drew her aside.

"Please, T.J., stay with him for a while. I don't want him to be alone. He needs to talk."

"I will," he promised, "but I needed ta give ye this." He handed her a yellowed envelope addressed to Catherine.

Catherine? "I don't understand."

"It's from Sarah."

How was that possible? "Sarah? But she died over twenty-five years ago."

"I only know she gave it ta me before she died. She said I'd know when the time was right. Nearly fergot aboot it, I did. I'll return ta the lad now."

Puzzled by the encounter, Chris went inside and dropped Sarah off with Judith before returning to the drawing room. As she broke the envelope's seal, the tinkling of notes on the piano came from the parlor. She unfolded the letter. The handwriting was shaky and scrawling. Her heart pounded. Sarah from her deathbed.

> *Catherine,*
> *Am guilty of heinous crime. Geoff had George's voice. Had his strength. I shot him trying to get gun. Win blames himself for keeping it in house. Rushed Geoff to hospital. Memories have always plagued him. Car skidded. He lies in coma. Thank God, he will survive. Need your help. She killed George. You tried to help him. Please help Geoff.*
> *S*

The ink streaked off the page before Sarah could finish her name. The notes in the parlor raised to a crescendo. The music and letter—both were cryptic. The lament had been Sarah's cry for help. Chris tried to make sense of the words. *She killed George.* Margaret? Chris dropped the letter from her fingers and raced for the gazebo. Laura was clearing away dishes, but Geoff and T.J. were gone. Out of breath, she pressed a hand to her chest. "Laura, where did Geoff go?"

"I'm not certain, but I think he went in the direction of the stable with T.J."

Chris charged after him. "Geoff!"

* * *

In the library, on wobbly legs, Geoff stumbled, but T.J. grasped his elbow to help steady him. "Thanks," he muttered. He eased into the leather chair behind the desk and switched on the computer. He couldn't recall his password. "I can remember things that happened over a century ago, but not my damned password. It looks like you'll have to wait until my head clears to check the schedule."

"That'll be fine."

Saber scratched on the door to go out. "T.J., can you let him outside?"

"Aye."

Geoff held out his hand. "Thanks for being here."

"Ye've always bin there fer me." T.J. shook his hand but eyed him. "Will ye be all right?"

"I'm fine," Geoff reassured the old man.

"I'll get Chris."

"I don't need a nursemaid." Saber scratched the door more frantically. "Please let the dog out before he pisses on the wall. I'd never hear the end of it from Judith."

T.J. waved at Saber to come along with him. As the pair left, Geoff returned his attention to the computer screen. Password? He tried again. The screen repeated the command. *Ask George.* He laughed to himself and tried 4thVirginia. He was in. A door creaked. No one entered the room. "T.J.?" No answer. "Chris?" The scent of honeysuckle was strong and sweet. He closed his eyes. "Aren't two in one week enough?"

Another creak. *Behind him.* He swiveled the chair.

Beth stood near an open panel along the bookcase.

"Beth."

Her black hair glistened against milky-white skin as she approached the desk. "Catherine tried to seal the entrance, but she didn't know about the one leading here."

Still a bit wobbly, he stood. "Beth," he said, hoping to break Margaret's influence, "what are you doing here? We can't be alone again. It's not right."

She grasped his hand and kissed his fingers. "Surely, you remember. You said that you recalled everything."

He withdrew his hand from her grasp. "I don't want to remember that life. I belong here."

A tear formed in the corner of her eye. "Then you no longer love me. George . . ."

George—he had to end it—once and for all. "Of course, I still love you. You were my life, my first love. I would have never survived prison without your love. But something happened between us. Margaret, why didn't you tell me about the Yankee scout and the baby?"

The tear spilled down her cheek. "I feared you would hate me. Georgianna was your daughter. It wasn't until I met Mary that I realized I had got with child before that monster . . ."

His sister, Mary, she had red hair, like the scout. No longer a dreaded signal of an impending seizure, the soft scent of honeysuckle was a delicate fragrance of the wife he had loved. "I could never hate you. I'm only sorry that I wasn't here to protect you when you needed me."

"Then why did you give this to *her?*" She held out the crystal necklace.

Catherine. He did remember. How would he ever explain to Chris? "You misunderstand. I gave it to her in *this* lifetime."

Her violet eyes blazed. "I found *you* with her."

"Margaret, I'm sorry. The distance between us had grown, and I had no idea how to help you. If there had been a way, please believe me, I would have found it, but it was impossible for life to return to the way it was before the war. There was so little money and almost no food."

Dropping the necklace, Margaret softened her gaze, and she sent him a forgiving smile. She retraced her steps to the panel in the bookcase, and he breathed out in relief. She vanished behind the panel. Deciding to seal the panel, he went to close it. Before he reached it, she reappeared. In her slender hands she held the scout's .44. Oh, God, he had blocked out the memory.

Her lip curled. "You shan't ever touch me again."

"Margaret, I won't hurt you. I'm not him!"

As he went reeling backward, he felt blinding pain. His head bounced off the wooden floorboards, and he came to rest near the desk. Light shimmered. Attired in a blue silk dress with glistening pearls, Margaret stood over him with the gun in her hands. Struggling to remain conscious, he drifted. She bent down and whispered. Unable to make out her words, he felt the murk carry him under, then nothing.

The gunshot had echoed through the house. *She was too late.* Upon entering the main hall, Chris tried to determine what direction the shot had come from. Winston came charging down the staircase so fast that he nearly stumbled, but he caught the banister to keep from falling. She now knew. "The library!" Where George had died.

They raced through the drawing room to the hall in the west wing. Down the hall, they finally arrived by the library door. Winston held up a hand to wait.

"But Geoff..."

He signaled again. "If he's not alone, we need to be careful." He cracked the door open.

Her heart thumped wildly, and she craned her neck over his shoulder. Beside the desk, Geoff lay on the rug in a pool of blood. Chris shoved past Winston but came to a quick halt. Beth knelt over Geoff, shaking him. "Now's not the time to sleep. George, wake up."

"Geoff..."

Beth raised her head and glanced around as if not really seeing her. Her eyes widened in recognition. In her hands was a pistol. She raised it. "Catherine? George mustn't be disturbed."

Winston hurtled across the room. The impact of his body against hers sent Chris sprawling. More gunfire. But Winston was on his feet, got a firm grip on Beth's arms, and pinned her to the wall. The pistol clattered to the floor. "Chris, check Geoff."

Where his head rested, the crimson pool widened. Her crystal necklace lay beside him. "Geoff, please forgive me. I found out too late." She crawled over to him and touched his hand. Still warm, but he didn't move.

"Chris?" Winston asked in a strangled voice.

Tears streaked her cheeks. She moaned. "I think he's dead."

"Are you certain?"

Tears were in Winston's eyes. Beth had stopped fighting him.

Chris grasped Geoff's wrist, checking for a pulse. Faint, but erratic. "He's alive!" She cradled his head in her arms, and blood spattered her jeans. "Geoff, please don't die. I'm sorry for being late."

His lips moved, but she couldn't hear what he was trying to say.

"Save your strength," she said, hushing him. "Don't try to talk."

"Catherine." His hand fell away and made a thump as it hit the wood floor. Whispering her love, she hugged him tighter and felt him slip away.

The banks of the James were warm under his bare feet. As Geoff strolled, he felt more agile than he had in a long time. Overhead, a gull squawked. Delighted by the calm river, he picked up a rock and skipped it over the water's surface. He snatched up another rock and poised to throw.

Drumming hooves echoed behind him, and the rock fell from his hand. A black horse with a woman riding sidesaddle came into view. The pair trotted closer, and the woman reined the stallion to a halt.

Her black hair was pulled tightly back in a chignon, and she had a milky-white complexion. Like a thin veil of mist, the apparitions stared straight in front of them as if unaware of his presence. "Margaret," he said weakly.

Her violet eyes met his. "Come with me."

"I can't. I have a wife and children in this time."

Margaret's face etched in sorrow. She stepped down from the horse. Raven—the stallion that he had ridden during the war.

"You weren't supposed to die, George. I loved you, but after the scout, I no longer knew how to show it."

"I know. If only you had told me, but I discovered what had happened too late."

A hand went to her throat. "I didn't realize what I had done until my own passing. Forgive me."

Like a smoke plume, Margaret's image wavered. Ears flicking, the stallion raised his head. The horse snorted and pawed the ground. The misty veil waved, thinner and thinner. Only the soft scent of honeysuckle remained.

"You're forgiven," he whispered. His mind drifted. Voices murmured in the gentle breeze. Someone called his name. He felt no animosity and reached out and grasped her arm. It wasn't *her*, but... "Chris." On the bed beside him sat Chris. Drab white walls surrounded him. He was in a hospital again. He groaned. "Seizure?"

She grasped his hand. "Not this time. You were shot."

"Feels like... a seizure. I think... my head's... been twisted off."

Her grip tightened. "The bullet grazed your head. You have a concussion. Because of your history and accident as a child, they need to keep you here a few days, but the doctor thinks you're going to be fine."

He reached up and felt a thick bandage near his temple. "Beth?"

"The police took her into custody. Judith brought Neal back to the house. She's upset because Saber has taken to sleeping in Neal's bed."

Too weak to laugh, he let his arm fall back to the bed. "Why does that not surprise me? Chris, I don't think Beth was aware of Margaret's influence. Will you have my father see that she gets the proper treatment?"

She frowned. "Of course, but he's here if you want to ask him yourself."

"I will." His fingertips lightly stroked her cheek. "You're still worried."

Chris forced a smile. "What about us? Was everything we

shared nothing more than a dead woman's nightmare? T.J. gave me a letter from your mother—addressed to me. How could she have known about me?"

Geoff held up a hand that she was asking too many questions at once. Should he reveal the truth? Time had passed—more than a hundred years. *Face it.* "Catherine . . . I don't know how, but you were there, as you are now. It's where I first fell in love with you."

She stared at him in disbelief. "Are you trying to tell me . . . That you . . . Me?" She shook her head. "Then you're telling me we were lovers during a past lifetime?"

He nodded.

"We had an affair? No wonder she was jealous. This whole time she wasn't sending me visions to let me know what had happened, but haunting me."

"Neither of us meant for it to happen. Margaret never regained her mental health after the baby's death. I could never make sense of what had happened to her until you came along. If only I had known earlier, maybe there would have been something I could have done to help her. You were there when I needed someone."

Chris squeezed his hand. "I finally understand what Beth meant by 'it's you' when she met me. But your mother—how did she know what was going on?"

"George told her, before the accident." Her grip tightened, and he closed his eyes. The memories were already fading, yet it was impossible to forget everything that had happened. Nor would he want to. They might need to retrace their steps a little, but George would always be a part of him. The past gave them hope. For the present, that was all he could ask.

Chapter Sixteen

DOGWOODS BLOOMED NEAR THE four-foot brick wall. The iron gate groaned on its hinges, and Chris crossed the brown winter grass, scanning headstones until arriving at George's grave. Although weathered, the modest stone was readable.

George Cameron
1836–1867

Three years had passed before she had mustered the courage to visit. Back where he belonged, George was a distant memory. Beside him lay Margaret and Georgianna. Geoff had made certain the baby had received a proper marker. Moving on, she knelt beside the graves and placed flowers there. After carefully arranging them, she smiled. Lilies for Georgianna, and red roses for Margaret—symbolic of the truly everlasting love she must have shared with her husband.

Chris touched the etchings of Margaret's name carved in the stone. In a bittersweet way, she felt kinship. Even though tragedy had nearly repeated, Margaret had given her much. Without the visions, she might never have shifted the direction of her career or fallen in love with Geoff. That was something she could never truly repay. Secretly, she hoped Margaret had finally found peace.

As if on cue, a cold breeze stroked her bare neck. Chris touched the crystal necklace and gathered her coat around her. Margaret's life was the past. Let it remain where it belonged.

She strolled from the cemetery. With Saber at his side, Geoff creaked the iron gate shut behind her. A warm wind ruffled her hair. Spring at last.

Like murmuring voices, the wind echoed, and honeysuckle filled the air. Starting slightly, she glanced over her shoulder. A single rose had drifted from the others. In the breeze, she thought she heard whispers from the grave. She grasped Geoff's hand. His blue eyes sparkled, reminding her the voices were only the wind.

Author's Note

The Civil War scenes depicted in Margaret's early "memories" are based on McClellan's Peninsula Campaign in April–June 1862. Her later war experiences are derived from Union raids and activities in 1864 leading up to the Siege of Petersburg. Many well-known historians maintain that the Civil War was a "low-rape" war due to the fact that few rapes were reported. Personally, I find this view shortsighted. For one, the historians fail to define what is meant by a low-rape war. Second, a circular defense of their position has been created by citing each other without any factual basis. U.S. National Archives and Records Administration reference archivist, *Prologue* magazine writer Trevor K. Plante makes this statement about the Civil War: "Army life was hard, and desertion, insubordination, cowardice under fire, theft, murder, and rape were not uncommon."

In modern society during peacetime, according to the U.S. Department of Justice statistics, more than two-thirds of rape/sexual assaults committed go unreported. In areas of the world where women have few rights, victims are even less likely to report the crime. Statistics during wartime are more challenging to document because they are often used for propaganda purposes. In addition to the emotional anguish and blame associated with the crime, victims during wartime fear for their family's lives and rejection from their partners and community, making disclosure less common than during peacetime.

To assert that Victorian mores somehow imposed gentlemanly restraint during wartime is preposterous. Sexually assaulting black women was not viewed as a crime by either side, and white women making an admission to being raped would have been systematically ostracized. As in modern warfare, fear would have been a powerful incentive for rape survivors to remain silent.

Acknowledgments

A special thank you goes to my editors, K.A. Corlett and Catherine Karp, my cover designer, Mayapriya Long, and Charles Holley of Holley Photography for providing the "ghost photo" for the cover art. And of course, I mostly wish to thank my family: my son, Bryan, and especially my husband, Pat; both are now convinced that I can indeed return to the twenty-first century on occasion, but only temporarily.